DARK SUMMER IN BORDEAUX

for Louis and Géraldine
with love

I

There are days, even in the bad times, even the worst of them, when you can still believe in the future, like that six o'clock in the morning three weeks ago when the bell rang and Dominique was there. Dominique, pale, wretchedly thin, exhausted, his hair cropped, but nevertheless Dominique. Lannes held him in his arms, neither able for a moment to speak. Then,

'Go to your mother, wake her gently. I'll make coffee.'

His hands trembled as he filled the pot. He lit a cigarette to calm himself. It was right to leave them alone together for a few minutes. He hadn't dared to pass on to Marguerite Edmond de Grimaud's promise to arrange for Dominique's return from the prisoner-of-war camp. 'I'm in his debt now, deep in his debt,' he thought and felt doubly guilty, utterly compromised. 'No matter,' he spoke aloud. 'The boy's home.'

Marguerite was in tears, but they were tears of joy and relief as she stroked Dominique's cheek.

'It's all right, Maman, it really is me, not a dream . . . '

'I can't believe it. It's so wonderful.'

Lannes put the cups on the little table beside the bed. They didn't notice him. They were like lovers. No, not that. Madonna and Child, sufficient for the moment to each other.

A morning like none since before the war, Marguerite singing and Dominique saying time and again, 'I can't believe it either, but I never gave up hope . . . '

Later Marguerite would want to know everything that had happened to him, everything he had endured. For the moment it was enough to see him there, to be able to touch him, stroke that cropped head. As for Alain and Clothilde, once the first expressions of delight were over, they didn't know how to speak to this brother who had been returned to them almost like Lazarus.

For Lannes himself the idyllic hour had been cut short, interrupted by a telephone call. Murder, but a banal one, calling on no investigative skills. A husband whose tether had broken after years of disharmony – the word he unexpectedly used as he sat, hands clenched between his legs, in Lannes' office.

'She's been asking for it for ages,' he said, 'and at last I've given it to her, though I never intended to do more than shut her up, stop her nagging for once.'

A poor thing, a clerk whose life had become impossible when he was compelled to retire from his office and spend days at home with his wife. Lannes had known other such cases, too many, revelations of the bleakness of life. It was a relief to hand the man over to the examining magistrate and to deal briskly with the paperwork. A miserable case, certainly, but there was a sort of normality to it; nothing to do with the war, the Occupation, the German presence, nothing therefore to present him with a test of conscience.

This was rare enough. His conscience had been oppressed since that day in Vichy when Edmond had offered him the bargain which he accepted: Dominique's extrication from the PoW camp and information which would allow him to checkmate the lawyer Labiche who was threatening his career, in exchange for his final abandonment of the investigation into poor Gaston's murder and the promise that he would hand over the compromising document that somehow linked Edmond to that case, should he ever happen to find it. He had been bullied, bribed and blackmailed: a humiliation and in his eyes a disgrace. He had other worries too: anxiety for Alain, the fear that his younger son's resentment of the Occupation would lead him to some rash act; apprehension for Miriam as a Jew and for her nephew Léon too. Yet these were as nothing to the shame which ate into him like a malignant growth. I'm not fit to be a policeman, he often thought, not worthy. When, over the days that followed, he heard Marguerite singing as she went about her housework, or saw her lean over Dominique and stroke his cheek, as if to reassure herself that he had really returned and that all was well, he couldn't experience to the full the happiness he should feel to see her restored to spirits.

There was a knock on the door and old Joseph the office messenger came in with a letter.

First published in 2012 by
Quartet Books Limited
A member of the Namara Group
27 Goodge Street, London WIT 2LD

A catalogue record for this book
is available from the British Library

ISBN   978 0 7043 7266 5

Typeset by Antony Gray
Printed and bound in Great Britain by
T J International Ltd, Padstow, Cornwall

Dark Summer in Bordeaux

ALLAN MASSIE

QUARTET BOOKS

'This arrived by hand,' he said. 'It's marked urgent, you see, which I daresay it isn't.'

'Who brought it?'

'Some street-boy. For a few francs or a couple of cigarettes I would guess.'

'All right, Joseph. I expect you're right and it's urgent only to whoever wrote it.'

All the same he waited till Joseph had gone before slitting open the envelope which was the cheap sort that a café will provide for its clients. The message was brief.

'Superintendent: it's important that we meet. Please be at the Bar Metéo, rue Fénélon, at 4 o'clock this afternoon. I shall present my credentials to you there. The matter is urgent. Destroy this letter.'

There followed an illegible signature.

Lannes lit a cigarette and applied the match to the corner of the paper, held it a moment burning and then let it fall into the ashtray when he watched it crumble.

Was it simply because he was bored that he resolved to accept the invitation?

*   *   *

The bar was quiet at that hour, only a couple of workmen in blue overalls drinking pastis and playing belotte. Lannes ordered a coffee and took a seat in the far corner where he could watch the door. The coffee was vile, the worst ersatz. He called for an Armagnac and lit a cigarette. A bluebottle settled on the rim of the coffee cup. A man emerged from the toilet, had a word with the barman, stood watching the card-players, sniffed the air, held himself just short of the door a moment, surveying the street, then turned and disappeared through a bead curtain to the left of the bar. A minute later the barman approached Lannes and said, 'Will you come this way, please, sir?' He led him through the curtain to a little room where the man was sitting at a table. He gestured to Lannes to take the other chair.

'I think we're all right,' he said.

Lannes said nothing. He sat down. The man had dark hair, shiny with some dressing, dark eyes, a thin mouth. He fitted a Celtique cigarette into a holder and lit it.

'You can call me Félix.'

'Latin for fortunate,' Lannes said.

'We must hope so . . . '

He drew on his cigarette, expelled smoke through his nostrils 'A misnomer,' he said, 'perhaps, these days. Which of us is fortunate?'

'Call no man fortunate till he is dead.'

'That's a quotation, isn't it?'

'Some ancient philosopher, Greek or Roman, I don't remember which.'

'So you're here,' Félix said. 'I think you are a patriot, superintendent.'

'A patriot? Aren't we all? – whatever being a patriot means, in our circumstances.'

'Oh quite. We all mean different things by the word. You've had dealings with Lieutenant Schussman, I think.'

'He's a patriot too,' Lannes said. 'A German one. Aren't you going to tell me who you are?'

'I don't think so. Félix is enough.'

'Not for me,' Lannes said. 'You mentioned credentials in your note. So I need a bit more than the assurance of a name that certainly isn't yours before I carry on this conversation.'

'Superintendent, you don't really want more than that name which is, as you surmise, a nom de guerre. Not at this stage anyway. Let's stop sparring and get down to business. Lieutenant Schussman is a queer.'

'If you say so. He's a decent enough chap actually.'

'All the better. A literary type too, isn't he? A regular customer of a bookshop in the rue des Remparts. Kept by your friend Henri Chambolley. But books aren't the only attraction, are they? Or so we believe.'

'We?' Lannes said, 'I don't know who you mean by your "we".'

'We? Oh, we're patriots, just like you, superintendent. I shouldn't be in Bordeaux, you know. I've taken a risk coming here. We're not really supposed or permitted to operate out of the so-called

Free Zone, not at present anyway. There: I've placed one of my cards on the table. Here's another. It's in our interest to have friends among the Occupying army, not friends, precisely, we can't have that, but men, a few anyway, who are bound to us. You understand?'

'Yes,' Lannes said. 'I understand now. I understand perfectly. But I'm a policeman. I don't like spooks.'

He had left it there, been, surprisingly, permitted to do so, the man Félix making no demur, as if, Lannes thought, he was content to have made only this brief preliminary contact, in the course of which he had, nevertheless, sown his seed. Walking away, leaning on his blackthorn stick, he was tempted to go straight to the rue des Remparts and warn Léon. Warn him off? Off what? The danger of being used as bait? Certainly, but . . . He couldn't be sure he wasn't being watched, spied on. He turned into a bar and ordered a demi, beer to wash the taste of the spook away. A word with Schnyder? Cover his back? Perhaps. But that would mean telling him more than he would care to divulge.

II

'Disharmony': the word that wretched clerk had used stuck with him. It so precisely described his state of mind, the state of France indeed. Bordeaux was a prison in which nevertheless he walked at liberty. It was late winter weather he had always liked, no leaves on the trees, a low sky, scudding winds, no hint of spring. As for the war, well, there was no war, and the Occupiers were mannerly. Sometimes, seeing German soldiers sitting at café tables, or chatting around one of the city's fountains, you might have thought they were on holiday.

He might as well be so himself. The case that had occupied him for months was dead. Nothing new claimed his attention, only routine matters which bored him.

But now, this 'Félix' – ridiculous name – had come to arouse him from his torpor. There was nothing for it, he must overcome his reluctance, speak to the boy Léon. All the same he waited till the streets were dark before making his way to the bookshop in the rue des Remparts.

Léon said, 'Oh, it's you. I was just about to close up. Henri's upstairs, but . . . '

'That's all right. It's you I've come to see.'

'What am I supposed to have done now?'

'I hope you've done nothing.'

Léon smiled.

'You look very serious,' he said. 'I could give you a cup of coffee.'

'Yes, why not? I'd like that . . . '

He sat smoking while the boy went through to the back room. It was very quiet. The place felt like sanctuary. Léon returned with coffee for both of them, sat opposite him, cupped his thin intelligent face in both hands and waited for Lannes to speak. When he didn't do so, he said,

'I haven't registered as a Jew. Should I have done so?'

'Not if you can avoid it, but . . . '

'Yes, it's a "but", isn't it? Otherwise I continue to behave myself, as you recommended. So?'

'Schussman,' Lannes said. 'I learn things I don't want to learn. Does he bother you?'

'Bother? What a strange word to use.'

'Don't play games, Léon. I'm too tired. You know what I mean.'

'He's a nice enough chap, you know,' Léon said and smiled. 'But I've made it quite clear, I think, that I'm not interested. That's to say, I've tried to choke him off. That's what you advised, isn't it?'

Lannes drank his coffee which was still of pre-war quality.

'His attentions have been noticed,' he said.

The boy flushed and looked away.

'I've spoken to nobody,' he said. 'But I can't help it if he . . . '

'If he . . . What?'

'Finds me attractive. Do you despise me, superintendent?'

'Despise you, Léon? No, why should I?'

'For being what I am, for being what I was to Gaston . . . '

Lannes sighed, lit a cigarette and pushed the packet over to the boy who took one and held his face towards Lannes for a light. Lannes looked him in the eyes over the flame till Léon lowered his.

'That's nothing to me,' he said. 'I despise nobody, except those who delight in power and misuse it. You're fond of Alain, aren't you?'

'We're friends, that's all. He's not like me, you know, so friends is all we can be whatever else I might want. You won't tell him, will you?'

His upper lip quivered and he looked close to tears.

'He thinks of you as a good friend,' Lannes said. 'I'm sure of that.'

'Thank you. So why have you come here?'

'It's difficult.'

'What isn't?'

'Yes, you're intelligent. You know that. Lieutenant Schussmann. The fact is, his attentions have been noticed, his inclination suspected. That's why you must be careful. Do you understand? People may want to use you. Try not to let them.'

'What sort of people? No, you don't need to tell me. I think I can guess.'

'I don't approve of them,' Lannes said. 'I have no time for these types who use other people as if they were pawns in a game of chess. Let me know if they approach you. That's as much as I can ask.'

'If they are who I think they are, how can I say no?'

'That's why I say to let me know, get in touch straightaway. I'll do what I can to protect you, but I have to warn you it may not be much. Not, certainly, as much as I would wish.'

'And this conversation, has it taken place?'

'I wish I knew the right answer to that.'

III

The body had been dragged into the bushes in the public garden. Incompetently. The feet protruded and one of the park attendants kicked them, assuming they belonged to a drunk who had passed out there. When he got no response, he parted the bushes to get a look at the man lying there. Then he hurried to call the police.

'His head's been bashed in,' he told Lannes. 'A very nasty mess, and it's not as if he's one of these young hooligans who get into fights. His hair's grey, white really, I could see that in spite of the blood. Dried blood it is . . . '

'All right,' Lannes said, 'we'll take a look at him. You didn't touch anything, did you?'

'Apart from giving him a kick because I thought it was a drunk sleeping it off, and pushing through the bushes to see why he didn't move, certainly not. I wasn't born yesterday, and I'm a good citizen. I called you straight away, and then came back here to lock the park gate again, seeing as I assumed you wouldn't want to have a lot of people gawking at you. Not to mention the kids. It's not a sight for them, I can tell you. If you think, superintendent, I'm talking too much, well, that's because I'm not accustomed to this sort of thing. To tell you the truth this is the first dead body I've seen since the last Armistice. Saw plenty before then of course. I'm not counting the wife's mother. She died natural, peacefully, just drifted away. Not that her death would have disturbed me however it happened. Here we are then. See for yourself.'

'Right,' Lannes said, 'thank you. Would you go back to the gate, please, and wait for the doctor and the technical boys? They'll soon be on their way. And yes, continue to keep the public out. Find some excuse. Or tell the truth. Whichever you prefer.'

'I've no doubt he'll lay it on,' Moncerre said.

'Doesn't matter. Let's go take a look then.'

Moncerre pulled a couple of branches aside.

'Not much doubt, is there?' he said. 'Our old friend, the blunt instrument . . . He looks a respectable gent though. That's a good piece of cloth.'

Lannes knelt and fingered the cuffs of the trousers.

'Indeed it is,' he said, 'good English flannel.'

He looked up.

'My mother's father was a tailor, remember. I learned about cloth as a boy.'

'I'd forgotten. Respectable gent,' Moncerre said again. 'Funny place for him to have copped it. I wonder what he was up to.'

The technical team arrived, followed almost at once by Dr Paulhan, Boyard cigarette in the corner of his mouth.

'Well, Jean, I can't examine him properly where he is,' he said, 'but the cause of death looks evident enough. No reason, is there, to think his nut was smashed in when he was already dead. No reason at all. I can tell you straightaway he's been lying there for hours, but you'll have come to that conclusion yourself, I've no doubt. Get him round to me and I'll do my stuff. But I'll be surprised if I can do much to help you. At least he is not one of our Occupying friends. That's clear. A good Frenchman and a man of some position, I would say. Wouldn't you? Spares you one complication at least.'

'An old-fashioned pre-war murder then,' Moncerre said. 'A robbery gone wrong. Let's hope so anyway. Then we're dealing only with our usual sort of client.'

Photographs were taken. Lannes set a couple of his men to look for the weapon, 'Which I doubt if you'll find.'

'Not unless chummy's a half-wit,' Moncerre said. 'Which of course he may well be.'

'He's had the sense at least to lift the chap's wallet,' René Martin said.

Lannes said, 'This suit's from a good tailor, hand-made. Look in the inside breast pocket and you'll find the tailor's name. He should be able to help us identify him. Of course, we may find he's been reported missing already. But I doubt it. Why, I don't know.'

'Léopold Kurtz, rue Xantrailles,' René said. 'The street Cortazar lived in.'

'I doubt if there's a connection with that murder,' Lannes said. 'The street's just a coincidence. Anyway, Mériadeck, it's where you'd expect to find a Jewish tailor. I'll go round there with the jacket when the technical boys have finished with it. Meanwhile there's nothing more we can do here for now.'

It was ridiculous, even, he admitted to himself, shameful; he felt a lightening of the spirit. It's only, he told himself, that I feel in need of work. And a crime such as this promised to be unconnected to the war and the Occupation.

'At least I hope that's the case,' he said when they were settled in the Brasserie Fernand and had eaten the pigeons with red cabbage Fernand had recommended.

'Could be sordid though,' Moncerre removed the toothpick from his mouth. 'The public garden, a head-bashing – if it's not just a robbery, what sort of crime does that suggest to you? One that stinks, in my opinion. Never mind, if it is that, we may even be permitted to solve it and bring the killer to what passes for justice.'

'Unless he's got protection,' René said.

'You're growing up, kid,' Moncerre said, 'getting wise to the ways of this wicked world. And suppose the old boy had made advances to one of our young Aryans who took exception to them and did for him. Would we be allowed to solve that? I think not, my friends.'

'We've no reason to suppose anything of the sort,' Lannes said.

$$* \quad * \quad *$$

The tailor was old and his wrinkled face was dominated by a big nose. He wore gold-rimmed pince-nez spectacles attached to the buttonhole of his jacket by a black ribbon. He sat cross-legged on a low table in the traditional posture of his trade. The light in his shop was dim.

'So,' he said, 'the police want help from an old Jew. We are not often approached so politely these days.'

'No,' Lannes said, 'and I'm sorry that is the case.'

'Nevertheless,' the old tailor said, 'I'm one of the lucky ones, am I not? Not one of those forbidden to practise my trade.'

He felt the coat, running his fingers over it.

'Nice piece of cloth, very nice.'

'English flannel, I thought.'

'Certainly, certainly. It's been well cared for since it is at least ten years ago that I made this coat.'

He took a pinch of snuff, reminding Lannes of Judge Rougerie's habit which he had always thought a tiresome affectation. It didn't seem so in the case of the old tailor.

'Can you tell me who you made it for?'

'So he's dead, is he, and nastily, since you're here to question me.'

'Perhaps,' Lannes said. 'Perhaps not, since the man you made it for may have passed it on to someone else.'

'Oh yes, I remember because I don't often get such cloth to work with. Most rich Bordelais, as you may know, who have a taste for

English cloth will get their suits made over there too. But in this case my customer had been given the material by his daughter – or mistress perhaps – I forget which, and brought it to me to be made up. That was natural enough. I'd made other suits for Professor Labiche.'

'Labiche? That was his name?'

'Certainly. A professor – I can't remember of what at the university – though he must have retired, I would think. This was the last suit I made for him, and, as I say, at least ten years ago.'

'But you still have an address?'

'Must have, though it may be out of date, of course. I'm sorry he's come to a bad end. These are bloodstains on the collar, aren't they. He was a gentleman, always well spoken, if reserved. A good client, I had a respect for him . . . '

He got off the table, stiffly, as he spoke, and hobbled to a roll-top desk which had certainly seen better days, for the wood was stained and scuffed. The inside of the desk was a mess too, but, after rummaging around, the old man came up with a note-book. He leafed through it, and said,

'Here we are. Professor Aristide Labiche, 72, cours de Verdun. 1 metre 75 tall, 82cm waist, used to be 87, but he lost weight before I made this flannel suit. It's the last thing I did for him. Does that sound like your man?'

'The height's right, but I suspect he had lost more weight in the years since . . . Thank you. You've been helpful.'

He hesitated, lit a cigarette,

'How are things with you?' he said. 'You haven't had any trouble, I hope?'

'I keep my head down and get on with my work. Most of my customers have stayed loyal. What else can I do? Besides, who's to bother with an old tailor even if he is a Jew?'

'I hope you're right.' Lannes gave him a card. 'If you're wrong, I'll see what I can do.'

IV

'Labiche?' the concierge said, 'Professor Labiche. No, there's no one of that name lives here.'

'It's the last address we have for him,' Lannes said.

'And when was that?'

'Ten years ago, I'm afraid.'

'Ah well,' she rubbed her hands on her apron. 'I've been here for five, and I tell you he wasn't a tenant here when I moved in. To tell the truth, I've never heard anyone of that name spoken of. Not that there's any reason why I should, is there now?'

'One of your other tenants might know something about him,' Lannes said.

'Indeed that's so, but then, again, this is a respectable house. There's none of the tenants would like me to call them to the attention of the police, if you know what I mean. I speak without offence, superintendent.'

'I understand perfectly,' Lannes said. 'Nevertheless, a man whom I have reason to believe used to live here has been murdered, and this is the only address I have for him, all I know about him . . .'

He paused, to let the woman think in the silence he imposed on her.

'Labiche?' Moncerre had said, 'that's the name of that bastard of an advocate. Maybe they're brothers. If so, it's the wrong one has caught it.'

The same thought had of course occurred to Lannes, the moment the old tailor produced the name. All the more reason to go warily.

'There's Madame Bouillou, first-floor right,' the concierge said. 'She's been here a long time, and she's alert as a hunting-dog. You could try her.'

*   *   *

'Yes, I'm Madame Bouillou, and you're police, you say. What have I done to deserve a visit from you?'

If she was indeed alert as a hunting-dog, Lannes thought, she was

18

one that was out of condition. She wheezed as she spoke and her big bosom palpitated as if the effort of moving from her armchair to the door had been almost too much for her. There was a whiff of port wine on her breath when she smiled and ushered Lannes in to an over-furnished drawing-room where a white cockatoo in a cage squawked to see him. She put a cloth over the cage saying, 'Naughty boy, be quiet or I shan't hear what the nice policeman has to say.' Then she sank into a high-backed chair which she filled, picked up her glass of wine and took a little sip.

'It's years since I have had dealings with the police,' she said. 'Quite like old times, this is. Take a seat, superintendent.'

She gestured with a hand which had a large ruby ring embedded in the fat of her finger, and a grey cat leapt off the chair she had indicated, arched its back and jumped on to her lap where it lay purring while she scratched it behind its ear.

'I know nothing about that,' Lannes said, 'and I can't suppose any dealings with the police you may have had are of any relevance. It's really some information I'm looking for, and I hope you may be able to help me.'

'Soft soap,' she said, 'but go ahead. It's a treat to have a visitor, even a policeman. Smoke if you wish. My doctor forbids me cigarettes but I do love the smell.'

'Thank you,' Lannes said. 'Do you remember a Professor Labiche who used to live here?'

To his surprise, she laughed.

'Give me another glass of wine and give yourself one. Poor Aristide! In trouble with you lot, and him such a careful man . . . '

'You knew him well then?'

'Seeing as we were lovers, or I was his mistress as he would have put it, I can't deny knowing him. You wouldn't think to look at me now that I was a beauty once, would you, but there you are, there's a photograph of the pair of us on that little table, and you can see I was a looker in those days. Well, that was nearer fifty than forty years ago. What's the old fellow done?'

'You sound as if you are still fond of him.'

'And why shouldn't I be? He's an old silly and he became an awful bore. Nevertheless . . . '

Lannes crossed the room and picked up the photograph which was in an Art Nouveau silver frame. More than forty years ago, as she said, but there was a resemblance to the dead man. As to the woman, yes, she was right, she had been beautiful in a blonde, buxom, chorus-girl way.

'It was politics,' she said. 'I couldn't be doing with his silly Communism. I was a businesswoman myself, you see. Yes, as you'll discover if you look in your files, it wasn't what most think of as a respectable business – I kept a house and I'm not ashamed to admit it. It embarrassed Aristide no end, he was very correct, even as a young man. Tell me why you're interested in him and I'll tell you our story.'

She laughed again and as she did so Lannes became aware of her charm and of how attractive she must have been when that photograph was taken.

'I've had lots of lovers, but there was always something about him,' she said, and emptied her glass.

Lannes hesitated. The smoke from his cigarette hovered in the still air of the room where it was probable no window had been opened for days. He had always hated this moment when you had to announce a death.

'I see,' she said. 'So that's why you're here. I didn't even know he was back in Bordeaux. How did you find me?'

Lannes said, 'It's the only address we have for him.'

'There's a time I would have wept,' she said. 'Now . . . ?'

She reached out for the bottle of port, and again offered it to Lannes, who declined because it was a drink he had never cared for.

'What was he a professor of?' he said.

'History, which has never interested me. The Commune was his subject, I believe.' She sighed and her bosom heaved. 'He was a shy and timid lover,' she said. 'Perhaps that's what attracted me, and held me for so long . . . '

Lannes said, 'Does he have family here in Bordeaux?'

'There was a wife of course. Perhaps she's dead too. I would be dead myself if I believed my doctor. And there's a brother, you'll know of him, I'm sure. The advocate, a good deal younger he is, a nasty piece of work. They didn't get on. Politics.'

'But he lived here with you, rather than with his wife?'

'He loved me, or said he did. So he moved in here when he left her at last, and stayed with me for I can't remember how long. Years anyway. Then he went up to Paris. On account of his stupid politics. I can't remember just why. Perhaps he went to write for a paper there. Yes, I think that was it. To tell the truth I wasn't much interested and I confess I had had enough of him really. Being under my feet, you understand.'

She picked up her glass and held it to her lips but paused before drinking.

'I can't think why anyone should have killed the poor chap. He was an innocent, you know.'

Lannes said, 'According to the tailor who gave me this address, the professor had a daughter. Can you tell me anything about her?'

'I never met her. That won't surprise you. He very seldom spoke of her, except occasionally as she had been when a little girl. He may have been fond of her, I don't know, it was a part of his life I didn't belong to. Though he was fond of me, as fond as he could be, I think, of anyone, it was ideas that held him, not people, and, as for the daughter, politics came between them. That's what he used to say. And perhaps she took her mother's side. I don't know. I was his mistress for years, you know, before he came to live with me. But there were sides of his life I knew nothing about. I preferred it that way, to be honest.'

Her hand stroked the grey cat. For a couple of minutes when she didn't answer its purring was the only sound in the stuffy room.

'I wouldn't have thrown him out, you know,' she said, 'not ever. Not even though he had come to bore me and I was past enjoying what we had had together. All the same, when he came to live here I gave him something he had never had before. Or so he said, though he never said what it was. But it wasn't enough. Evidently it wasn't. It was his decision to leave, for Paris and his politics, not for another woman, you'll understand. I could have seen off such a one, no matter who she was, if I'd chosen to, but I was helpless against politics. And to tell you the truth, superintendent, I didn't much care. As I said, he had become an awful bore. Give me some more wine, please.'

She held out her glass.

'All the same,' she said, 'I missed him. For a long time . . . '

'So you don't know where we might find the daughter.'

'No idea. You'll have to try the brother. As for me, I wouldn't demean myself by speaking to him. I'm a generous-minded woman, as won't surprise you knowing my milieu, but there are things I've no time for. Nor those whose tastes lie that way.'

'I'm with you there,' Lannes said.

He got to his feet.

'You've been helpful,' he said. 'I'm grateful. I'm sorry to have brought you distressing news. There's one other thing, a request. I've been speaking of the professor as the murdered man, and I've no doubt correctly. But actually we can't be sure until he has been identified. It's only the evidence of his suit and the tailor who made it brought me here. It's a lot to ask you, but . . . '

'It's the brother's job, surely.'

'You're right, of course, but I have reasons to think he may not prove co-operative. So?'

'Very well then, since you ask politely. And as for the brother, from all I've heard of him you may well be right. He's a bastard, my poor old boy couldn't stand him.'

*   *   *

'An innocent?' Moncerre said. 'A Communist and an innocent? Pull the other one.'

'Oh,' Lannes said, 'there are innocent Communists, you know, just as there are even innocent Fascists. We call them idealists and they cause a lot of trouble.'

He lit a cigarette and pushed the packet of Gauloises towards Moncerre. Then he got up, crossed over to the window. The sky was slate-grey, threatening rain and a little gust of wind threw discarded papers about the square.

'I liked her,' he said, 'and what she told me helps to give us a picture of our man. But she hadn't seen or heard of him for years.'

He took a bottle of Armagnac from his cupboard, filled two stubby glasses and passed one to Moncerre.

'There's the brother,' Moncerre said.

'Yes, there's the brother.'

'A bastard, isn't he?'

'Yes . . . '

Had he told Moncerre just how Edmond de Grimaud had arranged that Sigi, who was also known as Marcel and whom they knew to be a murderer, but one of those belonging to the category Schnyder described as 'untouchable', should apply pressure on the advocate Labiche to prevent him from continuing his campaign against himself? 'You're in deep shit,' Edmond had said – and got him out of it. By what was either blackmail or menaces. Or both. Lannes had been relieved and at the same time ashamed. Deeply ashamed. No, he hadn't been able to tell Moncerre everything, just made it clear he'd been heavily leaned on, bullied and bribed, though not with money.

He looked at his subordinate whose face was completely without expression. Lannes knew him to be loyal, thought of him as a friend as well as colleague, but was never sure that he had his respect. Not his full unconditional respect anyway, certainly not the unqualified admiration that he knew young René felt for him – which admiration, even reverence, was itself a cause for embarrassment.

'I want you to question him.' he said. 'There are things between us.'

'I see.'

'Frankly, apart from anything else, he would take pleasure in telling me nothing about his brother or even telling me lies, certainly making things as difficult for me as possible.'

'So you want me to twist his arm? It'll be a pleasure.'

'You might at least find out where our dead man has been living. That would be a start.'

Moncerre fingered his glass, then downed the brandy in one swallow.

'I've got itchy palms,' he said. 'It's like when I go home and find that my wife hasn't cooked a dinner because I've done something new to offend her and I've no idea what it is. So I've the feeling that this is not going to turn out to be a simple head-bashing. That advocate likes little girls, doesn't he?'

'So they say. There's no reason though to suppose his brother shared that taste. Certainly not if Madame Bouillou is anything to go by.'

'Never said there was.'

Moncerre laid his finger along his nose.

'But a bit of leverage, wouldn't you say?'

'Apply as much leverage as you care to,' Lannes said, knowing that Moncerre would take pleasure in doing so.

V

The judge appointed to supervise the investigation was new. Old Rougerie had been retired, or chosen to withdraw. Lannes didn't know which. He hadn't been sorry to see the old fusspot go. Nevertheless there had been this in his favour. You could always bamboozle or scare him; he hadn't been very bright and he was terrified of responsibility. The new man was more formidable, had come straight from Paris, and to make matters worse was several years younger than Lannes, maybe as much as ten. He wore a double-breasted suit in a harsh shade of blue. There was a gold watch on his wrist. He was tall and thin and his black shoes were highly polished. For a moment Lannes couldn't remember his name, which was Bracal. The first time they met, three weeks ago, he had begun by saying, 'I'm a good republican but we are where we are.' Lannes hadn't known what to make of that. Was it some sort of test? He had let it pass without comment anyway.

Now Bracal said, 'I could offer you coffee, but I wouldn't advise you to drink it.'

'In that case, no thank you.'

'So what do you know? Have you a suspect?'

'No suspect and we know very little. We have a name. Labiche. Professor Aristide Labiche. He used to be a resident of Bordeaux but we think he hasn't lived here for some time and has perhaps only recently returned. He has a brother. You'll know of him perhaps. An advocate. One of my men has gone to interview him, but I don't think they were close.'

'Why was that?'

'Politics,' Lannes said. 'The professor was apparently a man of the Left, a card-carrying Communist.'

The judge began to file his nails.

'Not a very prominent one,' he said, 'He took to journalism, didn't he? I rather think I've read some of his articles. Turgid stuff, no flair.'

Lannes let that pass.

Bracal said: 'I've no doubt you'll keep me informed. There's another matter.'

He kept his eyes fixed on the nail he was filing. Lannes waited. He wasn't going to help the man who seemingly preferred not to look him in the eye. The silence prolonged itself, broken only by the sound of the wind in the upper branches of the trees in the square.

'You had a visitor recently,' Bracal said. 'A visitor who had no authority to be here in Bordeaux.'

Lannes again made no reply.

'I'd be grateful,' – the judge laid stress on the word – 'if you would co-operate with him. We must all do our best in these difficult times.'

'I won't pretend I don't know of whom you're speaking,' Lannes said. 'But he gave me so little information I wasn't prepared to – what did you say? – co-operate. As you say. These are difficult times and one can't be too careful. A name – Félix – which certainly isn't his own – isn't enough to win my confidence . . . '

'You are wise to be cautious, superintendent. Nevertheless . . . he belongs to Travaux Rurales. Does that mean anything to you?'

'Rural works? Nothing at all.'

'He'll be in touch with you again and your co-operation will be appreciated. That's all for now. You'll keep me posted about the results of your investigation. Robbery with violence might be the best solution, don't you think?'

*   *   *

'Bracal?' Schnyder said.

'Yes.'

The commissaire rolled a cigar round between his thumb and forefinger.

'Our friend Schussmann gave me a box of these when he returned from his leave,' he said. 'They're German. Between you and me the Boches don't make good-quality cigars. Kind of him all the same. Just to show you collaboration isn't a one-way street, he said. He's not a fool, you know. I'm pretty sure he's not even a Nazi. Bracal now, he's a dark horse in my opinion. Vichy sends him here. So they must think well of him. But I don't know how well he thinks of Vichy.'

'Ah,' Lannes said. 'I wondered. And then I wondered again.'

'Who was the chap in the Bible who walked warily in the sight of the Lord?'

'Agag, as far as I remember.'

'Agag. You're well up in the scriptures. You're not a Protestant, are you?'

'I'm nothing,' Lannes said.

'Good. Best thing to be. Keep it that way if I were you.'

*   *   *

He hadn't been open with Bracal. Whoever Félix might be, Lannes knew very well that 'Travaux Rurales' was the designation of one branch of the Secret Services; a thin disguise indeed, doubtless penetrated by the Germans. He wanted nothing to do with them. Any decent policeman distrusted the spooks, disliked them too on account of their readiness to step outside the confines of law. It was true of course he had done that himself, on occasion. There was scarcely a senior policeman who hadn't. But exceptionally, only exceptionally, not as a matter of course. The spooks had no hesitation in using the innocent, as Félix intended to use Léon; with no thought of the consequences for the boy. Lannes smacked his blackthorn against the trunk of a plane tree in his irritation.

Miriam was behind the counter of the tabac.

'Stranger,' she said.

'I can't trust myself to come here too often,' he said, and was surprised to see her blush at what he intended as levity.

'Go through to the back room. I'll close up and join you.'

She brought him coffee and a nip of marc.

'You look tired.'

'So do you.'

'We're all tired,' she said, 'tired of this war which isn't being fought and tired of the conditions of this peace which isn't peace.'

Lannes knew what he had come to say, reluctantly, because it was bound to alarm her.

'You haven't been bothered, haven't had unwelcome visitors?'

'I don't know what you mean.'

'No, of course you don't. I've had such a visitor. It makes me uneasy. Since I don't know what to do, I was going to say nothing. But . . . I think you should know. There's a German officer I have to deal with, quite a decent type as it happens, who has taken a fancy to Léon. Well, that's natural enough, he's an attractive boy and an intelligent one. But it's been remarked on. There are people who want to use Léon to compromise the German. Do you see?'

'Oh yes, I see and I understand.'

'I don't like it. It puts the boy in danger. I've spoken to him and warned him. I think you should do so too.'

*   *   *

Moncerre was in the inspectors' room, paring his nails, when Lannes returned to the office.

'Well,' he said, 'that bastard was no help, no help at all. "So my brother's dead," says he, "murdered, you say. I can be of no assistance to you. We haven't spoken to each other for a dozen years. It's news to me that he had returned to Bordeaux. Why he should have done so is no concern of mine. Good day to you." And that was it.'

'You believed him?'

'Of course I didn't. He's a twister, that's obvious. I tried to press him. "Surely you must have some information?" "None at all," says he, "his death is a matter of complete indifference to me. As far as I am concerned he'd been dead for years." I asked him if it was on account of politics that they had fallen out. "None of your business," he said, "and none of Superintendent Lannes' either."

He stinks, but I suspect he may have been telling the truth. It's clear anyway that he doesn't give a damn about his brother's murder. Frankly I don't think we are going to get anywhere, and I have to say that I don't know that it matters. That's how browned off I am.'

Lannes usually enjoyed Moncerre's spurts of irritation, but this one depressed him. It wasn't like the bull-terrier – as they called Moncerre – to relax his grip on a case, not even, it seemed, to have applied the leverage of which they had spoken. And to hear him say that it didn't matter whether they found the old professor's killer or not, that was somehow symptomatic of the mood of demoralisation which had led so many to acquiesce in the extinction of the Republic and to accept the aged Marshal as their guardian, if not indeed as their saviour. That he should have accepted the advocate's refusal to interest himself in his brother's murder, and by his own account done so without demur – well, it didn't bear thinking about.

'Let's be honest,' Moncerre said, 'we've nothing to go on. Young René's been through all the hotel fiches and there's no record of our professor. Of course, as the lad says, he may have had false papers and another name, but that doesn't help us. We're stuck.'

'Agreed,' Lannes said. 'So we must find out more about him.'

It was something he had learned early. In any but the simplest of murders, it was knowledge of the victim that turned the key.

'What of the daughter?' he said.

'Denied all knowledge of her, hadn't seen her for years.'

'Did you believe him?'

'Not particularly, but, short of twisting his arm or beating him up, what could I do? He did say she wasn't married, or he believed she wasn't, but that was all, he shut up like a clam, except that he smiled, clearly taking pleasure in denying me any information. A bastard, as you said. It was all a waste of time.'

VI

The German officer was leaving the bookshop as Alain arrived. Indeed they almost collided in the doorway. Amazingly he apologised and then stood aside to let Alain enter. It had been raining and Alain took off his coat and shook it. The lock of hair that fell over his left eye dripped water down his cheek.

'That chap again,' he said, 'did he buy anything this time?'

'Not today,' Léon said, 'though he sometimes does. He's very keen on what he calls "good French literature".'

'Only on that?'

'What do you mean?'

'Nothing really. It's just suspicious the way he's always hanging around.'

'I think he's just bored.'

'I suppose a lot of them are. There's a young officer who is billeted on a family in our building. He's quite a decent fellow really. My brother has long conversations with him on the staircase.'

'How is your brother?'

'He's all right. We don't agree, however.'

'What about?'

'Things. Politics. He believes in Vichy's claptrap, the National Revolution and all that. He says we must take this opportunity to effect a moral regeneration of France. It's all nonsense. He talks about the iniquity of the money power and Jewish capitalism.'

'I'm a Jew,' Léon said, 'remember. I don't notice myself having much money, let alone money power.'

'And yet the strange thing is that Dominique's nature is sweet, much sweeter than mine.'

'I'll make some coffee.'

From the back room he watched Alain as he waited for the water to boil in the Neapolitan coffee-pot. His friend was frowning; he thought, he's really disturbed by this quarrel with his brother, that's why he's come here today. Nobody means more to me and yet every time I see him I feel more alone. He thought of how Schussmann had run his finger along the line of his jaw, and told him again, in German, that he had beautiful eyes, and had said, "You really are such a charming boy, I do wish you would consent to have dinner with me one evening." More, surely, was implied in that choice of verb, consent. I can't have what I want and I am being pressed to have what I don't want. And then he thought of the warning the superintendent had given him and felt uneasy, even afraid. A net was closing around him.

'What's this you've been writing?'

'It's a story. Don't read it, please, not in its present state, or I'm afraid I'll never finish it.'

Don't read it at all, he thought, it's too revealing.

He brought the coffee through, lit a cigarette, and, taking it from his lips, handed it to Alain. It was as close as he dared come to intimacy. He lit another for himself, and said, 'Henri has an old duplicating machine. I found it in the store-room. It hasn't been used for years, I should think. I thought we might . . .'

'Might what?'

'Do something with it. It's the only resistance possible just now.'

VII

The old man who looked like a colonel but had been a professor of literature was playing chess with his grandson, Michel, when the maid showed Lannes into the study.

'I apologise for calling on you unannounced,' he said, 'and I'm sorry to interrupt your game. Pray continue, I'm happy to wait.'

'Not at all,' the professor said. 'One of the beauties of chess is that one can lay the board aside and resume at the same point whenever one wishes.'

The boy turned in his chair and looked at Lannes, then got to his feet and made to leave the room. Was there suspicion in his gaze? Or animosity?

Lannes said, 'There's no call to go on my account. There's nothing confidential in what I've come to ask your grandfather. By the way, is your friend Sigi – Monsieur de Grimaud – still in Bordeaux?'

The boy flushed.

'I believe not,' he said. 'He was summoned to Vichy on business and hasn't returned, as far as I know.'

He leaned over and kissed his grandfather on the cheek.

'I think I resign anyway,' he said, 'You would have had me mate in three moves, wouldn't you? And I have this meeting. So I must go anyway. It's all right, Grandpa, I won't forget the curfew and I'll be back in time for supper.'

He inclined his head to Lannes.

'Superintendent,' he said, and hurried, awkwardly, from the room.

'He's a good boy,' the professor said, 'but he worries me. These political enthusiasms. Ill-judged and therefore dangerous. And he is devoted to the man Sigi, who is, as you told me, a criminal.'

'But one with friends in high places.'

'So much the worse, I fear, in the long run.'

The old man took a cigar from the box on the table by his side, saying, 'You prefer cigarettes, as I remember.' He rolled it in his fingers, snipped the end off, and put a match to it.

'I'm grateful to you, superintendent,' he said. 'There has been no more trouble regarding my granddaughter. The warning you gave the Comte de Grimaud seems to have been effective. So I assume it's some other matter that brings you here.'

The maid came in with tea and petits-fours. Lannes waited till she had left the room, and said, 'I've a corpse on my hands. A retired professor. Of history, I believe. I hoped you might have known him and may be able to tell me something about him. At present I'm at a loss. Not many professors get murdered after all. Labiche was his name.'

'Aristide?'

'Yes. You did know him then?'

'Years ago. He gave up his chair. For journalism. To tell the truth I rather think he was happy to do so. Why should anyone kill poor Aristide? An inoffensive person.'

'A Communist, I've been told.'

'Certainly. But that's no reason to murder anyone. Or wasn't, I suppose. How was he killed, if I may ask?'

'Hit on the head, and the body left in the bushes in the public garden, not two hundred metres from here.'

'So . . . A robbery with violence perhaps?'

'Perhaps, it's an obvious explanation, but there are reasons why it doesn't satisfy me.'

The old man drew on his cigar and closed his eyes. Then he pulled the Paisley shawl more tightly around his shoulders. Lannes sipped his tea which was scented with bergamot. He felt tired and would have been content for the silence to prolong itself companionably. The rising wind threw rain against the shutters. The black-and-white fox-terrier came and settled on the old man's slippered feet. Wouldn't it be simpler, Lannes thought, to accept that explanation – robbery with violence – and be done with the case? Was it only obstinacy that prevented him from doing so?

'You'll know his brother, the advocate,' the professor said.

'Yes, he has been no help at all. Says he hasn't been on terms with his brother for a dozen years, even denies knowing the married name of Professor Labiche's daughter, which I find hard to believe.'

'There I can help you. He's lying, of course. She's quite a distinguished person, famous indeed. You will certainly know of her, superintendent, as the actress Adrienne Jauzion. I don't believe she has ever married – Jauzion was her mother's name. She excels in romantic comedy, but fails in tragedy. Hasn't the voice for Racine. A matter of breath control, perhaps. That's only my opinion, you understand. Not that this can be of any significance to you.'

VIII

'The fair Adrienne,' Moncerre said. 'That complicates things, doesn't it?'

'You think so?'

'Seeing as the Alsatian has been chasing her tail and may have caught it for all we know, I should say it does. What'll you tell him?'

'Nothing. It's not as if she's a suspect. That would be ridiculous.'

'All the same, he won't be happy. He'll think you're hassling his girlfriend, interfering in his private life . . . '

'But that's precisely what it is, private. You and I know nothing of his relations with La Jauzion. He's never spoken of them, has he? To either of us? So we know nothing.'

This was true enough, but he guessed when he called to make an appointment for later that afternoon that she would be on the telephone to Schnyder within minutes. As indeed she was, for here was Schnyder coming into his office, cigar in mouth, and perching himself on the corner of Lannes' desk. He blew out smoke.

'These German cigars really aren't up to much,' he said. 'But there are no Havanas in the shops now. It hadn't occurred to me that being condemned to smoking poor quality cigars would be one of the penalties of losing a war.'

'There are more severe ones,' Lannes said.

'True, of course, but it's the minor ones that irritate. You don't happen to have a smuggler chum who could run some over from Spain? I'm sure fat-arse Franco isn't short of them. The pleasures of neutrality.'

'Might have,' Lannes said. 'I'll ask around.'

'Kind of you. You know the ropes as I don't, me being still an outsider here . . . Any movement in your case?'

'Not much, not much at all.'

'Robbery with violence gone wrong by one of our usual customers seems the most probable, doesn't it?'

'Convenient too.

'So why not wrap it up then?'

'Just what Bracal suggested. I hope I can do so. Unfortunately there may be a political angle. Meanwhile,' he lit a cigarette; it really wasn't fair to tease Schnyder who was evidently desperate to know why he had made that appointment with La Jauzion, but was reluctant to put the question. 'Meanwhile,' he said, 'I've arranged to see the murdered man's daughter this afternoon.'

'His daughter?'

'Yes, the actress Adrienne Jauzion. I think I pointed her out to you in a restaurant once, the first day you were here, was it?'

Schnyder stubbed out his cigar.

'There's really no pleasure in these things,' he said. 'Do look out for your smuggler, there's a good chap. Adrienne Jauzion, yes, I remember, good-looking woman. Actually I've met her since, at a race-meeting. And you think she can tell you something?'

'Probably not. Just help tie up loose ends. Then perhaps we can agree on the solution everyone seems to favour.'

*   *   *

The apartment overlooking the Place de l'Ancienne Comédie was itself like a stage set, though the elderly maid who admitted Lannes was long past playing the 'soubrette'. Heavy dark-blue velvet curtains were drawn in the salon, where La Jauzion reclined on a chaise-longue in the style of a First Empire beauty. Lannes had last seen her in 'La Dame aux Caméllias' in which dated weepy she had given a performance at least as moving as Garbo's in the film version. She wore a silk Japanese jacket and loose white cotton trousers, and there was a little bunch of cattelyas pinned above her left breast. It was at least five years since Lannes had been called to investigate an attempted burglary in the apartment, but he would have sworn that nothing had changed, that the furniture and objets d'art were in the same precise places, and that the actress herself didn't look a day older.

'Your call intrigued me,' she said. 'I can't imagine that I have done anything unlawful to attract your interest . . . '

She spoke slowly with an affected stress on the word 'imagine'.

He handed her a photograph of the dead man.

'This is your father, I think.'

'But certainly it is. Poor Papa.'

'Why do you say "poor Papa"?'

She fitted a cigarette into an amber holder at least eight inches long and waited for Lannes to rise from his chair and light it for her.

'Because he has been "poor Papa" to me for thirty years, for as long almost as I remember.'

The air was heavy with the scent of flowers.

'I'm sorry to say that I have bad news for you.'

'About poor Papa?'

34

'I'm afraid so.'

'I see . . . And since you are here?'

'Since I am here, yes. Not a natural death.'

'If I was on stage,' she said, 'I would know how to weep, but as it is . . . '

'As it is?'

'You see that I have no tears. How was he killed?'

Lannes told her, sparing nothing, and she listened as if unconcerned or perhaps wondering how to play this part that had been so suddenly assigned her, one for which, he supposed, there was no rehearsal time.

'Did you know he had returned to Bordeaux?'

There was a pause – was it hesitation? – before she said, 'But certainly. He came to see me two, perhaps three weeks ago.'

'What did you talk about?'

'What should a father and daughter talk about when they haven't met for four years and then only briefly? Does that sound bitter, superintendent?'

She stubbed out her cigarette, removed the remnant from the holder with a pearl-headed pin, inserted another and again waited for Lannes to light it. She rang a little hand-bell which stood on the table beside her, and the maid entered followed by an orange Pekingese which leaped onto its mistress's lap and stretched up to lick her face.

'Bring us a bottle of wine and two glasses, Berthe.'

She stroked the dog which now settled itself.

'He wanted money.'

'And you gave him some?'

'Naturally.'

'Did he say why he needed it?'

'Because he had none. Poor Papa, he had scarcely thought of money all his life, but now he had none, so of course he had to think about it, and who else should he approach but the daughter he had abandoned and seen perhaps half-a-dozen times since she was a little girl? Again I ask you, do I sound bitter, superintendent?'

'That's no concern of mine,' Lannes said.

The maid returned with the wine and poured two glasses. It was better wine than Lannes could afford: Château St-Hilaire, given Adrienne, doubtless, by the count of that name who had been her acknowledged lover for years. The attachment was convenient; she let it be known that it was on account of St-Hilaire that she had chosen to pursue her career in Bordeaux rather than in Paris.

'And besides asking for money, what did your father have to say? Had he some other reason for remaining in Bordeaux?'

'I know nothing of that,' she said. 'What he was doing, or hoped to do, here, was no concern of mine, but I can tell you he wasn't a well man. Indeed I shouldn't have recognised him from the photograph you showed me if he hadn't made that visit. He told me he had spent a year in one of Franco's prisons, but I have no idea whether this was so. You must understand, we had nothing in common.'

'Nothing?'

'Apart from the accident of my birth.'

'And you didn't see him again after that visit?'

'No. I made it clear to him he would not be welcome. He was a Communist, you see, and these are not good times to consort with Reds.'

'And so you have no idea who might have killed him?'

'None at all. How should I have? I expect it was on account of politics.'

'Was he at ease when he came here?'

'He was never at ease. There was always some so-called injustice he was railing against. But I will add this. I think he was afraid.'

'There's one other thing,' Lannes said. 'Did he mention where he was staying in Bordeaux?'

'Some hotel, I suppose.'

'There's no record of him doing so.'

'Then I can't help you.'

'It didn't occur to you to ask him?'

'No. Why should it? You must understand, superintendent, he meant nothing to me. He used to have a mistress, I believe, but perhaps she's dead too. I knew nothing of her except that my mother said she wasn't respectable.'

* * *

36

'And that was all I could get out of her,' Lannes said to Moncerre. 'She's an actress of course, so you can't tell when she is playing a part and you know that if she chose to lie to you she would do so uncommonly well and convincingly. Still, I can't believe she knows anything and it's evident that she doesn't care either.'

'Doesn't take us anywhere. Write it off as robbery with violence? That's what they want, don't they? So everybody can be happy. It's clear nobody gives a damn who killed the poor sod.'

'I don't envy Schnyder,' Lannes said. 'She's a copper-bottomed bitch.'

'She ought to meet my wife then, they'd get along fine.'

IX

Henri wasn't drunk, not quite, just a little tipsy as he had been most times Lannes called on him since his twin Gaston's murder. They embraced. He was one of Lannes' oldest friends and the only man he greeted in this way.

'There's no Johnnie,' he said. 'There'll be no more Johnnie till the English come to liberate us. Or the Americans when they enter the war.'

'You think they will?'

'At the eleventh hour, as before. I'm drinking white wine instead.'

He poured Lannes a glass.

'Graves,' he said. 'It reminds me of Gaston. You remember that English joke he was fond of repeating: only sextons drink Graves . . . Byron. It doesn't of course make sense in French, but what does, these days? You look tired, Jean.'

Lannes took the glass and sat down.

'Not tired,' he said, 'not so much tired as empty.'

'You too?' Henri said. 'Do you know, I scarcely ever go out at all now, except to take Toto for his constitutional.' He leaned down to pat the little French bulldog which was sleeping at his feet. 'And some days I ask Léon to do that. Seeing Germans in the streets, it's too distressing, even though they're polite and well behaved. Actually that makes it worse, it's as if they despised us so deeply that they don't even feel the need to act as conquerors. Which sadly they are. But at least you have Dominique home. That must make Marguerite happy.'

'Yes,' Lannes said, and thought of the tension that was developing between Dominique and Alain, Pétainist and Gaullist, and of how Marguerite hated to hear Alain express his opinions because they frightened her.

'He speaks of becoming a priest – Dominique, I mean – after the war, he says.'

'And that displeases you?'

'It pleases Marguerite.'

'But not you?'

'It's not what I would have chosen for him, but . . . '

'But it's his life?' Henri said. 'I've often been glad Pilar and I had no children, though, do you know, I've come to think of Léon as a substitute son?'

Lannes wondered if Henri knew of Schussman's attentions, and whether he should speak of them and of the spook who called himself Félix. Instead he said: 'Did you know Aristide Labiche . . . ?'

'You use the past tense. Does that mean?'

'I'm afraid it does.'

'So you're here as a policeman, Jean?'

'I'm always here as a friend, but . . . yes, that too. He's been killed, murdered. I'm being urged to write it off as an unsolved crime, robbery with violence gone wrong. I'm reluctant to do so . . . '

He remembered how when he brought Henri news of Gaston's murder he had said murder shouldn't go unavenged, and how he had failed there, and felt ashamed again.

'Poor Aristide,' Henri said. 'Pilar thought highly of him. Their opinions were not exactly the same, for, as you know, she was an Anarchist while he was an orthodox Communist party member, but she trusted him. I thought he might be dead in Spain, like her, poor girl.'

'According to his daughter, he was in one of Franco's prisons for a year, but he had been back in Bordeaux for some weeks.'

'I wish he had come to see me,' Henri said. 'It would have been a link.'

Had there, Lannes wondered, been political reasons why he hadn't?

X

Alain was sitting at the table writing. His black cat, which Clothilde had nicknamed 'No Neck', lay beside him purring. When Lannes entered, Alain closed his notebook and looked up.

'Don't let me interrupt your work,' Lannes said.

'It's nothing, Papa, just notes for an essay.'

'Where are the others?'

'Dominique's at one of his meetings, the *Légion of the Youth of Aquitaine*, or some such nonsense. Clothilde went with him. I wish she wouldn't. And Maman's in church, praying I suppose.'

'So it's just you and me.'

'Yes.'

Lannes had always been able to talk more easily with Alain than with Dominique, but now there was some constraint between them. Curiously it was because they took the same view of the Occupation and of Vichy, and this made Lannes afraid. Anything he said on the subject might encourage Alain to do something rash. No doubt the time might come when acts of resistance were not futile as well as dangerous, but, even if this was so, he knew that he would still hope that Alain did nothing. Love makes cowards of us, he thought. How much better if the boy was to content himself with his rugby, his books and his cat. It wasn't the hour for d'Artagnan and heroics.

'Do you still see Léon?' he said.

'Yes of course, he's my best friend now. Why do you ask?'

Why couldn't he reply? Because I suspect he's in love with you, and that's dangerous. Because people want to use him and I'm afraid for him and afraid too that somehow you may get caught up in the complications of his life, and this thought makes me ashamed too. Because you are both being robbed of your youth by the stupidity of politicians and the viciousness of the men of power.

He couldn't say any of this.

'I'm glad you're friends,' he said, 'I'm sure he needs you and your support. Perhaps you need him too. But be careful. Don't get involved in anything rash.'

'You sound mysterious, Papa. But we're not fools, you know. We both realise there's nothing much to be done now. If you want my opinion, it's Dominique we should be worried about. Vichy can't last, I'm convinced of that, and when it's over there will be a reckoning with those who took its side and engaged in collaboration. So I think you ought to speak to him. And if he's involving Clothilde . . . '

'Yes,' Lannes said, and would have continued but at that moment Marguerite returned.

'I found eggs in the market,' she said. 'Alain, I want you to take three round to your grandmother. She likes an egg and I know she hasn't had any for days.'

'She'd prefer Dominique to do it,' Alain said.

'Yes, but he's not here, he's at his meeting. If you hurry you can do it and be back before the curfew. Besides, she was saying the other day that she never sees you now. So hurry along.'

'All right, all right,' he said, putting his notebook in his pocket and making a face at his father.

When he had gone, she said, 'It's good for him to do something for other people. I don't understand him these days. He used to be so eager and lively and now he seems to spend all day moping. Do you think he's jealous of Dominique? It's as if he resents his return.'

'Not jealous, no,' Lannes said. 'It's just that they have different ideas.'

*　　*　　*

Actually Alain was pleased to have an excuse to be out of the house. He calculated that if he delivered the eggs quickly and cut short his grandmother's usual litany of complaint by telling her he was only stopping off on his way to an urgent appointment, he would have time to call on Léon in the bookshop and hand over the notebook in which he had been writing what he intended to be the editorial for the first edition of their underground paper; he thought of the editorial as their manifesto. He hadn't quite lied to his father; 'nothing much to be done now' wasn't exactly the same as 'nothing to be done'. The old woman tried to detain him, but he managed to get away.

Léon read what he had written while this time it was Alain who made coffee.

'So?' he said, 'What do you think?'

'It's terrific . . . '

'Terrific, but . . . I hear a "but" coming . . . '

'Two "buts", actually. Everything you say is true, that's to say, I agree with it entirely. But, first, I think we should tone down your criticism of the Marshal.'

'All I say is that he's a vain old fool.'

'And that he has betrayed France.'

'So he has. You can't deny it.'

'I don't. Only if we are to have an effect, then we have to remember that lots of people who loathe the Occupation and don't like Vichy, nevertheless have a high regard for the Marshal and don't think of him as a traitor. So it'll get their backs up. There are some who think of him as our shield and of de Gaulle as the sword. So let's say that, while the Marshal's patriotism can't be questioned, his policy is misguided and in Vichy he is subject to evil counsels. Something like that?'

Alain pushed the lock of hair away from his eye and lit a cigarette which he passed to Léon before lighting another for himself.

'Pity,' he said, 'I enjoyed writing that, but maybe you're right. You've a better political brain than I have, Léon. What's your other "but"?'

'What you say about the anti-Jewish laws . . . '

'I thought you'd approve of that.'

'Of course I do. How couldn't I? But, again, some of those we want to stir up don't much like the Jews. It may even be the one bit of Vichy they approve of. So again, let me tone it down, just a bit.'

'Well,' Alain said, 'you're the Jew. So your word on the subject's law. How soon can you get it typed and run off on your duplicator?'

'Tomorrow, I hope. Then we've the problem of distribution . . . '

'For this first one, let's just scatter it about,' Alain said, 'and see if we get a response.'

'It's good to be doing something. At last.'

'Good and necessary. Now I must fly to beat the curfew. It's exciting, isn't it?'

'Don't forget it's also dangerous. We must be careful . . . '

They both got to their feet. Alain gave his friend a hug. Léon brushed his cheek with his lips.

'I love you,' he said aloud as the door closed behind him. 'If only I had the courage to tell you.'

*   *   *

A couple of times Léon had spent the night on a couch in the back-room of the bookshop. Henri wouldn't mind, even if he knew. He was tempted to do so this evening, to type and duplicate Alain's article, but then he thought of how on the other occasions his mother had been alarmed when he hadn't returned, afraid that something had happened to him – an accident, even an arrest; there were all sorts of things to frighten her now, especially since her nerves were weak and she never spoke as she used to of what they might do next month or next year. So he had better go home, and get there before the curfew too. He put Alain's notebook where it wouldn't be found, surely, on a shelf behind volumes of eighteenth-century sermons which nobody was ever likely to be interested in. As he locked the bookshop door, he heard singing. A lorry full of German soldiers lurched down the street. He pressed himself into the shadows and waited there till the singing died away. He was shivering, though it wasn't a cold night for the time of the year. It would have been so easy for them to scoop him up; and then what? He lit a cigarette to calm himself, and found that his hands were shaking. It was absurd.

A figure stepped out of a doorway across the street and approached him. Léon's fear sharpened but the man only asked him for a light.

'I'm late,' he said. 'But glad to have caught you.'

'What do you mean? Who are you?'

'I think we go back into the shop. Unlock the door, will you?'

Léon hesitated. The man gripped his arm hard, just above the elbow, pressing on a nerve.

'Just do as I say. That's better. Switch on a light, only one. Let's make it look as if you are working late.'

42

'I have to get home,' Léon said, 'the curfew . . . '

The man slapped his cheek hard, open-palmed.

'Sit down,' he said.

Léon obeyed and the man took the seat occupied so recently by Alain. Léon's cheek smarted and he felt tears filling his eyes.

'Who are you?' he said again.

'You don't need to know who I am. You can call me Félix, which isn't naturally my name. I don't like your sort, Léon. You're a Jewboy and a pervert who goes with older men, a little tart, aren't you, and I daresay you think of yourself as an intellectual – all this, these books – and I don't like intellectuals either. I'd quite enjoy beating you up which is what you're afraid of, so afraid that you're near pissing your pants, aren't you? But you're lucky. I need you and I need you for all the reasons that make me despise you. What do you say to that? Lost your tongue, have you?'

He leaned across the table, took hold of Léon's hair and tugged his head down so that his nose was being pushed against the wood.

'If I'd followed my instincts I'd have slammed your face down hard, but we don't want to spoil your pretty pussy-boy looks, do we now? They're your only asset, remember that. And remember this too: I could have you sent to an internment camp, Jewboy, as easily as I could bang your face down hard. Do you follow me? Answer.'

Léon said, 'I follow.'

The man who called himself Félix relaxed his grip on Léon's hair and Léon .lifted his head.

'Are you a patriot, Léon? Would you call yourself that?'

Léon nodded.

'So you are ready to serve France . . . like an obedient little Jewboy? Lieutenant Schussmann now, he fancies you, doesn't he, not knowing of course that you're a Jewboy. He doesn't know that, does he, but we both know what he does want, don't we? And you're going to oblige him, that's what you're going to do. He's no beauty, I grant you, but you'll go with him – for France, you understand. And I daresay that being the little pervert you are, you'll enjoy it.'

'I . . . I can't . . . '

'Oh yes, you can, and you will. Close your eyes and think of the internment camp, for yourself, and your mother and your Aunt Miriam. You see. There's no real choice, Léon, is there? Get up now.'

Léon obeyed. Félix came up close to him, looked him in the eyes, kissed him hard on the mouth and spat in his face.

'You're mine,' he said. 'Mine. Don't forget that. So you'll do as I say.'

He seized Léon by the hair again, swung him round and threw him over the table. He took off his scarf and tied it round Léon's face, forcing it to his mouth and gagging him.

'We don't want the old drunk upstairs to hear us, do we now?'

Holding Léon's head with one hand, he tore his trousers and pants down, gave him two stinging blows on the buttocks, and raped him.

He was only panting a little when adjusting his own trousers he said, 'That's what you wanted, isn't it, and now you'll do just whatever Lieutenant Schussmann wants too, won't you, and you'll say nothing of this to your policeman friend. Oh yes, I know all about him too. I think that's everything. I'll give you a fortnight to be in Schussmann's bed. Worse things would happen to you in that camp. And to your mother and your aunt. Just remember, Léon, I'm the only real friend you have now.'

XI

'So,' Bracal said, 'there's really no progress? It sounds to me as if the case is a dead one.'

Was there a note of satisfaction in his voice?

Lannes said, 'I'm never willing to write a case off.'

'But you know nothing of what the victim was doing back in Bordeaux, where he was living or who he was associating with. Really, superintendent, from your own account you have learned nothing, or nothing of any significance since we last talked about the matter. Isn't that so?'

He sounded not only superior but bored. Lannes remembered that the judge had described himself as 'a good Republican', which he had taken as a hint that he might not be whole-heartedly committed to Vichy. He wished he knew something of his background.

The silence prolonged itself. Bracal seemed content to wait. Was he inviting Lannes to fall in with his opinion or to raise an objection? The judge's first and second fingers beat an almost silent little tattoo on the desk. His signet ring glinted in the shaft of sunlight that had appeared to light up the room. Behind him the Marshal's portrait seemed like a summons to a duty that could not be fulfilled. Lannes lit a cigarette.

'That's not exactly so,' he said.

Bracal raised his left eyebrow. No doubt it was a well-practised display of scepticism.

Not exactly so, it seemed to say, pray enlighten me.

'There's an interesting mystery,' Lannes said. 'The dead man, Professor Labiche, had evidently been in Bordeaux for some weeks. We know this from my conversation with his daughter who is, however, the only person we have come upon who admits to having seen him, and this for only one afternoon. He wasn't registered in any hotel, and, since he didn't call either on his old mistress – and I don't think she is lying about that – why should she be? – it is reasonable to assume that he was here incognito, certainly that he didn't wish to make his presence known. He visited his daughter only because he needed money. So it seems likely that he had provided himself with false papers or had been provided with them. If so they have disappeared. They certainly weren't found on his body. So we may assume his killer removed them. Then we know that he had been in Spain, and, again according to his daughter, had spent time – a year, she said – in one of Franco's prisons.'

'He may have been lying to her,' Bracal said, 'in an attempt to win her sympathy.'

'That's possible, certainly. But in any case, you see, we have learned quite a lot about him, even if all we have learned makes it clear how little we know. And that – by which I mean, this sort of ignorance – is always interesting.'

'It doesn't alter the fact that a robbery with violence which went wrong or too far remains the most likely solution.'

'A likely solution? Undoubtedly. But the most likely? That's open to question. Given that he seems to have gone to some trouble to keep his presence here secret – not calling on old friends or associates, for example – and given what we know of his history, it is equally reasonable to suppose that there may be a political aspect to the case. Meanwhile I have my young inspector, Martin, taking his photograph round hotels, pensions and lodging-houses in the hope that someone may identify him.'

Bracal's fingers resumed their drumming, more firmly.

'I can't quarrel with that, though for various reasons I hope you are wrong. Still I admit that you are right in thinking we shouldn't yet file the case away. On another matter, has our friend from the Travaux Rurales been in touch with you again.'

'No,' Lannes aid, 'I rather hope my lack of enthusiasm has choked him off.'

'I doubt that. I very much doubt that. These fellows are persistent, you'll know. You'll keep me informed – about both matters.'

XII

Léon had spent the night in the shop. For a long time after the man who called himself Félix had left, he couldn't stop shaking. He felt filthy, dishonoured, wretched and afraid, very afraid. He washed himself thoroughly, all over, at the sink in the back room. The water was cold and he was still trembling. Nausea seized him and he vomited, retching till his mouth tasted of bile. He drank a glass of water and almost at once spewed that up too. Then he lay down on the couch. The springs were broken and there was no comfort there. He began to cry, sobbing as he hadn't since he was a small boy. There was nothing he could do. He had been found out, found guilty, and sentenced: guilty of being what he was and could not be other than.

He had been living in . . . what? A make-believe dream? Ridiculous, being who and what he was. But the shop had been a refuge, sanctuary, and Alain . . . Alain's face and the way his hair fell on the back of his neck . . . his voice, light, mocking, strong, indignant . . .

now his tears flowed unstoppably. How could he face Alain after this?

It was a few weeks since he had learned of the Institut des Questions Juives being established here in Bordeaux and had read in the newspaper what was described as its purpose: 'Our goal is to rid France, as far as possible, of the criminal influence of the Jews, and our desire is to pursue a closer collaboration between France and Germany.' He had tossed the paper aside with a casual 'bastards'. But the collaboration Félix demanded of him was of a different sort.

He lay very still, trying slowly to collect himself. Outside the city was silent. Day was far off, it was the hour of suicide. There had been blood on the towel when he wiped himself. But the physical pain would pass. It was less searing than the other pain, the contempt and hatred in everything said and done to him and this fear which had not left him, would never leave him, would be part of him for ever. And the self-disgust which had the refrain 'Why am I like this?' throbbing in his mind. He had never been ashamed of what he knew himself to be and now shame had been forced on him. He had known horror before: when he had been told of Gaston's murder, when he had learned of the mutilation inflicted on him, when he imagined, as he only too vividly had imagined, Gaston's terror as he realised that this was it, death in the form which he had perhaps always dreaded now being inflicted on him. But this was worse. He would never walk the street confidently again, would never again feel desire without the contamination of terror. This was what he had been reduced to.

There was no sleep for him, but gradually he composed himself. It was still possible to think. Of running away, going into hiding, finding his way across the border into Spain and then to England to join de Gaulle or to North Africa where there were no Germans. With Alain? Why not? They had talked of it, it had been on their minds, not as a solution but as a duty. But if he did so, if they did so ... there was the threat which would certainly be carried out, of an internment camp for his mother and aunt ...

Was what was demanded of him so dreadful?

He got up from the couch. His legs were still shaky and he

stumbled, preventing himself from falling over by reaching out his hand to the table to steady himself. He heard footsteps above, Henri getting up for a pee.

Schussmann was a decent enough chap and fond of him perhaps, besides the other thing he wanted. So . . . so? But he was being asked to betray him, to go with him to compromise him . . . Well, he was a German, a member of the Occupying army. He and Alain had agreed that when it came to it, when the day arrived, they would not hesitate to shoot a German soldier. But Schussmann with his crinkled apple face and his enthusiasm for French literature and the gentleness with which he told Léon he had beautiful eyes, that was a different matter surely. He rather liked him after all, could imagine that if they had met in peacetime, well, who knew?; and when he spoke so tenderly of his home and summer evenings on a terrace overlooking the Neckar and of how perhaps one day he and Léon might enjoy such evenings together . . .

'Are you a patriot, Léon . . . ? Would you call yourself that?'

And he had nodded agreement and not only because he was terrified. He was a patriot. He was French. He was a French patriot.

Yes, indeed, but . . . but indeed: France was rejecting him and his tribe.

Normality was returning, if normality could ever be restored to him.

He made himself a cup of coffee and drank it and did not vomit.

Alain's father, the policeman, who was kind and had taken care of him after Gaston's murder, who knew what he was and did not condemn him, had said to tell him if he was approached and asked – told? – to do what he had now been ordered to do. He would try to protect him. But he had also said there might not be much that he could do for him.

And there was nothing. Léon was sure of that. There was nothing. There would never be anything again. Why was he what he was? He had known one part of it early, but the other, his Jewishness, had been forced on him. And there was no way out. There would never be a way of escape.

But . . . suppose he was to speak to the superintendent? And if he was to warn Schussmann off? What then? Or if he told Schussmann himself what had been demanded of him? Félix would be back. He still felt the press of his lips, the first kiss he had ever received which was an expression of contempt and hatred.

XIII

Miriam said to Alain, 'I think this must be the last time.'

'What do you mean? Have you tired of me?'

'No,' she said, stroking his cheek and running her fingers along the line of his lips. 'No, it's not that . . . You're lovely and desirable, you'll be that to me for ever and I'm grateful for what you've given to me.'

'So? I don't understand. I love you, Miriam, you know that.'

'Oh you think you do, and you're grateful yourself for the experience I've given you, but . . . get dressed and I'll explain. It's too distracting lying here with your young body.'

She had determined on this before he came and on finding some adequate reason for him, but when they had both dressed and she had made coffee and they were in the room behind the tabac which had been her father's living-room, the speech she had prepared in her mind refused to form itself into words she could speak. The boy looked miserable, white-faced, like a child who is being punished for some offence that he doesn't recognise as such, and all she could say was, 'Believe me, my dear, it's for the best, for both of us.'

'I don't see how it can be,' he said. 'I don't see that at all.'

'It's the times,' she said. 'They're difficult enough as it is without . . . '

Her voice tailed away.

'All the more reason to take such pleasure as we can,' he said, and smiled for the first time, as if he sensed that she was weakening . 'I love you,' he said again.

'You love the idea of me,' she said, 'and making love to me, certainly, but oh, it's too complicated.'

What she couldn't say: certainly that first time I found you intoxicating and I was so happy that a beautiful boy like you wanted to make love to the middle-aged woman that I am. And I enjoyed it, of course I did, not only because nobody had made love to me for so long, and you restored something in me that was dying, it was wonderful, you were so young and ardent and indeed it's still wonderful, but less so each time because when you kiss me I think of your father whom I can't have, because he would feel guilty.

Well, of course she couldn't say any of that. It was all she could do to think it.

So she said, 'I'm Jewish, remember, it will make trouble for you.'

'That's nonsense,' he said. 'How could it? Nobody knows about us, and even if they did, I wouldn't care.'

'Oh yes,' she said, 'you're brave as well as sweet, but it's impossible to keep secrets in this town. And besides, it involves us both in deceit.'

'I don't understand.'

'Well, perhaps it's better that way. And in any case an affair like ours, it's better to end it while it's still fresh, before it withers and turns sour, as it would, believe me, my dear. We're not characters in a novel or a romantic drama, Alain.'

'You're tired of me. That's what it is,' he said.

'I'd end it more easily and less painfully if that was true,' she said. 'But consider. Your father's a friend of mine, he's done me more than one good turn. But now when I see him I'm embarrassed, because of us. And that's not right. Then there's Léon . . . '

'Léon?'

'What would he say if he knew about us?'

Again: there was what she couldn't say, couldn't possibly say: that Léon was in love with Alain. He hadn't of course told her this, but all she had to do was to see how his face lit up when he looked at Alain, even if Alain didn't recognise it himself.

'You're the only friend he has now, the only real friend,' she said, 'and I'm his aunt. What would he think if he knew? He needs you, my dear.'

'You're tired of me. That's what it is. I'm too young for you.'

'Well, of course you are, but, since that's one of the reasons I love you, it's not why we must break this off.'

*   *   *

50

When at last she had persuaded Alain to leave, she smoothed the front of her dress with her hands and thought, 'Well, that's done, at least it's done.' There was more that she might have said and couldn't. Shouldn't too, come to that. Truth and plain-speaking were to be avoided. If she had told him how the advocate Labiche, whom she had always found repulsive, had come to the shop and informed her, with that air of triumph, that he had been made a member of the new Institut des Questions Juives, and that her friendship with Superintendent Lannes could now avail her nothing – if she had said all that, then Alain would have been still more defiant. He was a chivalrous boy, she knew that, it was one of the things she loved in him. 'Am I expected to congratulate you?' she had asked the advocate. 'Oh I don't look for congratulations from anyone of your race,' he had smirked, 'it's a warning I am giving you.' It wasn't a warning at all of course, rather a display of power. Well, she had taken one other necessary step, and perhaps shouldn't have delayed so long in doing so. She had gone straight to Henri in his bookshop and accepted the offer he had made months ago to have the tabac and its licence transferred to his name. You may be safer as an employee, nominally that is, he had said. She didn't know if it was true. Really she couldn't believe it was. There was no promise of safety that could be kept. She was all but sure of that. If her husband, the old count, had still been alive, perhaps the title, Madame la Comtesse, might have served as some protection. And the old man had influential friends, wicked old thing that he was.

It was a fine evening. She took a chair out on to the pavement to enjoy the spring weather. In times like these, you should snatch what small innocent pleasures remain. A band was playing in the Place Gambetta and there was sadness in the music. She turned the wedding ring on her finger. Her neighbour, Madame Clouzot, brought a chair out and sat beside her.

'There are times when you can forget it all,' she said, 'but the truth is, Miriam, I can't see an end to it. It's a long time since we played together as children, but I often find myself thinking of those days now. We didn't know how lucky we were to be happy. That's what I say.'

'Have you news of Jean-Pierre?' – her son who was a prisoner-of-war somewhere in Germany.

'A postcard saying he's working on a farm. I don't know what he'll make of that, he was never the outdoor type. I'm knitting him these socks, he was always an awful boy for wearing them out.'

Her needles worked rapidly, with assurance.

XIV

When he had good news young René Martin looked like a schoolboy who had just passed his exams or kissed his first girl.

'It's a pension in the rue Xantrailles,' he said, 'a few doors as it happens along from the house where the Catalan was murdered. There's no doubt in the proprietor's mind that it was our man. He recognised him when I showed him the photograph, though at first he pretended not to. But I could tell he was lying and eventually he gave way and admitted he had had a room there, then left without warning.'

'What about his bill?' Lannes said.

'Well, that's the interesting thing. A couple of days ago someone came to settle it and collect his luggage – not that there was much of that, apparently. It's odd, don't you think?'

'You've done well,' Lannes said, and young Martin blushed, a reaction to praise he couldn't rid himself of, so that once again he seemed too young to be in the police force.

Lannes motioned to him to sit down.

'It almost certainly rules out our robbery gone wrong,' he said.

'It seems that the dead man had a Swiss passport, with another name – Braun it was – which is of course why we didn't find his name on the hotel fiche.'

'Did you get a description of the man who paid the bill?'

'Yes, I did, but it's not a very precise one. I really think, sir, you should come and speak to the proprietor yourself, Mangeot's his name. I'm sure you would get more out of him than I did.'

'Seems to me, you've got quite a lot. Enough certainly to enable us to keep the case alive.'

The Pension Bernadotte was on the corner of the street, two floors up, according to the imitation-marble plaque on the wall. There was a bar on the ground floor and, above it, the offices of a company with a Jewish name; its windows were boarded up. Lannes and young Martin went up the narrow stairs – there was no lift – and found the reception desk deserted. There was a bell on the counter and Lannes pressed down hard on it; the ringing was faint. Eventually a small man with a moustache that was as white and assertive as the Marshal's emerged from a back room, hooking one strap of his braces over his shoulder. The look he gave young Martin was heavy with resentment.

'I should have known better than to talk to you,' he said. 'That's what the wife said and for once she was right. And now you've gone and interrupted my lie-down, which I need at my age, and you've brought your boss, as I suppose this gentleman is, which is also something I could do without. I've told this young fellow all I know,' he said, turning to Lannes, 'and if he don't remember it but needs it repeated, well, that's how it is, but don't think I've more to relate because I don't.'

Lannes took a packet of Gauloises from his pocket, thumbed out a cigarette and offered it to the little man. It was accepted without a word. Lannes lit it and one for himself, then gestured across the little hallway to a sofa and chairs that stood behind a low table.

'We'll be more comfortable sitting down,' he said. 'You've a bit more to tell us, you know.'

'Nothing I haven't said to the young fellow.'

'Nevertheless, Monsieur Mangeot, we'll take a seat.'

'If you say so, if you say so . . .'

The little man dipped into a cupboard below the desk and brought out two bottles of beer. He unclipped the tops and offered one to Lannes.

'A drop of wet won't come amiss, friendly-like,' he said, coming out from behind the desk and taking one of the chairs. He sat on its edge, took a swig of beer and placed the bottle on the table and the cigarette in the corner of his mouth.

'I've never had trouble with the police,' he said. 'I run a decent establishment, which is why it disturbed me to see you, not forgetting that I'm never at my best if my kip is broken. So you'll pardon me if I seemed unfriendly. What I will say is that my fiches are always in order and delivered on time to your colleagues. They'll confirm that, I'm sure.'

'I don't doubt that they will. Now my inspector here tells me that Mr Braun was travelling on a Swiss passport . . . '

'Nothing amiss with that, is there? The Swiss are neutrals, welcome everywhere, aren't they? And it was Doktor Braun. Herr Doktor Braun.'

'So he was Swiss-German then.'

'As I supposed, though he spoke French very well.'

'Any accent?'

'Well, now, since you ask, superintendent, that's the funny thing. If I'd met him, just casually, you know, I'd have said he was a born-and-bred Bordelais.'

'Which, as it happens, he was,' Lannes said, 'and this didn't make you suspicious?'

'Why should it? None of my business. He said he was Swiss, his papers and passport said he was Swiss. Why should I question it?'

'And the passport?' Lannes said.

'What do you think? I handed it over with the rest of his stuff. No reason not to, was there? He was entitled.'

'Ah yes, your mysterious visitor.'

'Nothing mysterious about him, not to my mind. He had authorisation for collecting the stuff, showed me a lawyer's letter. So I'd no reason not to hand it over to him and no reason at all to hold on to it. I was glad enough to be rid of it, that's all. And to have the bill paid.'

'A lawyer's letter?' Lannes said. 'Can you remember the lawyer's name?'

'No, I can't and it's no use pressing me. It was no concern of mine, see.'

He picked up his beer bottle again and turned it round in his hands.

'And the man who handed it over. The description you gave my inspector was vague. I'd like you to be more precise.'

'If it was vague, it's because he made no impression on me.

54

Young chap, in a suit, fair hair, what they call nicely spoken, bit prissy in my opinion, but that's all I can tell you.'

Voices came from along the corridor. A woman calling 'au 'voir' and adding, 'any time you want, darling, I'm always up for it.'

A door closed and a young blond German soldier came into sight, buttoning his tunic. He passed them without a look or word, a touch hurriedly, and descended the stairs.

'So you keep a decent establishment, Monsieur Mangeot,' Lannes said. 'Who's the lady? A professional? Maybe the Vice Squad would be interested. What do you think, René?'

'Looks as if they might, chief.'

'Or perhaps you may remember a bit more, Monsieur Mangeot. For instance, did Doktor Braun have any visitors?'

Mangeot took a grubby handkerchief from his trouser pocket and dabbed his forehead.

'There's no need to talk of the Vice Squad, superintendent. Like I say, I keep a respectable house, and if that girl chooses to have a friend in her room, it's no concern of mine, is it? I'm not the Gestapo, am I? And as for Doktor Braun, there was nothing of that sort with him. Very quiet gentleman. Kept himself to himself. Respectable, like I said. Never thought he would cause me this sort of trouble. All the same, now you mention it, I do recall one visitor. It was a couple of days before he, well, disappeared. A Spanish gentleman, I think it was. Tall, dark fellow with a thin moustache. Very abrupt in his manner. Course, I don't know what he wanted or what they talked about. As a matter of fact they went out together, not for long, maybe just down to the bar below, for all I know, but I will say this, Doktor Braun seemed a bit disturbed after. And that's all I know or have to say.'

'Right then,' Lanes said. 'Take a statement from him, René, please. Meanwhile I'll have a word with the lady along the corridor. Which room is it?'

'If you must, you must. I should have kept my trap shut when this young fellow showed me the photograph. But that's my trouble, I've always been too obliging. The wife always tells me that, time and again. Seven, that's where you'll find her.'

She answered his knock immediately. Perhaps she thought it was her German returning, or old Mangeot come to demand his cut.

She was a pretty girl, not much older than Clothilde, with wavy brown hair, a lock of which fell over her forehead, brown eyes, a wide mouth and generous breasts which were disclosed by the negligée she was wearing.

'Police judiciaire,' Lannes said. 'Put some more clothes on.'

'That's funny. Most gentlemen tell me to take them off.'

'You surprise me,' Lannes said, handing her a dressing-gown that was folded neatly on a chair at the end of the bed. 'What do you charge your Boche?'

'Who says I charge him anything? None of your business, is it? He's a nice kid and good looking. I might even be in love with him.'

'Might you now? Bad luck for you if you are. There's a new term for it, you know. It's called "horizontal collaboration".'

'We're meant to collaborate, aren't we? That's what the Marshal says, isn't it?'

'So it is.'

'Well then . . . '

'What's your name?'

'Yvette. I've done nothing illegal. Got a fag?'

'Certainly.'

He lit one for her and another for himself. She lay back on the bed, letting the dressing-gown fall away to give him a good look at her legs.

'I'm not interested in your Boche,' he said, 'though for your own good – and safety – I would advise you to have done with him. The day will come when people will get rough with girls like you. You'll be a scapegoat for their own shame, but that won't make it easier for you.'

'Depends, don't it?' she said. 'The Boches are here and look like staying if you ask me. Besides, why shouldn't a girl have a good time? Like I say, he's a nice kid.'

'You're only a kid yourself.'

'I'm of age. I could give you a good time too.'

She lay back with her arms folded behind her head, a smile spreading and the dressing-gown falling further away.

'Forget it, Yvette. I'm not interested in what you have to offer.'

'Like that, is it? One of those, are you?'

'Don't be silly, and rude. Doktor Braun. See anything of him?'

'The old gentleman? That's funny. He was just like you.'

'What do you mean?'

'What I say. Just like you, one day when Wolfie – that's my Boche – left he rapped on my door and tried to warn me off. Just like you, like I say.'

'And then?'

'Then, not just like you, I gave him a blow-job, he really wanted it badly. "So long as you don't tell Wolfie," I said. So?'

'So then what?'

'Then, nothing much. We talked a bit. He got in the way of dropping in and we talked and I gave him what he wanted. He was a nice old thing really. I was sorry when he moved out.'

'He didn't exactly move out,' Lannes said. 'You might say he was moved out. In fact he was murdered, hit on the head with a blunt instrument.'

'Oh no,' she said. 'I don't believe you. You're kidding.'

'I'm afraid not. That's why I'm here. I'm investigating his murder.'

'Oh no,' and to his surprise she began to weep, genuine tears and sobs. He thought how strange it was: Adrienne Jauzion dry-eyed and indifferent to the news of her father's murder and this little tart in floods.

He let her have her cry out. Then she said, 'There's a bottle of wine in the cupboard. Give me a glass. Take one yourself.'

'That's better,' she said. 'It's his wine. He gave me half a dozen bottles. This is the last.'

'What did he talk about?'

'The state of the world. The war. Communism. He went on a lot. Over my head, most of it. He wanted to educate me. That's what he said, that it wasn't safe being an innocent in the world today.'

'He was right there.'

'Not so safe for him either, from what you say.'

'Oh I think he was quite an innocent in his way himself. Did he ever seem frightened?'

'Only after the Spaniard came. Then he said he was going to have to disappear. Disappear again, he said. That's why I wasn't surprised when he left. But I did think he might have come to say good-bye . . . '

'He didn't go when he meant to, of his own accord. Otherwise I daresay he wouldn't have left without a word to you. Did you see the Spaniard?'

'No, but he frightened him. I know that.'

'You've been helpful,' Lannes said. 'And remember: his advice was good. Take care.'

'That's all right, he was a nice old boy. Can't oblige you?'

Lannes shook his head.

'Another time,' she said, and smiled. 'Whenever you're needing.'

XV

'The lawyer's clerk,' Lannes said, 'Labiche's young man, do you think?'

'Seems possible,' Moncerre said. 'I never thought the bugger wasn't lying to me.'

There were more Germans than French in the Brasserie Fernand where the food was still of pre-war quality and abundance, doubtless because Fernand cultivated the chiefs of the black market. Sometimes, when Marguerite complained of the difficulty of feeding the children adequately, Lannes felt guilty because he had eaten so well at lunchtime. Today's saddle of lamb for instance – it was impossible for Marguerite to buy anything like that. It had been a triumph to find a dozen eggs the other day. Lannes had eaten very little of the pipérade she had cooked. 'The children need it more,' he had said.

'I'd like to shake the truth out of him,' Moncerre said. 'I don't care for his sort. Pity he's one of the Untouchables.'

'For the time being . . . I think, though, the clerk is a job for you, René. See if you can strike up an acquaintance with him. We'll keep this unofficial just for now.'

'And what about the Spaniard?' Moncerre said. 'The description fits our old friend Sombra. Or would that be too much of a coincidence? Mind you, it fits every second goddam Spaniard too.'

'Take his photograph to the pension and check it out,' Lannes said. 'And ask in the bar too. Things may be beginning to move.'

As they left the restaurant he remembered Schnyder's request about Havanas, and drew Fernand aside. Sure, Fernand said, with a smile. It was possible. Anything was possible if you were prepared to pay.

'It's playtime for those who step outside the law,' he said. 'Must make your life more difficult, Jean.'

The sun was shining as he limped back to the office. A spring afternoon, with women in pretty frocks for the first time that year and the candles on the chestnut trees. Before the war it would have raised his spirits and he would have been happy to stop off and sit for half an hour on the terrace of a café, enjoying the scene. But now he felt only a tightening of the knot of apprehension, as if the sweetness of the day mocked its reality. A year ago, he thought, the 'drôle de guerre' had been exploded by the German blitzkrieg, and now they were living through a 'drôle de paix'. Phoney war, phoney peace. But hadn't the inter-war years been no more than that?

There had been an anonymous letter on his desk that morning. A single sentence: 'Superintendent Lannes, don't you want to know who your real father was?' Madness: as if his poor pious mother would ever – could ever – have cuckolded his father? They had been as decent and loving a couple as you could imagine. It's vicious, intended to disturb me, he thought. Only that. In any case, how could it matter? His parents were dead. His father had been his father.

Paperwork, paperwork, paperwork: an afternoon of the utmost tedium lay before him. Perhaps that was what he needed, the re-assurance that he was only a functionary. If only he could believe that, could be content to go through the motions! But he was weighed down by responsibilities, oppressed by perplexities. And everything was going to get worse. That was his one certainty. Nevertheless he settled at his desk, reading, annotating, ticking, signing his name, going through the motions as if any of it mattered, profoundly bored, but finding that the routine of bureaucratic duty was indeed a sort of soporific.

Old Joseph interrupted him: the Alsatian would like to see him.

Schnyder was at his window gazing out on the square. His desk was clear, uncluttered by papers. Lannes had the impression, doubtless mistaken, that his chief had had nothing to do all day, and was only waiting for the hour when he could decently leave the office, perhaps even to call on La Jauzion.

'Are you still working on the Labiche case? You got nothing from the daughter, did you? So can we write it off?'

'That's what everyone seems to want,' Lannes said, 'but I can't oblige. We're making progress. Or perhaps we are.'

He brought Schnyder up to date, briefly recounting the visit to the Pension Bernadotte.

'Young René Martin's done good work,' he said.

'Well, I suppose you'd better carry on. But it's something else. I've had a visitor, not the kind I like. He was inquiring about that Chambolley case which I thought we'd agreed was dead and buried. I told him it had been your business. So he wants to see you. When I say I had a visitor, I don't mean here. He preferred to meet me out of the office, summoned me really. What does that say to you?'

'Nothing good.'

'Exactly. Anyway, if you don't mind, I've arranged for you to meet him. In an hour's time. In the public garden, he'll be on a bench by the statue of Montaigne, and he'll have a copy of his essays. They're so childish, the spooks. I hope you can get rid of him without any trouble. That's the last thing we want.'

'Very well,' Lannes said, 'I suppose I've no choice. By the way, I've put out a request for your cigars.'

'Kind of you.'

'My contact thinks he can get them. May take a week or two.'

'Good, these German ones are really no pleasure to smoke.'

* * *

The man on the bench was wearing a dark suit and an Italian straw hat. He got up to shake Lannes' hand and then motioned him to share his bench.

'I'm told you're honest,' he said.

Lannes made no reply.

'Cards on the table. My bosses would prefer that I don't give you my name, but I think they're wrong. If we're to work together . . . '

'Are we?'

'I hope so. Lionel Villepreux of the Bureau des Menées Anti-nationalistes. Does that mean anything to you?'

'The Bureau does, but . . . '

'You mean anyone might make that claim?'

Lannes lit a cigarette and waited.

'Of course they could, but for the moment you'll have to take my word for it. It can't surprise you that I don't carry identification. If I did we wouldn't be meeting here, but in your office. Last autumn you made a visit to Vichy, which is unusual and which was probably, given our circumstances, unauthorised. Not that that matters to me. You saw Edmond de Grimaud and had a long conversation with him in the Hôtel des Ambassadeurs. Subsequently he arranged for your son Dominique to be repatriated from his prisoner-of-war camp. Correct?'

'Yes. You're well informed.'

Villepreux – if this was indeed his name – took a tobacco pouch from his pocket and filled a pipe, pressing the tobacco down hard, with his thumb, lit it with a wax match and emitted a couple of puffs.

'A pipe's reassuring, isn't it? You can trust a man who smokes a pipe. That's why I prefer it. What did you give de Grimaud in return? A promise to close down the Chambolley case, wasn't it?'

'If you say so.'

'I don't care about that. The Chambolley case doesn't interest us, not directly. Beautiful these gardens, aren't they? So peaceful. You wouldn't think there was a war on. Not of course that there is, just now. Do you think that will last?'

Villepreux took off his hat and fanned his face. His fair hair was thinning. He had a Norman accent and a big mottled nose. His eyes were a very pale blue.

'Unwilling to commit yourself?' he said. 'I like that. I do indeed. It's a rash man who is ready with an opinion these days. So anyway

I don't need to know what you think, but I tell you this. Things aren't going to continue the way they are. We must prepare for a change. Vichy won't last for ever. Will it now?'

'If you say so.'

'France has lost a battle. France has not lost the war. You know whose opinion that is, don't you? The general who is currently in London. Do you think he's right?'

'You don't want my opinion,' Lannes said. 'Tell me instead what you do want.'

'Cards on the table, eh? Even if you choose to keep yours close to your chest. Fair enough, I like a careful man. Bureau des Menées Antinationalistes, that's who we are, like I say. But there's more than one interpretation of what might constitute anti-national goings-on, plots or machinations. Wouldn't you agree?'

'There's more than one interpretation of most things,' Lannes said. 'I'll grant you that. But the wind's blowing from Vichy.'

'Quite so. But winds change, don't they? That's the thing about the wind, it only blows for a certain time from the same direction. Your friend, Edmond de Grimaud now – is he your friend, by the way, or merely someone you've found useful? No, don't bother to answer. He's sitting pretty at the moment – as long as the wind doesn't shift. But, you see, if it does – I won't say "when" – there are questions that will be asked about his activities before the war as well as now. And they may not be questions he can answer with any comfort. You see what I mean? We've quite a dossier on Monsieur de Grimaud.'

'I suppose you've a dossier on many people . Even one on me doubtless.'

'Certainly on you, superintendent. I have you marked as a good Republican. Not like your friend – if he is indeed a friend – Monsieur de Grimaud. Your Chambolley case turned out to be somewhat different from what it seemed. Isn't that so? And now I'm told you have another murder on your hands.'

Lannes looked towards the bushes where the professor's body had been found. Two children, boy and girl, were playing ball with a ginger-coloured terrier which was in a state of high excitement. When it succeeded in catching the ball, the boy, who wore a sailor-suit, threw himself on the dog and persuaded it to release its trophy while it responded with mock growls which the child did not take seriously. The children's mother sat knitting on a nearby bench, and now looked up to smile at them.

'There's no connection,' Lannes said. 'Murder comes my way, from time to time. As you might suppose.'

'But if you were to discover a connection, would you feel obliged to report that to Monsieur de Grimaud?'

'It seems unlikely.'

'I'm glad to hear it.' Villepreux put another match to his pipe and said: 'Naturally you are wise to have a friend at Vichy. We all have friends at Vichy. Even the general who is now in London has friends at Vichy. But friendships can be dangerous. And you would be wise to have friends also who are – how shall I put it? – not perhaps entirely of Vichy. You follow?'

'I understand what you're saying.'

The little dog had seized the ball again and this time disappeared with it into the bushes, followed by the boy calling out its name.

'Cards on the table,' Villepreux said again. 'I'll be frank with you. Before the war Monsieur de Grimaud paid several visits to Berlin. He was friendly with Admiral Canaris of the Abwehr. You know what that is, of course – Military Intelligence. Well, that's the sort of thing that interests me, do you see? Canaris is an interesting case himself – a German patriot who doesn't, we believe, love the Nazis as they think they should be loved. All the same, when a French politician who is also the proprietor and editor of an influential review has relations with a man like Canaris, questions are bound to be asked by people like me.'

'People like you,' Lannes said, 'but I don't see that this is any concern of mine. I'm a cop, not a spook.'

'But a patriot?'

'Whatever that means today. Like you I'm a servant of the Republic.'

'Quite so,' Villepreux said, 'even if we are no longer supposed to speak of the Republic but only of the French State. And Edmond de Grimaud is a pillar of that State who has close German friends. I need more for my dossier, superintendent, and I trust you to help me. Who knows? If you do so you might solve both your cases. I'll be in touch. Now, if you'll excuse me, I think my sister is ready to take the children home. And that tiresome little dog.'

So that's your cover, your excuse for being here in Bordeaux, Lannes thought, damn you. He watched Villepreux approach the woman he said was his sister. The little boy ran up to him and clasped his hands round his knees. Villepreux swung him up and round and on to his shoulders and the boy crowed with pleasure. The family party moved slowly away. The little dog now trotted at his mistress's heels accepting that playtime was over. Lannes watched them drift out of sight. Out of sight wouldn't be out of mind, unfortunately. Should he pass on a report of this conversation to Edmond? Was that part of the agreement he had reluctantly made with him, inasmuch as there was any agreement? No reason to do so. Besides, if the Bureau was interested in Edmond's activities before the war, there wouldn't be much he could do about that. Except cover up; you could always try to cover things up. It was the one thing at which the political class really excelled.

He would go home, perhaps stopping for a drink on the way. A glass of beer on an early summer afternoon. But home too was uninviting. It was a long time since he had been able to shelve his guilt opening the apartment door.

Crossing the Place de l'Ancienne Comédie, he saw Clothilde. She was sitting at a café table with the young German lieutenant billeted on their neighbours. For an instant they caught each other's eye, then, simultaneously, both looked away in denial.

XVI

Léon slipped the duplicated sheets into his satchel and called up the stairs to Henri to say that he was closing the shop and going home. He checked both ways to make sure the street was empty before locking the door. It was a week since his humiliation, and in that time Schussmann had not visited the shop and there had been no sign of the man who called himself Félix. Perhaps Schussmann had been transferred from Bordeaux, and he would be safe. But he couldn't persuade himself that this was so. Fear had laid a frost-chilled hand on him. Two or three times he had resolved to speak to Alain's father, but his nerve failed. If he had come to the shop, even if to call on Henri, he might have dared to blurt it out. Not all of it, certainly; he would never surely be able to speak of the worst, of the shame.

The terrace of the Café Régent in the Place Gambetta was crowded. Two tables were occupied by German officers drinking beer. The prosperous Bordelais acted as if their presence was normal, as if they had accommodated themselves comfortably to the presence of the Occupiers. Léon entered the café and was relieved to find Alain already there, alone at a table at the back of the room. He was reading a book. So Léon was able to watch him for a moment unobserved. He wasn't sure he could trust his voice. If Alain knew what he must never know, would he despise him or be indignant on his behalf? Either would be intolerable. Either would reduce him to tears. He swallowed twice and approached the table. Alain looked up and smiled.

'I couldn't sit outside,' he said, 'watching the Boches drink beer as if they were in Bavaria. Are you all right? You don't look all right.'

Léon sat down.

'Seeing them made me nervous,' he said. 'That's all.'

Alain closed his book. 'Kafka,' he said. 'Appropriate, don't you think? "Someone must have been telling lies about Joseph K because without having done anything wrong he was arrested one morning." That's the first sentence, you know. It's the way things are now, isn't it? You've brought the stuff?'

'Yes.'

'Give me one. I'll leave it in the toilet. I brought some drawing-pins.'

When he returned, he said, 'That's a start. It looks good. But we shouldn't hang around.'

When they came out into the square, Alain said, 'I'd have liked to watch people going in and out and see the expression on their faces, but . . .'

'But it's a luxury we have to deny ourselves.'

'Exactly. Come, we're going to meet a couple of mates from school who've agreed to help.'

'Is that wise?'

'We can't do it all ourselves and they're good mates. Of course they know nothing about the production side. It's better they don't. We're meeting them at the railway station. It's a place where nobody knows us, where it's natural to meet by chance.'

The two boys were waiting at the station entrance as if on the lookout for girls. Alain clapped one on the back and said, 'This way.' He led them through side-streets and down to the quai, without saying anything. The quai was deserted. Alain heaved himself up on to the parapet and sat there swinging his legs.

'Good,' he said, 'introductions. This is Athos,' he said, indicating Léon. 'And this is Porthos and this is Aramis.'

'And you're d'Artagnan, I suppose,' said the large solid youth he had called Porthos.

'What's the point of this?' Aramis said. He was a slim fair-haired boy with a sulky mouth. 'We know each other.'

'You don't know Athos,' Alain said, 'and you don't need to know him as anything but Athos. He's the brains of our network.'

'Network?' Porthos said.

'That's what it's going to be. When you find a new recruit, you give him a false name. That way, if we are taken, we don't know his real name and he doesn't know ours and so neither can give the other away.'

'But we know each other by our real names,' Aramis said.

66

'That's unavoidable. We have to start this way, but from now on, we know each other only as the musketeers, and I'm our only link in common.'

Léon gave them each a leaflet to read. They expressed approval; 'This is incendiary,' Aramis said. Léon blushed with pleasure and handed each a sheaf.

Alain said, 'Never put them up where you can be seen. Always post them where they will be seen. This is just a start. We have to encourage people to see that things don't have to be the way they are. All right?'

'All right.'

'And remember this isn't a game. It's dangerous. We're still in the war, or rather we're renewing it. We'll meet tomorrow to see how it's gone. The municipal swimming-pool would be a good place. Four o'clock?'

As they were about to part, Aramis turned to Léon.

'I've seen you before, Athos, but I don't remember where.'

'It's better that way,' Léon said.

When the others had left, he said,

'I'm going to make a drawing of the Cross of Lorraine and duplicate it. Then we can just scatter it around to show that de Gaulle has supporters here in Bordeaux.'

'Great idea.'

'Tell me about Aramis. He thinks he knows me from somewhere, but I don't recognise him.'

'Doesn't matter, but, as you said, keep it that way. Now let's start our own distribution. It feels good to be doing something, doesn't it?'

'Yes,' Léon said, 'as long as all four of us remember to be careful.'

'Are you afraid, Léon?'

Léon lifted his gaze to look his friend in the eye.

'Yes,' he said. 'I admit I am.'

'Good,' Alain said. 'So am I. Fear makes you cautious, which is what we have to be.'

XVII

Lannes remembered how most mornings when he was a boy his mother had had to call him several times to get up and ready for school. Occasionally she had stripped the bedclothes off and even given him a smack on his thigh to wake him up properly. Now, sleep deserted him long before the early summer dawn and he slipped out of bed quietly so as not to wake Marguerite. He put on a dressing-gown. In the kitchen he filled the coffee-pot and set it on the stove. His clothes were over the back of a chair; he had taken to undressing there in order not to disturb his wife. It was a long time since they had made love. Perhaps they would never do so again. There must be many marriages like theirs in France now where nothing was said because what might be said was painful or frightening. Their last time of real intimacy had been in the weeks when he was recovering after being discharged from hospital following the shooting outside the Hôtel Splendide. Even Dominique's return had only brought them together again for a few days. Perhaps if he had explained his role in securing it, things might have been different, but he could not claim credit for the shameful deal he had made with Edmond de Grimaud. And now he was perplexed by his conversation with the spook which meant he must choose one betrayal or another.

The coffee was sour. In the years of peace he had learned to prefer coffee without sugar, but this ersatz stuff, more chicory than coffee and God knows what else, needed sweetening, even though the sugar ration was small. Another compromise; he restricted himself to the shallowest of spoonfuls, and lit his first cigarette of the day. He opened the window and leaned out to savour the cool clear air of early morning, and to watch the swallows, martins and swifts swooping and diving like demented acrobats. He surprised himself in a moment of happiness. Usually he shaved in the kitchen, in cold water. Today he would stop at the barber's on his way to the office. He dressed and drank another cup of the vile coffee which this time he improved with a slug of marc.

Clothilde came in, barefoot and in a dressing-gown, and kissed the top of his head. She took a glass of milk from the press and settled herself at the table cupping her chin in her hands.

'You saw us, Papa, didn't you?'

He thought how much he loved her, how much he was afraid for her, and didn't pretend not to understand.

'He's very nice,' she said, 'he's sweet actually. Dominique likes him too. You disapprove, don't you?'

'Nothing good can come of it, nothing but unhappiness I'm afraid.'

'You'd like him, I'm sure, and, though he's a German, he's shy and polite. Besides, this war – well there's no war, is there? Nobody's fighting, not here in France, or anywhere much as far as I can see. Manu is in the army just as Dominique was, not through his own choice. He doesn't even like Hitler much. When I ask him about him, he just makes a face. Rather a funny face. Maman wants to ask him to dinner, or lunch on Sunday. When you meet Manu I'm sure you'll like him, really sure.'

'Clothilde darling,' he said, 'things won't stay the way they are and then what?'

Then what indeed, he thought, as the barber stropped his razor, He wondered if Schnyder would ask him about his meeting with the spook. But of course he wouldn't. The Alsatian was cagey, no cards on the table for him. Lannes remembered that he had been born a subject of the Kaiser's Reich. He might not like the Nazis and the Occupation. Lannes was pretty sure he didn't. He might not care for Vichy and have no enthusiasm for either collaboration or the new European Order of which they spoke. Again Lannes was confident this was so. But Schnyder was going to avoid engagement either way. The fence might be uncomfortable, but that was where he had prudently settled his buttocks. Lannes didn't blame him. Was his own position any different, any braver or more honourable? He got a photograph of the Spaniard, Sombra, from his desk, called Moncerre in and told him to take it to the Pension Bernadotte and to the bar below, and see if he could be identified as the man who had called on Professor Labiche.

'Sure,' Moncerre said, 'but he's not the killer. The garotte's his method, remember. The blunt instrument's a bit too crude for chummy.'

'You're probably right, but it would be nice to make the connection.'

There was another pile of paperwork to be dealt with, passed on by Schnyder with a note which almost contained an apology. If Moncerre did get the answer he hoped for, he would himself call on old Marthe, the housekeeper in the rue d'Aviau, and see if Sigi was indeed back in Bordeaux. He was sure that anything Sombra did was authorised by him – and that led the trail back to Edmond in Vichy. He wondered if he should have said something about this case to the spook.

* * *

The young man who emerged from Labiche's office fitted the description Mangeot had given, vague though that had been. René Martin hesitated for a moment, unsure whether it would be wise to accost him in the street. However, the clerk turned in the opposite direction, stopping at a kiosk to buy a newspaper, doubtless to read over his lunch. Martin followed him at a distance till he saw him turn into a brasserie in the Cours du Chapeau Rouge. He quickened his pace and was relieved to see that his quarry had taken a seat at a table for two against the wall in the back of the room. Without an apology he settled himself opposite the clerk who was evidently a regular customer, for the waiter greeted him with a handshake.

'The usual?' the waiter said. The clerk nodded, and Martin said, 'Bring me the same.'

Martin showed him his identification and said, 'We can talk here, which will be more convenient for you, or you can accompany me to the station.'

'I can't think that we have anything to talk about.'

The words were bold, but there was uncertainty in the tone of voice and he did not look Martin in the face.

'Doktor Braun and the Pension Bernadotte,' René Martin said. 'What's your name, by the way?'

'Jacques Bernard. I see no reason not to tell you that, since I have done nothing which can interest the police, but I have to say that these names you mention mean nothing to me.'

'Oh, if that's so, we had better continue this conversation at the station, with my boss, when we've eaten our lunch. He will certainly want to see you. He is interested in your boss after all, Monsieur Labiche. You won't deny you're his clerk. On the other hand, if you're sensible, we can deal with this matter over our meal and I hope that can be the end of it as far as you're concerned. It's up to you. Ah here's our soup.'

He smiled at the young man who was a bit younger than himself, a mere child, René Martin thought, and who hadn't even started to shave, probably because he was fair-haired and his skin was very pale. He had long fingers and when he lifted his spoon to his mouth was so nervous that he spilled some of the soup. René Martin picked up the carafe the waiter had placed on the table and poured them each a glass of wine.

'Doktor Braun,' he said again, 'Pension Bernadotte. You collected his things, didn't you?'

'That's not an offence.'

'Of course it isn't, that is, if you didn't know that Doktor Braun had been murdered.'

The clerk's hand trembled. He stretched it out to pick up his glass, then drew it back.

'Murdered?' he said, and wiped his mouth with his napkin. 'I know nothing of that.'

'So you say, so you say, but your master now . . . '

'Said nothing of that to me. I swear it. Doktor Braun was a client who had left instructions for his things to be collected and his bill to be paid. I did as I was told. I know nothing of any murder, you must believe me.'

Moncerre would have seized happily on the clerk's evident nervousness. René Martin felt ashamed. He thought, what a horrible trade mine is.

'Drink your wine,' he said. 'Doktor Braun was no client, but your master's brother. He left no instructions for him, but someone bashed his head in. Your master knew that, even if you didn't. What can you tell me about this man?'

71

He passed the photograph of Sombra across the table. Bernard looked at it, and pushed it back.

'Your face tells me you recognise him,' Martin said.

Bernard kept his head lowered, unwilling to look Martin in the face, and crumbled a piece of bread.

'You called me a clerk,' he said, 'which makes me sound more important than I am. I've no responsibility, I'm just the office-boy used to fetch and carry messages, that's all. And I've only been in the job a few months, since I left school because my father's a prisoner-of-war in Germany and it's necessary for me to earn a wage. So I had to leave school. If my boss, Monsieur Labiche, finds out I've been speaking to you, I'll get the sack, That's sure as eggs is eggs. He's a holy terror.'

René Martin put his finger on the photograph.

'Come on,' he said, 'I don't want to make trouble for you. We know quite a bit about the advocate Labiche and we don't like him. We're not going to be sharing confidences with him, I can assure you of that. So, this chap now . . . '

The boy still hesitated.

René Martin smiled and said, 'Look, I understand how you feel, but if I have to ask you to accompany me to the station, then you can be sure that your boss will learn of it. On the other hand at present it's just between you and me, and need go no further.'

'I suppose I have to trust you. I don't know his name, but he came to the office once, that was a couple of weeks before I was asked to fetch Doktor Braun's things, and that's all I know. I never spoke to him or heard him speak.'

'Good,' Martin said, 'that's all I need to know. Now, enjoy your lunch . . . '

'All the same,' he said to Lannes, when he reported the conversation, 'there's something that doesn't ring true. Because if he took this job as an office-boy because his mother needs him to earn a wage, which certainly won't come to much, I don't understand how he can eat lunch regularly in that brasserie which equally certainly isn't particularly cheap.'

'No doubt you're right, but it's no concern of ours. Moncerre says the barman has identified our friend Sombra as the man who had a drink with Aristide. So the connection's established. I think we are almost ready to have a word with our precious advocate. We'll call him in tomorrow. There's someone else I want to speak to first.'

*   *   *

Lannes' hip ached as he limped, leaning heavily on his stick, towards the rue d'Aviau. He was oppressed by a sense of futility. Moncerre was surely right in refusing to believe that Sombra had killed Aristide Labiche; murderers stuck to their favoured and practised method. But his involvement in the case not only brought back sour memories of Gaston's murder and his own failure; it meant that he was morally bound to pursue a case which he couldn't now believe he would be permitted to bring to court. If Sombra had had dealings with Aristide and with his repulsive brother, then so had Sigi, and so, at one remove, had Edmond de Grimaud; and therefore he himself was compromised. None of it made sense. If Edmond was involved, even at one remove, with the advocate Labiche, why had he stepped in to protect Lannes against him?

He stopped at a bar for an Armagnac. And Clothilde and her German officer – what had she called him? Manu? Short for Manuel, he supposed. If he was a proper father, he would force her to break that friendship for her own good. But he was weak, he couldn't bring himself to hurt her, even to save her from future pain. As always he would take the path of least resistance, in the hope that things would turn out all right. Which they wouldn't.

Old Marthe greeted him as sourly as ever, but led him into the gloomy cavern of her kitchen.

'I suppose it's me, not the Count you want to speak with, seeing as you've come to the back door. Not that you would get any sense out of him, he's back at the brandy, sip, sip, sip, morning and night and making no sense.'

'Do you still have Germans in the house?'

'That we have, though I've naught to do with them. I've made that clear. Not like Madame, she's all over them, silly woman.'

'And Sigi?' Lannes said.

'God knows where, or rather the Devil. I take no notice of him since he killed his own father, which you failed to prove.'

'And the Spaniard?'

'That long streak of nothing! He's in and out, why I don't know. Madame is thick as thieves with him.'

Lannes showed her the photograph of Aristide Labiche.

'What about him?'

Marthe took it over to the window and shut one eye to examine it. She nodded her head twice, laid the photograph on the table went to the cupboard and brought out a bottle of marc, less than a quarter full, and two little glasses. She passed one to Lannes and settled herself in her chair holding her glass in both hands

'He used to come here,' she said. 'The old count liked him, or came as near to liking him as the old devil liked anyone. They would talk for hours, don't ask me about what, because I don't know or care.'

She had been the Count's mistress for years, through his several marriages, and even in his feeble old age he would have his hand up her skirts. Her voice softened as she spoke of him, then resumed its habitual harsh brusque tone as she said,

'Since you're here with this picture I suppose something's happened to him. He's dead too, is he? Well, I know nothing about that. He was a gentleman, however, I can tell you that.'

'Yes,' Lannes said, 'not only dead, but murdered. You may have heard of a body being found in the public garden. That was his. It's the Spaniard I'm interested in. He was seen with the dead man.'

'I know nothing about that,' she said again. 'But there's wickedness in this house, always has been, always will be. That's why that poor sot sitting in his father's chair drinks himself into a stupor, day after day, to drown the wickedness.'

Lannes had no reply to that. The old woman got up, took a lump of dough from a bowl and put it on a board, sprinkled flour on it and began to roll it out. She sniffed, twice. Then she wiped her hand on her apron and drank her marc.

Lannes said, 'The Count knows the dead man's brother. He's his client, perhaps his friend. They're two of a kind.'

'That's nothing to me,' she said. 'Nothing's anything to me, since the old devil died. I never thought I'd say this to anyone. Now go away.'

Léon was the first of the musketeers to arrive at the swimming-pool. He felt nervous, on edge. Lieutenant Schussmann had called at the shop for the first time in ten days, and had again pressed him to accept his invitation to have dinner. 'It would please me so much, Léon,' he had said. 'I seek refreshment. So much of my work here is boring. Of course, I understand that you may resent our presence here. When I was your age I would have hated to see a French Army of Occupation in Würrtemberg. But such things are accidents of politics and history. They are no reason why you and I should not be friends. It would give me such great pleasure.'

And for the first time Léon hadn't said 'no'. He hadn't accepted the invitation either, but he hadn't dared to refuse. It wasn't possible of course that the man who called himself Félix could know that Schussmann had renewed his request. But he might know he had visited the shop – he might have someone tailing Schussmann – anything was possible. At the thought of Félix Léon felt as if he was at a door that would open on a house of desolation . . . And what would Alain and the other musketeers think if they learned that he was being solicited by a German officer? They would condemn him as a spy. Certainly they would never trust him again.

He began to strip and thought how Gaston had liked to unbutton his shirt and run his hands over his body, murmuring lines of verse, sometimes Rimbaud, but more often English poets. Would Schussmann do that too? He had just put on his bathing-trunks when Aramis came into the changing-room.

'Are we the first?' he said.

'I don't know. The others may be already by the pool. I'll wait for you.'

Aramis chattered as he changed, then said, as if shyly, his eyes averted from Léon, 'I thought what you wrote was brilliant.'

'It was mostly Alain's work.'

'I'm sure it wasn't all his, that you had a hand in it. Anyway, you mean, d'Artagnan's.'

They both found themselves giggling. Aramis put his arm round Léon's shoulder.

'I'm sure we're going to be great friends,' he said. 'But I wish I could remember where it was I saw you before.'

'In the bank perhaps,' Léon said. 'I used to be a counter-clerk.'

'Not possible. I've never been in a bank in my life.'

Again they both laughed and with Aramis' arm still round his shoulder went through to the pool.

Aramis said, 'Well, we are the first. Do you want to swim? It looks more natural if we do.'

Léon blushed, 'I can't actually. I've never learned.'

'I'll teach you. It's not difficult. Really, it'll be a pleasure. Some day you may have to swim for your life and think how embarrassing it will be if you can't. Come on.'

They entered the pool at the shallow end where the water came just up to their waist. It was colder than Léon expected. Aramis put his arm on Léon's middle and told him to kick his legs up. Then he cupped his other hand under Léon's chin and said, 'Now arms and legs like a frog.' To his surprise Léon found himself buoyant. He made a few strokes and with Aramis supporting him, felt the tension leaving him and was almost swimming. Then he looked up and saw Alain standing on the poolside. Alain dived in, swam a couple of lengths and stopped beside them.

'All right?'

They clambered out. Porthos was standing watching them. He was still fully dressed.

'I hate swimming,' he said, 'except in the sea. Before the war we always went to Biarritz for the holidays every summer. I suppose that's off this year too.'

He talked for some time about Biarritz and what a bore it was that they had been confined to the city last year, and how it looked like being no better this one.

'So that's how it is,' Aramis said. 'We're accustomed to going to the Côte d'Azur, to Nice where my grandparents live. Now we can't even cross the demarcation line to the Unoccupied Zone. What about you, Athos?'

Alain intervened, sparing Léon the embarrassment of admitting that he had never gone away on holiday because his father was dead and his mother couldn't afford it.

'This is not what we're here to talk about,' he said, and led them to the little gallery above the pool. They spread towels and lay down.

'So . . . ' Alain said, 'how did we do?'

All the posters had been distributed.

Aramis said, 'I've got a confession though. I was pinning one to a tree in the public garden and thought I was alone till an old lady who had been asleep on a bench came up and stood by my shoulder. I don't mind admitting I was scared stiff in case she called a police-man – not that there was one about but I wasn't thinking straight – until she clapped me on the back and said, "Bravo, young man, but you really must be more careful. Vive la France all the same!"'

Alain told them about Léon's plan to scatter copies of the Cross of Lorraine around the city.

'I like that,' Aramis said, 'that's brilliant.'

Porthos said, 'My father says de Gaulle's a madman, crazy, vain and conceited. He was in a prison camp with him in the last war, and says he wouldn't trust him an inch.'

'Well, my father thinks the Marshal the saviour of France,' Aramis said. 'We just have to accept that we can't trust our fathers' generation. After all, it's they who have got us into this mess.'

'De Gaulle may be a madman,' Alain said, 'but perhaps a madman is what France needs just now.'

'Absolutely,' Aramis said, 'Joan of Arc was probably crazy and think what she achieved.'

'And Hitler's a certifiable lunatic,' Léon said, 'who hasn't done badly, I'm sorry to say.'

Two men approached.

'Yes, that's him,' one of them said.

Léon looked up and recognised Monsieur Dupuy who had been an assistant manager at the bank.

'You're sure?' the other, who was wearing white drill trousers and a white shirt, said.

'No doubt at all.'

The man in white stepped forward, seized Léon by the arm and hauled him to his feet.

'Out,' he said, 'and don't try this on again. Out.' He shook Léon, and said, 'Just think yourself lucky I don't give you a boot up the arse.'

'What the hell is all this about?' Alain leaped to his feet. 'Leave my friend alone. Who do you think you are anyway?'

'I'm the pool supervisor and Jews are not welcome here, not only not welcome, but prohibited.'

Aramis said, 'Surely you're speaking the wrong language, my dear man? Don't you mean "Juden sind verboten"?'

The supervisor swung his arm and caught Aramis on the mouth as he got to his feet. Blood spurted from his lower lip.

'I give you two minutes to be off, all four of you, or I call the police.'

'Do that,' Alain said, 'and I'll give you in charge for assaulting my friend.'

'Like I say,' M. Dupuy addressed the crowd that was gathering around, 'it's always the same, wherever they go, Jews cause trouble. Jews and Jew-lovers. Lice, that's what they are, lice and sexual perverts, take my word for it. Well, their time's up, here in France, just as it is in Germany. You can't deny that Hitler knows the way to deal with them.'

'Do you know what you are?' Alain said, 'You're a fucking Fascist, and what's worse, I expect you're proud of it.'

Porthos laid his hand on Alain's arm.

'Come on,' he said, 'don't make things worse. It's all right,' he said to the supervisor, 'we're going.'

'And don't come back, any of you.'

Outside Léon struggled to hold back tears of anger and shame. When Porthos said, 'Are you really a Jew, Athos?' all he could do was nod.

'And if he is,' Alain said, 'does it matter to you?'

'Never said it did, did I? I just like to know what's what.'

'Bastards,' Alain said. 'Now you know what we're fighting against.'

'I thought we were fighting against the Germans,' Porthos said.

'There's no difference,' Alain said, 'between the Germans and French Fascists.'

'I'm not very bright,' Porthos said, 'as you've often made clear to me, old chap, but as I see it, there is a difference. The Boches are a foreign army of Occupation and our enemies. French Fascists are whether you like it or not French. And there seem to be quite a few of them.'

Léon said, 'I'm sorry if I have embarrassed you.'

His voice was unsteady and he felt ashamed again, to be apologising, or seem to be apologising, for what he was.

'Not at all, old chap. Just like to know where I stand. Hadn't occurred to me that you were a Jew. That's all.'

'And does it matter to you, now that you know?'

'Not a lot. I don't think so. You seem all right and Alain here vouches for you. That's good enough for me. It's just that I don't know any Jews, except a few rich ones whom I don't much care for. That's all.'

'Aramis,' Léon said, 'your poor mouth. It's still bleeding. Here, take my handkerchief.'

Aramis took it and dabbed his mouth.

'If I've got a scar,' he said, 'I'll wear it as a badge of honour.'

XIX

Lannes had tried to persuade Schnyder to send a summons to the advocate Labiche.

'He'll find some excuse to ignore it, or will simply ignore it without any excuse if it comes from me,' he said.

'Have you cleared it with Bracal?'

'I don't think that's necessary.'

'I don't know,' Schnyder said. 'Labiche is a man of some influence. Hasn't he been appointed to that body – I forget its name – set up to handle what they call the Jewish Question. I know it's absurd, and I don't like it myself, any more than you do. But if we are to retain our independence we have to walk warily – what did you say that king's name was?'

'Agag.'

'That's right, Agag. After all it's not as if you suspect Labiche of any crime, do you?'

'He's withholding evidence, I'm sure of that.'

'Clear it with Bracal then, and I'll sign the letter.'

It was all Lannes could do not to slam the door behind him. He talks of retaining our independence, he thought, but as far as he's concerned it's independence to do nothing.

Nevertheless he sent a note through to Bracal and Joseph soon returned to say the judge would be happy to see him straightaway.

Bracal filed his nails as Lannes explained his reasons for wanting to question Labiche.

'Why don't you just call on him?' he said.

'One of my inspectors – Moncerre – a very good man – has already done that, and was given the brush-off. We've learned more about the case since, as I have just told you, and I think we are more likely to get answers if he realises I am not acting on my own, not merely conducting what we call a fishing exercise.'

'Very well. I'll take the responsibility of signing the letter myself. Labiche is well thought of in Vichy, I believe. That's no reason why we shouldn't disturb his comfort of course. Between you and me, superintendent, and please don't repeat this, from what I've heard of the advocate, I'll be quite happy if you do just that.'

So, Lannes thought, I was right, you're not much in love with Vichy.

Bracal smiled. Then, as if he had read Lannes' thoughts, or more probably because he realised that he had spoken rashly, he said, 'As I'm sure you know, superintendent, Vichy is not a monolith. There are different opinions as to what constitutes patriotism, even there.'

The sun was shining and there were only a few fleecy little clouds in the deep blue of the sky as Lannes left the office. He felt almost happy. Even his hip wasn't hurting. In the Rugby Bar his friend, the journalist Jacques Maso, was drinking pastis.

'For me,' he said, 'it's a sign that summer has arrived. Swallows mean spring, pastis summer. They say Vichy is going to prohibit its manufacture, but, for now at least, there's a good supply here in the Occupied Zone. Something to thank the Boches for? I don't think! Same for you, Jean?'

'Why not?'

'You have something for me?'

'If I had,' Lannes said, 'it would almost certainly be something you couldn't use.'

'We can still write about crime, providing . . . '

'Providing there are no political angles?'

'Precisely, and, since there are so often such angles, we can't write anything. That's life.'

'As we have to live it now,' Lannes said. 'Take me. I'm presented with a case that looks like a straightforward pre-war murder.'

'The corpse in the public garden?'

'How did you guess? Jacques, you still have friends in the Communist Party?'

'Friends, no. Contacts, yes. You want me to ask around about your professor?'

'I want to know if he was considered a reliable party member.'

'That might be possible.'

'Meanwhile, here's something for you. His brother, the advocate, sent his office-boy to collect the professor's goods and papers, though he told one of my inspectors he didn't know the professor had returned to Bordeaux. Does that interest you?'

'No end,' Jacques said, 'but I can't write about the advocate, can't even hint that he might know something about his brother's murder.'

'I suppose you can't, but you may like to know that I've summoned him for examination tomorrow.

Jacques lit a cigarette and asked the barman for two more pastis.

'Be careful, Jean,' he said, 'that bastard's close to the Power.'

'Quite so, but would it also interest you to know that someone in Vichy gave me ammunition to use against him?'

He didn't like lying to his friend, even if the lie was only an exaggeration. Edmond de Grimaud had certainly brought the advocate to heel the previous autumn, but he hadn't supplied Lannes with the weapon he used.

'Oh,' Jacques said, 'so you know about the photographs.'

'I know they exist. But I haven't actually seen one.'

'Well, as it happens,' Jacques said, 'I can help you there – so long, old man, as you realise I have had nothing to do with it. They arrived one day in our office, eighteen months ago, before the war anyway. Sent anonymously. We couldn't use them of course and anyway the editor . . . Well, you know what his politics are – so he ordered them to be destroyed. But I managed to get hold of a couple and hid them away, for future use, if things turn out the way I hope they will. I'm happy to let you have them, that bastard needs to be stitched up. So I'll have an envelope left for you at the bar here. It'll be marked "To be collected on behalf of the emperor". How'll that do? Don't pick it up yourself. Send a minion. And enjoy what you find – even though it'll disgust you. How's Marguerite? She'll be happy now, won't she, that you've got your boy home. Stroke of luck. Well, you deserve a bit of that, Jean.'

'She's as well as can be, given the times we live in. You should come to see us, Jacques. She'd like that. She remembers the dancing.'

'Long time ago,' Jacques said. 'My dancing days are over.'

*   *   *

You might have thought the old tailor hadn't moved from his cross-legged pose on the work-table since Lannes' previous visit. Little eyes peered smokily through his pince-nez spectacles. The needle moved in and out as though by its own mechanical accord. He sniffed loudly and emitted a throaty cough. He offered no greeting, waited – it seemed politely or perhaps without interest – for Lannes to speak.

Instead Lannes settled himself in the rocking-chair that stood by an empty grate, and waited in his turn. The silence prolonged itself and it felt almost companionable to him. At last Lannes said, 'Of course he came to see you, didn't he?'

The tailor drew out his thread and nipped it with his teeth.

'And if he did?'

'He wasn't only your client, was he? You were comrades. I checked up on you.'

'Naturally you did. And what did you find?'

'That you were expelled from the Party in '32.'

'So long ago,' the old tailor said. 'It means nothing to me now.'

'Professor Labiche spoke in your defence.'

'So he did, so he did.'

The tailor laid his work aside, and with a nimbleness that was surprising descended from the table and hobbled to a cupboard from which he took a dusty bottle of brandy and glasses that were grey with dust too. He gave them a perfunctory wipe with his apron and poured them both a drink.

'Trotskyism, that's what they accused me of, but really it was because I could no longer subscribe to faith in the Revolution. You want to know what we talked about? Why not? It can't matter now, not now that Stalin in the Kremlin and Hitler in whichever ante-chamber of Hell he inhabits are as one. What did we talk about? We talked about the girl. Of course we talked about the girl.'

'Pilar?'

'Pilar, though naturally she went by other names as well. Of course she did. They thought she was a spy too. And of course she was. But you must know all this, superintendent.'

'Some of it,' Lannes said.

The brandy was Spanish, at once fiery and sweet.

'She was betrayed and murdered,' he said.

'Liquidated. They don't use the word "murder". There would have been a trial.'

'In absentia,' Lannes said.

'The outcome would have been the same whether she was present or not.'

'But it was the Fascists who killed her,' Lannes said.

'And who gave them to her? You know the answer as well as I do, Mr Policeman. Get the devil to do your own dirty work.'

'So the professor came to tell you about it?'

'Not at all. There was no need to tell me. She came to see me before she left for Spain. I told her it was foolish. She knew that but she still went. She still believed, you see.'

'In the Revolution?'

'That too, but worse. She believed in Justice. In this world – Justice! – I ask you. How can anyone believe in Justice? Do you, a policeman, believe in Justice?'

'I try to. Sometimes it's difficult. Always it's difficult.'

'For the old Jew it's impossible,' the tailor said. '"Ruat coelum, fiat justitia" – that old crazy hopeful lie – believe me, the sky falls but there is no justice. I told her that. She wept but she still believed.

She was very young, you see. And innocent as only someone who believes in the Revolution and Justice and Fraternity and the Rights of Man can be innocent. Me, I believe in getting through the day, one day at a time, and in my needle and thread.'

'No God?' Lannes said. 'No God of Israel?'

'No God, even of Israel. Have some more brandy. Sometimes I believe in brandy.'

Not very often, Lannes thought, looking at the dust-smeared bottle.

'There was a paper,' he said. 'I think the professor entrusted it to you.'

'And if he did, should I break his trust?'

'Is there trust between the living and the dead?'

'More perhaps than between the living since there is only one who can betray it. Still you are right, not so foolish after all. But you are also wrong. I refused.'

'You refused? Why?'

'Because there is nothing left for me but refusal. Perhaps that was why. I don't know. Perhaps because I have had enough. I don't know. Perhaps because I was afraid, but that is not why. When I'm afraid I drink brandy. That is why a bottle lasts me a long time. I am too old to be afraid. What is there for me to be afraid of? Death? There is nothing fearful in death. In the moment of death? Perhaps. But death itself? No. I refused because it is my habit to refuse. So I can't help you, Monsieur Lannes. I won't say I would if I could, because it is unnecessary for me to tell a lie. I can't help you and I no longer care. That is why I refused. Perhaps.'

*   *   *

'Nevertheless,' Lannes said, later, to Moncerre and René Martin, 'we have made progress. We know the two cases are connected – through Pilar – and we know that the professor had a paper which he wanted to hide – and I think that he came to this decision after his meeting with Sombra. The question is whether he found a hiding-place, someone to entrust it to, or whether it was among the papers your office-boy, René, collected for his master. Tomorrow we'll act as if we are sure that's the case.'

XX

There were three customers in the shop when Aramis entered.
Léon was startled, then pleased, and was about to speak when
Aramis smiled and gave a small shake of the head. His mouth was
still swollen. Then he turned away and began to scan the shelves,
removed a book, and settled himself on the floor. He was wearing a
high-necked pale-blue jersey and loose fawn-coloured trousers.
Sunlight slicked through the window, making particles of dust
dance, and lying restfully on the boy's blondness. Léon was both
pleased and alarmed to see him, and eager for the other customers
to make their purchases, or grow weary, and leave; in any case
leave. When at last they did so, Aramis seemed for a moment not
to notice that they were now alone, then was on his feet with a
dancer's lightness, and held out the book to Léon; it was Alain-
Fournier's *Le Grand Meaulnes*.

'Don't you love this?' he said. 'I don't know how many times I've
read it but I don't believe I could ever tire of it. Surprised to see me?'

'Did you know I worked here?'

'Hoped. Suspected.'

'But why?'

'My mother's a friend of Henri. She was in here last week – you
won't remember – why should you? – and happened to say he had
a nice boy working for him. I hoped it might be you.'

'Why should you have thought so?'

Aramis looked away.

'It's a bit shameful, I'm afraid. She said someone had told her the
boy was Jewish. She's not really anti-semitic, you know. She did
say you were nice. You don't mind, do you? You don't mind that
I've come?'

Léon said, 'No, not at all. I'm pleased really. Only . . . '

'Only what?'

'Our incognitos, noms de guerre. We're supposed, aren't we, not
to know each other, so that . . . .well, you know. What would Alain
say if he knew?'

85

'D'Artagnan you mean.'

And again, as in the changing-room at the swimming pool, they found themselves, simultaneously, giggling.

'It's a bit silly,' Aramis said, 'when we all know him. But of course, if you like, we can remain Aramis and Athos to each other. But I really wanted to see you, that's all. You don't mind? Truly? You are pleased?'

'Yes, of course I am. I'll make some coffee, shall I?'

Aramis followed him through to the back room. When Léon had filled the pot and put it on the little stove, he felt Aramis lay his hand on his shoulder, and turned round.

'Your poor mouth,' he said. 'It's still sore, isn't it?' and touched it with his finger. 'You were brave to speak as you did.'

'I just didn't think. The words came out. If I'd thought I might have remained silent.'

'All the same, it was brave. I was frightened. I think I'm a coward really.'

'That makes you all the braver, to be doing what we are doing. Especially since you're Jewish.'

He took a piece of blue chalk from his pocket.

'Do you know what I did on my way here? Chalked V for Victory on a number of walls. I would have drawn a Cross of Lorraine too, but I couldn't remember how to do it. Isn't that silly?'

'I've duplicated lots of them,' Léon said. 'I'll give you some to scatter about. But carefully.'

'Carefully, of course. Actually I wanted to speak with you about Porthos. I hope he didn't offend you. He's a bit of an ass, you know.'

'I wasn't offended but I didn't much like him.'

'Can't say I do either, not much anyway, but he's all right really. He's one of Alain's rugby-playing mates.'

'And you're not?'

'Certainly not. Do I look as if I might be?'

'I suppose you don't.'

They took their cups through to the bookshop and sat opposite each other at the table. Aramis leaned forward and cupped his chin in his hands, looking Léon in the face.

'I've a confession,' he said, 'that's the other reason I wanted to see you alone. You remember I said I thought we had met somewhere? I was wrong, but I did recognise you. My grandmother – my other one, not the one who lives in Nice – has a house in Bergerac. I often visit her there. One day she took me to see her friend Gaston – she was very fond of him – and there was a photograph of a boy on his desk. That's how I thought we'd met. Poor Gaston, it was horrible what happened to him.'

Léon felt himself blushing. And it was extraordinary surely that Aramis should have taken note of that photograph and remembered it.

'It's all right,' Aramis said, 'I understand. I understand completely. My mother wanted a daughter. I've always done my best to oblige.'

He brushed his hair off his brow.

'You're in love with Alain, aren't you? There's no need to be embarrassed. I was myself, two years ago, but it was no good.'

'No, it's no good, it's hopeless, I know that,' Léon said. 'How did you guess?'

'The way you look at him.'

'You won't tell, will you?'

'No, of course I won't. I didn't tell him I was, so I certainly won't say you are. It's our secret. I often thought, if I'd been a girl instead of being girlish, he might have guessed how I felt, and even responded. But there you are, that's life.'

Léon thought, I could tell him about Félix and Schussmann, and my fear, and he would understand, but of course I can't and so I won't, and even though he would understand, he would feel obliged to tell Alain that I couldn't be trusted even though he might not say why or how he knew.

'Alain's so innocent,' Aramis said, 'so single-minded. You and I know more about ourselves, because we've had to ask questions. That's our penalty for being what we are and our reward and our strength too. I've thought a lot about it. I expect you have too. That's because we're outcasts. They call us inverts.'

'I don't like the word,' Léon said. 'But at least you're not a Jew, Aramis.'

He pushed a pack of Gauloises across the table.

'Take one.'

'Are you sure you can spare . . . '

'It's all right. My aunt keeps a tabac. So cigarettes are one thing I'm not short of.'

Aramis took one, lit it, and, turning it round in his hand, stretched over the table and put it between Léon's lips. Then he lit another for himself.

'No,' he said, 'I'm not a Jew. I don't know any, not really, you're my first Jewish friend. But I hate these laws. They're disgusting.'

'You won't be surprised to know that I agree,' Léon said, and remembered how he had spoken that exact sentence to Alain, months ago, perhaps the first day Alain came into the shop, and they got talking and Léon had hoped he would never leave, which was absurd.

'It makes it natural for me to want to engage in resistance,' he said. 'I hate Vichy almost as much as I hate the Boches. Maybe I hate it even more. The Boches are at least our enemies, but Vichy just makes me sick. What about you, though? Didn't you say your father thinks the Marshal is our saviour?'

'Stepfather actually, though I call him Papa and think of him as that really, because I was only four years old when he married my mother after my real father was killed in North Africa. He was an officer in the Chasseurs d'Afrique. I suppose I would have been a disappointment to him with my pansy manners. Fortunately Gilles – that's my stepfather – is more tolerant. He's a novelist, not a very good one, I'm afraid, you won't have heard of him, I'm sure. Mostly about priests who have a crisis of conscience or fear they are losing their faith. No, my whole family's on the Right, Action Française and all that, bring back the monarchy, France needs a king, that's how I was brought up.'

'And so?'

There was a touch of mischief or mockery in the smile Aramis offered to Léon, as if to say that these attitudes were nonsensical. Then, before he could continue, they heard footsteps on the stair and Henri came in with Toto on a lead. He was bleary eyed and unshaven.

'Léon, Toto needs to go out. Would you mind taking him? I don't feel up to facing the world outside.'

'Of course,' Léon said, getting to his feet.

'Why, Jérôme – it is Jérôme, isn't it?' Henri said. 'I didn't know you two knew each other.'

'We don't really,' Aramis said. 'I was just browsing and we fell into conversation.' He held up the book. 'About this.'

'Ah,' Henri said. 'Ah yes.' His jowls shook. He coughed several times, rackingly, and his eyes filled with tears. 'The lost domain, the enchanted estate, how we all dream of such a place now, long for it precisely because we know it is unattainable. And how is your mother, dear boy? Well, I hope. Please give her my best regards. Does she still read books? Not that there is much new to appeal to her. Thank you, dear boy,' he said, handing Léon Toto's lead. 'Lock the door behind you, please. I'm not up to dealing with customers, especially if they should turn out to be Germans. To think how I used to love Germany and German literature. I suppose that barbarian has burned most of the books now.'

Outside in the street, Léon said, 'Toto doesn't like to go far, he's a lazy old thing. We might just go to a bar in the rue du Vieil Temple. I'm quite welcome there. Of course we don't yet have to wear a yellow star like in Germany.'

There were tables outside the bar. They ordered lemonade. Toto snuffled and sniffed busily around the chair-legs.

'Henri's in a bad way,' Léon said. 'I don't know what I would do without him, but the only people he likes to see now are my Aunt Mirian and Alain's father, and he spends most of the day drinking. Go on with what you were saying. About your family and why you . . . You know. There's no one who can hear us.'

'That's how I was brought up then,' Aramis said, 'to believe that France was being ruined by corrupt politicians, by the money power and – I'm sorry to say this, Athos – no, it's too silly when we are alone, Léon – by the Jews. So when we heard that the Marshal had replaced Reynaud as Prime Minister, I was overjoyed. We might have lost the first battles of the war but now France would be saved. The Hero of Verdun would deliver victory – the Loire would be a second Marne. With Pétain in power, everything was possible. And then came his broadcast. You heard it, we all heard it. And I had an immediate revulsion of feeling. We are betrayed. The

89

Marshal has betrayed us. It was appalling. You were probably wiser than me and never trusted him, but for me, it was as if someone had picked up my idol and dashed it to the ground. You understand?'

'I understand.'

'But I must tell you because I want you to know and because I wouldn't want you to hear it from someone else, that I remain a member of a Cercle Charles Maurras and that, at my father's suggestion, I signed up to join the Légion des Jeunes d'Aquitaine which, as you know is devoted to the service and person of the Marshal. I'm happy with this, Léon. If we are serious in our resistance – and we are, aren't we? – it's good cover. Porthos refused to join – he says, 'I don't like associations' and Alain also, of course, though his brother Dominique is now favourable. But I think it wise and, besides, I have a conspiratorial nature, I've discovered.'

He laughed.

'Now you know everything, you know the worst. Except one thing. There's a boy there in the Légion I'm mad about, hopelessly because he is equally mad about girls and anyway I fear he despises me. What's more, he's a Fascist, a natural one, I'm afraid. And yet I adore him. Isn't life stupid?'

XXI

To Lannes' surprise the advocate Labiche presented himself at his office as requested and only half an hour late. He settled himself, dark-suited, squat and assured, in the chair where so many suspects had found themselves sweating with anxiety.

'So,' he said, 'I have come even although your summons was unnecessary as well as an impertinence. I have already told your inspector I know nothing about my unfortunate brother's death. We had no dealings with each other.'

'You also told Inspector Moncerre that you knew nothing about his daughter. Nothing about the celebrated actress, Adrienne Jauzion?'

Labiche smiled.

'He irritated me, your inspector, and I saw no reason why my niece should be troubled.'

'You can hardly expect me to believe that.'

'As you like, superintendent. It's no concern of mine. May I say it is only out of respect for the French State which we both serve that I have presented myself here today. You know very well that I have sufficient influence to have enabled me to ignore your summons with impunity. If I have not done so it is because I am curious to know why you are acting so rashly. You must be as aware that I have been appointed a member of the Institut des Questions Juives as I am that you have Jewish friends, superintendent, your pretty Jewboy in the bookshop and his aunt, the widow of the Comte de Grimaud, in her tabac. I really wonder at your audacity.'

'We are not here to speak about Jews,' Lannes said.

'Nevertheless you would do well to bear them in mind.'

Lannes pushed the photograph of Sombra across the desk.

'Do you know this man?'

'Certainly. He presented himself at my office some days after my brother's death and said he had information which he would let me have at a price. I told him what I told your inspector – that my brother was of no interest to me, dead or alive. So I sent him away. I don't know his name. He spoke French fluently, but with an accent, Spanish perhaps. Does that satisfy you?'

'Are you sure that visit was after your brother's death, not some days before it?'

'I am not in the habit of making mistakes.'

Lannes lit a cigarette, got up from behind the desk and looked out on to the square which was bathed in sunshine. A party of schoolgirls passed, chattering like starlings.

'The present Comte de Grimaud is one of your clients, I believe.'

'He has been in the past. An unfortunate man. I have done what I can for him.'

'The man in that photograph frequents his house. He is a friend, or associate, of the Count's illegitimate nephew, who calls himself Sigi de Grimaud, though that is not the name on his birth certificate. Do you know him?'

'Superintendent, you are wasting my time. Your time too, though that is no concern of mine. I fail to see the relevance of your questions. As for this Sigi de Grimaud or whatever, I may have seen him. I don't know. I have never spoken to him, though I have heard the Count speak of him. Does that satisfy you?'

'I take note of what you say. If your brother – and his murder – are of no interest to you, Monsieur Labiche, how did you know the name of the pension where he had been staying and why did you send your office boy to collect his possessions from it?'

'Because it was natural and proper I should do so. Superintendent, my brother was a fool and his politics were not mine. Nevertheless he was my brother. I am not devoid of family pride, for we are, as you must know, a family of some position here in Bordeaux and have been for generations. Naturally I was anxious lest my brother had some papers which were – shall we say? – discreditable. The Spaniard – if he was a Spaniard – let slip the name of the pension where my brother had been living since his return to Bordeaux. So naturally I sent one of my clerks to retrieve his belongings.'

'And did you find anything discreditable?'

'Nothing at all, and nothing of interest either. My brother had led a wasted life, somewhat pitiful indeed, engaged in political foolishness and futility. His effects were meagre. Tell me – since I am being frank, I am entitled to expect frankness in return – do you suspect this Spaniard of complicity in my brother's murder?'

'It seems unlikely that he killed him,' Lannes said.

'Very well then. I fail to see the relevance of your questions. As I said, we are both wasting our time. Naturally you must investigate his death and I admire your pertinacity. But it has nothing to do with me, and I would advise you to accept what is surely the obvious conclusion: that some lout attacked my brother with intent to rob him and hit him perhaps harder than he intended. It is surely among the scum of the criminal world that you will find his killer – if he is to be found at all.'

He leaned back in his chair, and for the first time smiled, a man at ease with the world. No doubt it was calculated to demonstrate his indifference to the conversation.

'There are however complications,' Lannes said, 'which have led me to reject what would, I agree, be a comfortable solution.'

Labiche took a gold watch from his waistcoat pocket, snapped it open, and said, 'I have another and more important appointment.'

There was a knock on the door. René Martin came in with an envelope in his hand.

'Collected on behalf of the emperor,' he said, and passed it to Lannes, who slit it open and extracted two photographs. They showed the same scene: the advocate Labiche sitting on a couch beside a little girl. A black mask concealed her face. Otherwise she was naked. She looked no more than twelve. The advocate's hand rested between her thin thighs. Lannes passed one copy across the desk.

'You will of course have seen this before,' he said. 'Who was the little girl? Is she still alive? And who took the photograph? Jean-Claude who is now the Comte de Grimaud?'

The advocate held the photograph in both hands. The tip of his tongue moved very slowly across his lips.

'This is evidence of nothing,' he said.

He tore the photograph across, then tore it again and again, till it was reduced to scraps which he let fall on the floor.

'I knew you were a fool, superintendent, but I didn't know you were also a hypocrite. You and Gaston Chambolley and his Jew boy, your Jew boy. As for the girl she gave for money what she was ready to give for free to any "voyou" in a back-alley.'

'Is she still alive or was she disposed of?' Lannes said.

'How should I know?'

Was he indifferent or indignant? Lannes couldn't tell. He knew only that he felt disgust at being in the same room as the advocate. He had felt pity for many who had sat in that chair, resisting him for hours before breaking and confessing to their crime, sometimes with relief, as if he had been a priest. They weren't seeking absolution, merely to be known at last for what they were. If Labiche was unconcerned, it was surely because guilt was foreign to him. And of course he was protected.

'Superintendent,' he said. 'Allow me to make something clear. These Jews – your Jews – are at my mercy. One word from me, and they will be arrested and taken to an internment camp. I am told conditions in the camps are not agreeable. If you interfere further in my affairs, I shall make good my threat, and take pleasure in doing so. Pray bear that in mind.'

He clamped his hat on his head and left. Lannes opened the window wide.

XXII

'Sometimes your beautiful eyes look so sad.'

Lieutenant Schussmann leaned across the table and pressed his hand on Léon's.

'Of course,' he said, 'we all have reasons to be sad. I understand that. I told you once, Léon, of my dearest friend who was killed and of how, because I loved him, I married his sister. That was not right of me, nor of her. We both knew it soon, that our marriage was a mistake, because it was founded in loneliness and pity, not in love or desire.'

He paused and drank some wine. He had drunk most of the first bottle and had already drunk one glass from the second.

The restaurant was emptying as people looked at their watches and thought it was time to be home. They were mostly French and, though Schussmann was not wearing his uniform, which was probably in breach of regulations, and therefore was not obviously German, Léon had had the uncomfortable feeling that people had been looking at them throughout the meal. But perhaps it was the key to the hotel room which Félix had given him that made him think this. The memory of that second visit and the way Félix had smiled when he confessed that he had agreed to have dinner with Schussmann made him feel sick.

The waiters were clearing tables and rolling up the paper covers, and still Schussmann talked. Probably he was nervous too and being nervous wanted to postpone the moment when they would have to leave and he would put the question he so much wanted but feared to put.

After all, Léon thought, he can't be sure, he can't be sure of me or of how I will answer. And I know how I would answer him if I didn't have to give him the reply I've been instructed to make.

94

He slipped his hand into the pocket and felt the key.

He can't even be sure, not absolutely sure, I am as he hopes I am, he thought. Perhaps he won't dare, perhaps his nerve will fail him at the last minute and we shall say good-night and I'll thank him for a pleasant dinner.

It was what he wanted, but what he was also afraid of, because Félix would not believe it was Schussmann whose nerve had given way.

How Alain would despise him if he saw him now, knew what he was doing and was about to do, Alain who was so angry that his mother had invited a young German officer to lunch with the family that he had said he certainly wasn't going to be there. Alain must never know. He couldn't speak to him of his shame.

'So my marriage did not last because I am not made for marriage,' Schussmann said. 'On the other hand we are not divorced because Greta thinks it is better we maintain the appearance of marriage. Mine is not a good country now for men of my inclination. You understand, Léon, what I am saying. But when the war ends, things will be different, and it is only the stupid obstinacy of England which prevents that. Yes, after the war, we can all relax and be ourselves again and I hope you will visit me in Tübingen which is very beautiful. But for now, Léon, there are only a few moments such as this evening when I can be what I truly am.'

Léon felt sorry for him, but also that he was a bore, as Gaston had never been. Gaston had been full of jokes as well as poetry and intelligence. He had set himself to educate Léon and the education had been fun. He had opened his eyes to so much and he had been full of mischief. He had loved to tell scandalous stories about the distinguished and eminent. He had laughed at himself, even if, quoting an English poet, he had said, 'and if I laugh at anything, 'tis that I may not weep.' His favourite Byron, Léon thought, Byron who had, Gaston told him, loved boys as well as women, his last infatuation being a Greek boy called Loukas. 'I like to think you resemble him,' Gaston said, 'though, alas, I know I am no Byron.'

I can't go through with it, Léon thought. Gaston would despise me as much as Alain. No, he wouldn't, he would despise the action, what I've been ordered to do, but not me, he wouldn't despise me.

Maman and Aunt Miriam in an internment camp – he would understand how . . .

'You are distracted,' Schussmann said, 'perhaps I have been boring you . . . '

'Not at all, but when you spoke of your dead friend, it set me thinking of one of mine who is also dead.'

The waiters were piling chairs on the tables.

Schussmann leaned forward,

'Léon, I would so much wish . . . Have you, I wonder, a room we could go to . . . '

Léon felt his hand begin to tremble. He thrust it between his legs.

'Yes,' he said, 'we could do that.'

* * *

The clerk in the mean hotel – Hotel Artemis – across the road from the Gare Saint-Jean did not look up from his newspaper when Léon and Schussmann passed him. In the lift, mounting slowly and unsteadily to the second floor, Schussmann stroked the boy's cheek.

'I have so much wanted this.'

Léon took the key from his pocket and unlocked the door. The little room was bare, the only furniture the bed, a chair and a table on which stood a jug and basin, and a couple of tumblers.

'So this is not where you live?'

Léon, tense, made no reply.

'And you have used this room before, for this purpose.'

Léon couldn't bring himself to look Schussmann in the face. He was on edge, ashamed and afraid. He slipped his jacket off and began to unbutton his shirt.

'No, please, allow me the pleasure of undressing you.'

He let his hands fall to his sides. Schussmann kissed him on the mouth.

'Oh Léon . . . Sit on the bed, please.'

He knelt down and removed Léon's shoes and socks. Then he unbuckled his belt and pulled down his trousers. Léon shifted aside to help him. Then he lay back on the bed and closed his eyes.

Schussmann, still on his knees beside the bed, ran his hands up and down Léon's thighs and brought his head forward. Léon felt his tongue go to work and heard him moan with the anticipation of pleasure. The door opened.

'Act One: curtain,' Félix said.

He stood there smiling, and closed the door behind him. He put a paper bag on the table, and said, 'We have matters to discuss, Lieutenant. Léon, pick up your clothes and get out. You've done your work, Jewboy. Oh yes, lieutenant, it's even worse than you feared. Not only are you caught *in flagrante delicto* but your catamite is a Jew. You didn't know? Doesn't matter. What would Himmler say? I can guess, can't you? Dachau or some other holiday camp? That would be your fate, wouldn't it?'

He took a bottle of brandy from the paper bag and poured two glasses. He handed one to Schussmann.

'You've gone white as a sheet,' he said. 'Drink this. It need not come to that. It's not in my interest that you are sent to Dachau. Léon, take your clothes and get out. You can dress in the lobby. Your work here's done.'

Léon obeyed. With his hand on the door handle, he turned and said, 'I'm sorry. I had no choice.'

It felt feeble. It was feeble.

He opened the door and hesitated a moment in case Schussmann should reply. He wanted him to say, 'I understand, I don't blame you,' but instead heard Félix say, 'Really, you've nothing to worry about. Why, when we've come to an agreement, there is no reason why you shouldn't have the opportunity to finish what I interrupted. They say pleasure delayed is pleasure enhanced, don't they? That's of course if it's what you still want. I don't care how perverted your pleasures are, and I'll admit this. The Jewboy's right. I gave him no choice.'

XXIII

Marguerite had gone to the early Mass so that she would have more time to prepare lunch. Not that there was actually much to do. She had managed to obtain an old fowl and it would simmer for hours in the pot with the vegetables.

'Just what Henri Quatre wanted every Frenchwoman to have for Sundays,' Dominique said on their way back from the cathedral. He linked his arm in his mother's.

'It's going to be all right,' he said, 'don't worry, Maman.'

There had been a scene, a fierce argument anyway, the night before. Alain had said it was all wrong, they shouldn't have a German in the apartment. Admittedly he had spoken to him on the stairs and found him pleasant enough. But it was a matter of principle. It was wrong to collaborate with the enemy. He had nothing against him as an individual, but he was nevertheless the enemy. At this point Clothilde burst into tears and accused her twin of always trying to spoil anything. Why did he always think he was right and everybody else wrong?

'He's not the enemy,' she screamed. 'He's Manu and I'm in love with him,' and fled to her bedroom, banging the door behind her.

'It's all right, Maman,' Dominque now said, giving her arm a squeeze, 'she's not really in love with him, you know. She just likes him and she was in a temper. As for Alain, if that's his attitude, well, we'll all be more comfortable if he's not with us at the table. Besides, Manu really is a nice chap. You'll like him, I'm sure. And Papa doesn't object.'

Actually Lannes did object. His sympathies were with Alain. That's to say, he agreed with him and shared his distaste. He was compelled as a police officer to collaborate with the Occupier, but collaboration shouldn't get past the door of the family home. On the other hand, he not only adored Clothilde and hated to see her disappointed or unhappy, but he knew that she was every bit as obstinate as Alain – or indeed as he himself was; and so he suspected that opposition might actually convert her idea of being in love into a reality. Yes, she's 'thrawn', he said to himself, happy to employ the dialect word which had been a favourite of his peasant grandmother in the Landes: she had applied it time and again to her husband. Yes, she's thrawn, it's a family trait, and at the right moment I'll remind her that she and Alain quarrel so bitterly because they are two of a kind. Marguerite often recalled how they had, as she put it, kicked each other in her womb. As for the lunch, if the young German was indeed as well mannered as Dominique said, it would no doubt pass off quite smoothly, and perhaps seeing him at the family table Clothilde might think him quite ordinary, with nothing special, certainly no glamour, about him.

He would tell Alain later: 'If you really want your sister to be set on him, then present him as forbidden fruit.'

'Alain should be ashamed of himself, upsetting Clothilde like that,' Marguerite had said when they were in bed together. 'He's so selfish and wild. You will speak to him firmly, won't you, Jean? He really needs to learn to have some consideration for others. Mother was very hurt that day when I told him to take her some eggs and he just dumped them on her kitchen table and was off with barely a word to her.'

'I'll speak to him,' Lannes had said, making a mental reservation as to what he would say.

*   *   *

Alain sat on the parapet above the Garonne listening to the cry of gulls. There was little traffic on the Sunday river. He watched it flow, towards the sea, towards a world beyond imprisoned France, towards, with a tilt of the map, England, de Gaulle and the Free French. He should go. The resistance in which he and the musketeers had engaged – was it anything more than play-acting? There were copies of Léon's version of the Cross of Lorraine in his pocket – he had already scattered a few, almost careless, in his ill-temper, if he was observed. But what did such action amount to: a mere statement of childish defiance? And how could he stay when his family home had become a nest of collaborators and his sister was in love with a German? Who would care if he went? Not Maman certainly. She was content with Dominique, always her favourite. Papa? Papa might even admire him for doing what he didn't dare to do himself. Poor Papa, chained to duty. He lit a cigarette, only one left in the packet. In London he would be made welcome. Why have you come here, young man?, the General would say. To fight for France, sir. Magnificent.

Two German officers passed, laughing. Laugh on, he thought, one day we'll laugh in Berlin. He would have liked to hand each of them a Cross of Lorraine – as a promise, a warning?

I'm eighteen, he thought. It could be like this for years. Stepping aside on the pavement to make way for the Boche, condemned to hurry home to beat the curfew imposed by the Boche, watching the Boche with French girls on their arms – why, if it lasted long enough Clothilde might even marry her Manu – ridiculous name! And listening to that senile dotard on the wireless telling us we are paying for our laxity – what had he ever denied himself? – that was good – and telling us that we must endure suffering in expiation – him and his precious Maginot Line. The truth was that all these bastards at Vichy, from the Marshal and Admiral Darlan down, wallowed in humiliation like pigs in muck. *Maréchal, nous voilà* – not me – not bloody likely.

He felt alive again and was hungry. No money in his pocket. Miriam would feed him – and give him cigarettes. She might deny him her bed, and it no longer mattered, now that he had decided he would be off as soon as the opportunity presented itself. With Léon and Jérôme and Philippe whom he had called Porthos? Why not? Dumas' musketeers had gone to England, more than once, d'Artagnan several times. He had put the English General Monk in a box and carried him across the Channel. What a jest to take Admiral Darlan on the reverse journey! But that was day-dreaming. He must be practical and find a way. His mind was made up.

*   *   *

Clothilde was nervous. She had made a fool of herself last night. It was Alain's fault. He always knew how to provoke her into saying more than she meant. She should have insisted that Manu was merely a friend, a nice boy in a foreign land. Instead she had burst out with that cry 'I'm in love with him,' and seen sadness creep over her father's face. Sadness like river mist, she thought now. And it wasn't even true. Or she didn't know if it was. Manu was sweet, with his pale face and mouth that never seemed sure of itself. And his gentleness, the sudden burst of enthusiasm when he spoke of music, the church choir he used to sing in, or the beauty of his home in the Black Forest, and said how much he missed his mother and little sister and their two shepherd-dogs. But they had never even kissed, he had never held her in his arms, and she didn't know what he wanted – he was always so polite and restrained. So she had never spoken to him of her feelings and anyway she wasn't sure what they were. She would never have met him if it wasn't for this beastly war, which might any day take him away, so that they never saw each other again.

She laid the table with hands that trembled a little, with excitement and uncertainty, and buried her nose in the sweet scent of the bowl of red roses which she placed as a centre piece. She was aware of Maman and Dominique in the kitchen. They at least were on her side. Dominique was anyway; she was never sure of what her mother really thought about anything. Still, she had agreed readily to invite Manu, adding only 'if it makes you happy, Clothilde.'

The doorbell rang. She let Dominique answer it, heard him greet Manu as if there was nothing remarkable in his presence. She pushed a lock of hair away from her eye. As she did so, she thought, that's one of Alain's gestures.

He was carrying a bunch of freesias.

'For your mother,' he said.

She stretched out to take the flowers from him and for an instant their fingers touched. He had left his officer's cap in the hallway. His light brown hair was close cropped. Once, at the café where they had eaten ice-cream and talked, he had shown her a family photograph in which he wore his hair curling over his ears and his face had seemed even softer. But, even with his brutal military cut, he looked so gentle.

'It is so kind of you to invite me,' he said.

For a moment she found nothing to say. It was a relief when Maman came through to be introduced.

*　　*　　*

It being Sunday, the iron shutter of the tabac was drawn down, but Alain rang the bell for the apartment.

'It's all right,' he said when Miriam opened the door. 'I've accepted your decision.'

'It really is for the best,' she said. 'How are you?'

'Hungry actually.'

He explained why he hadn't been able to endure the thought of a family lunch with Clothilde's friend.

'He's a decent enough chap, but I won't eat with a German officer.'

'Then you'd better eat with me, not that I've much to offer you, only bread and cheese and some dried figs from last year's crop.'

'And I'm out of cigarettes,' he said.

'Well, that's something else I can supply.'

She looks older and sadder, he thought. Even in the weeks since we were lovers, she has aged. She'll soon be an old woman. It's very strange.

'I can't stand it here any longer,' he said.

'What do you mean?'

'The humiliation. It's intolerable. I have to do something.'

'Is this because of Clothilde, or me?'

'I don't know. I don't know anything for sure except that I hate our position and have to do something, get out.'

'Eat something first. Drink some wine. Then we'll talk. You look exhausted. I suspect you didn't sleep much last night.'

*   *   *

At least the young man didn't click his heels as he stood up to shake hands. That was Lannes' first thought. He seemed nice. This made it worse. When he saw how Clothilde looked at him, and, so often a chatter-box, was lost for words, apprehension gripped him. However things turned out she was going to be hurt. As for himself, all he could manage was to ask polite conventional questions about the lieutenant's home and family, all of which he answered in a manner which suggested a proper depth of affection and respect. If the young man had been a visitor from abroad before the war, Lannes would have asked him how he found Bordeaux and would have talked about the city himself. He couldn't bring himself to do so; he couldn't forget what had brought him here. Fortunately Dominique took charge of the conversation. He spoke about literature and films with a naturalness which impressed Lannes. Manu responded. They found a common enthusiasm for Thomas Mann and for Joseph Roth's novel, 'The Radetzky March.'

'Of course Roth's books are banned in Germany now,' Manu said, 'but that doesn't prevent this one from being one of the great German novels of the century, and my father, who is a professor of literature in a Hochschule, says these things will pass, but Art remains. I would like to believe it is so.'

He smiled.

'I am happy to be able to say such things to you. There are places where I would not have the courage to speak like this.'

'These are bad times,' Dominique said, 'but your father is right, they will pass. That's what my faith tells me. Men – and women, Clothilde – of goodwill must come together in peace and fellow-ship. I am sure of that. These quarrels between our two countries can't continue. We must learn to work together so that we may live in peace. Think of it: Louis Quatorze, Napoleon, Bismarck, the Kaiser, 1870, 1914 and where we are now. It's too much.'

'Yes,' Manu said, 'we are the two great nations of Europe and we must stand together against atheistic Bolshevism and the power of international capitalism and the forces of the money power.'

Lannes said, 'I'll make coffee.'

In the kitchen he gave himself a glass of marc and drank it quickly. Clothilde joined him there.

'He is nice, Papa, isn't he? You do like him? You could come to like him, couldn't you? You see how well he and Dominqiue get on, how they think the same way.'

'Yes,' Lannes said, 'I see that, and, yes, he seems a nice boy. But don't throw your heart at him, darling. If there was no war it might be different, but the war . . . well, we don't know how it is going to end.'

He thought of the young tart Yvette and her Wolfie, the warning he had given her, and how she lay back on her bed displaying her legs to him.

After lunch Dominique suggested they go for a walk. Lannes was pleased to see them off. Marguerite said, 'Well, he is a nice boy, well mannered and gentle. But you don't need to worry, Jean, as I see you are ready to do. It's not serious. It won't last. It's calf-love, nothing more.'

'I hope you're right.'

He wished he could be sure she was.

XXIV

Léon passed a miserable Sunday. He had slept badly, disturbed by dreams and waking early. He was reluctant to leave his bed, lying on his side, his knees drawn up against his chest, the sheet pulled over his head against the sunlight which seeped through curtains that did not meet in the middle. He heard his mother moving in the kitchen, and this deepened his shame. There had been a moment before Félix opened the door and said 'Act One: Curtain' that he had felt himself responding to Schussman's eagerness. He told himself he had done only what was required of him – 'Are you a patriot, Léon?' – but it was shameful nevertheless. What more would Félix require of him? I am doubly punished, he thought, for being what I am. Might Schussmann have believed him when he said, 'I had no choice.' Said? Whimpered.

There was no one he could tell. Not Alain. Not Alain's father. Jérôme – Aramis – would understand, but . . .

'Aren't you going to get up?'

He didn't move, pretended to be asleep.

'I've brought you coffee.'

He heard her place the bowl on the little table by the bed, and the door close behind her. There had been anxiety in her voice. She knew something but not what it was.

He remembered how when he had first met Alain's father in the Buffet de la Gare, months ago, after Gaston's murder, when he had realised he had information to offer, he had been self-assured, cocky, even defiant, and now . . .

When at last he got up, drank the milky coffee on which a skin had formed, flapped cold water on his face, brushed his teeth without succeeding in ridding himself of the nasty taste in his mouth, dressed, and dragged a comb through his hair, his mother greeted him with an attempt at naturalness.

'Lazybones.'

Then without looking at him, she said, 'I wish you wouldn't . . . '

'Wouldn't what?'

'Take risks with the curfew. I was frightened listening for you. I won't ask what you were up to because I would rather not know, but you might have some consideration . . . '

'I'm sorry, Maman.'

'Easy to say "sorry". What am I going to do with you?'

What would she reply if he said, 'What was I up to? Saving you from an internment camp'?

But of course he couldn't.

'You look peaky,' she said.

'I'm all right. Don't fuss.'

'You don't make it easy for me,' she said. 'Eat something.'

'I'm not hungry.'

He had to get out, but once in the streets had nowhere to go. The sun shone, but Bordeaux was a desert. He walked aimlessly for a long time. Once in the Cours du Marne, near a restaurant where he had eaten with Gaston, a middle-aged man wearing a white linen suit and a broad-brimmed straw hat looked at him searchingly, hopefully, till he turned away and resumed his walk. Outside the station a motherly woman beckoned to him. He hesitated. He had never gone with a woman; it might be a solution. But he had no money and in any case he shrank from it. He wanted what he couldn't have, and didn't want what was available. He looked across the road to the Hotel Artemis. The key was still in his pocket. Again the clerk did not trouble to raise his head as Léon passed him and entered the lift. The room hadn't been cleaned. The glasses Félix had produced were still on the table and there was a little brandy in the bottle. Léon rinsed a glass from the water jug and poured himself a drink. He lay down on the bed holding the glass in both hands. It was ridiculous to think that the brandy tasted of corruption and betrayal, but it did. He stretched out and wondered if Schussmann was as miserable and afraid as he was. In a little he fell asleep.

*   *   *

The letter was waiting for him in the bookshop on Monday morning. There was no stamp; it had been delivered by hand and bore no address, only his name, Léon, underlined twice.

He made coffee before opening it.

My dear Léon – I think too well, too fondly – no, let me be honest – too lovingly of you to believe you betrayed me willingly. So, when you say that you had no choice, I understand that though this was not literally true, for there is always a choice, only it may be so framed that in reality there is none, or none that is tolerable, I know' – underlined twice – 'that the alternative presented to you was even worse than what you felt compelled to do. And now that I know you are Jewish, which – believe me – is no matter to me – I can guess what that alternative was.

For my part I yielded to the tender feeling I have developed for you. I do not regret the feeling or apologise for it – we are what we are, you and I – and what we are does not make for happiness. I regret only that I yielded and that the consequences of my indiscreet behaviour should be unhappy for both of us.

As for me, I am faced with a choice of three courses of action, none of them agreeable. Fortunately only one of them is dishonourable. You will understand which that is.

This war destroys so much.

I have been foolish, not in falling in love with you, but in seeking to give expression to that love, to that form of love which the world and those I serve regard with disgust and contempt. To me of course it is neither of these things, as it should not be to you, my dear Léon.

We shall not meet again, but I truly hope you can find happiness and remember me with affection.

E. S.

The letter, intended to acquit him of blame and free him of guilt, caused Léon to dissolve in tears.

XXV

It was a beautiful morning. An old woman had set up a little flower-stall by the newspaper kiosk in the Place Gambetta.

'A rose for your button-hole, superintendent,' she called out when Lannes paused to admire the display. He recognised her, the widow of a burglar, the old professional sort who never carried a weapon or resorted to violence. Lannes had arrested him more than once. He had liked him, a man who made light of his inter-rogation, and recognised that Lannes had his metier as he had his. He had died in prison.

'So people still buy flowers, Jeanne, even in these hard times?'

'If there's no food to put on the table, or little enough of it, a bowl of flowers cheers the room up. Here,' she said, holding out a yellow rose, 'for your button-hole. We've known each other long enough. Frédéric always spoke well of you, said you played fair with him. So compliments of the house.'

'I'll pay for it all the same,' Lannes said, taking the rose and the pin she offered, and handing her a couple of coins.

'Makes you look quite handsome,' she said.

In truth he felt uncommonly cheerful, partly because of the sunshine, but also because yesterday had passed off without too much embarrassment, and because Alain had returned home well before the hour of the curfew and, without prompting, had apologised to Clothilde for upsetting her the previous evening. They had settled to play bridge, Lannes and Clothilde in partner-ship against the boys. There had been no quarrelling and Clothilde had brought off a little slam thanks to an audacious finesse, while Marguerite sat darning Alain's socks and they played Charles Trenet records on the gramophone. It had been like an evening before the war and they had felt like a family at peace.

Even the rue Xantrailles in Mériadeck had an air of gaiety. Lines of washing were strung across the street and women, having completed their housework, had brought chairs out to the pave-ment so that they could sit and gossip with their neighbours. Even those whom he recognised as Jews looked at ease.

It's the right thing, he thought, to take advantage of the day and find such happiness as may be.

He stopped off at the bar below the Pension Bernadotte for a glass of beer. The proprietor greeted him by name.

'He was a gentleman, that professor,' he said. 'Of course he was here only for a few weeks and he wasn't what I would call a regular. But he liked his glass and there was no side to him. An intellectual, which is something I respect, and politically sound. That's my opinion and I don't care who knows it. Hope you catch the swine that did for him. I suppose you're going up to question old Mangeot again. Don't believe a word he says, superintendent, until you've checked it, if you don't mind a bit of advice from the likes of me. We get to be good judges of people in my line of business, just as you do in yours, and that one would sell his own grandmother for a shekel.'

Mangeot was at his desk, at work with a toothpick which he removed when Lannes offered him good morning.

'Which I hope you haven't come to spoil,' he said. 'There's nothing more I can tell you, superintendent, except that I wish I had turned Doktor Braun away when he came asking for a room. If I'd known he was going to cause me so much trouble, I'd have sent him off with a flea in the ear. I don't like it when my customers attract your lot's attention. My nerves are bad enough as it is.'

'Don't disturb yourself, Mangeot. It's Yvette I've come to see. Is she in?'

'Well, she wouldn't be up and out at this hour, the slut. I've a good mind to send her packing too. You know the way to her room. I think she's alone, unless she slipped someone in last night when my back was turned. No doubt she'll make you welcome.'

He closed his eyes and returned the toothpick to his mouth.

*   *   *

Yvette was stretched out naked on her bed. There was dance music on the wireless and her right foot jiggled up and down in time with it. The sunlight gleamed on her pink-varnished toenails and her thighs looked as warm as a Renoir nude.

'I knew you'd come again,' she said. 'Needing?'

'Don't be silly, Yvette,' Lannes said, and, as before, tossed her the dressing-gown which was folded over the end of the bed. She let it lie where it fell across her middle, and raised her arms up behind her head to give Lannes a fuller view of her breasts.

'All right then,' she said, 'if it's not that, it's a bit early to disturb a girl. Not that I mind, not really.'

Lannes switched the wireless off and sat down. She pushed her foot against his thigh. He lifted it away.

'Stop playing games,' he said.

'Don't you like games? I could give you a good time. Seriously.'

'I've no doubt you could. Nevertheless . . . '

'Have you found out who killed the old gentleman yet?'

'Not yet.'

'Shame. A clever policeman like you.'

'Not so clever it seems, I'm sorry to say. Has anyone else come to ask you questions about him?'

'Not counting your young inspector? He's quite a dish that one, I'm surprised you let him out on his own.'

'I'll pass on the message. Now, be serious.'

'I was being serious,' she said.

She drew up her legs and hugged her knees. A strand of hair fell over her face. She nibbled the end of it.

'All right,' she said. 'There was the Spanish gentleman.'

'What did he want?'

'Can't you guess? Not that I gave it to him. To tell the truth I wanted him out of my room as soon as he entered. There was something about him.'

'What?'

'I don't know, do I, but he looked the sort to keep clear of.'

'And he asked you about Doktor Braun?'

'You are a good policeman after all. Give me a cigarette and I'll tell.'

She took the cigarette, put it between her lips, and held her face towards Lannes for a light. She put her hand on his as he held out the lighter, and looked over it into his eyes.

'He asked what you didn't ask first time: if the old gentleman had entrusted anything to me. Have you a daughter, superintendent?'

'Yes. What did you say to him?'

'Is she about my age?'

'More or less, I suppose. A year younger perhaps.'

'Is that why you won't?'

'Answer my queston.'

'Answer mine first and then I'll answer yours.'

Lannes smiled. 'You do like games, don't you?'

'Doesn't everyone?' she said, smiling in turn.

The smile revealed that she was missing a front tooth.

'All fathers want to fuck their daughters, don't they,' she said. 'Mine certainly did.'

'And did he?'

'That would be telling. I'm not your daughter, am I?'

'Now answer my question,' Lannes said.

'Forgotten it.'

'What did you reply to the Spaniard?'

'Can't remember. Might if you were to help me.'

'All right then, perhaps this will help. You were right to think he's a man to keep clear of. In fact he's a murderer.'

'Fancy that now. Did he kill the old gentleman?'

'No. I don't think so. His method's the garotte.'

'Nasty,' she said. 'I don't like that sort.'

'So? What did you say to him?'

'I wouldn't tell him anything. He spoke to me as if I was dirt. But I don't mind telling you.'

She got off the bed, letting the dressing-gown slip away. There was nothing coquettish in her movement now. She opened a drawer in the chest, revealing a tangle of underwear, and rummaged among it to bring out a long brown envelope.

'The old gentleman said he could trust me to keep it for him, and there was nobody else he could trust. "No family?" I said because I knew he had a daughter, he'd spoken of her, apparently she's quite a distinguished person. I think he was proud of her but disapproved also. "No," he said, "only you, kitten" – that's what he'd taken to calling me, kitten. But it's no use to him now he's dead, and, frankly, in case that Spanish bastard comes back, I'd just as soon be without it. So . . . '

She held it out, then, with a swift gesture, put it behind her, out of Lannes' reach.

'Kiss first,' she said.

'I'm more inclined to slap your bottom.'

'Oh, if that's your style . . . I have a friend who would oblige.'

'No, thank you.'

'Right then. Kiss first,' she said, and settled on his knee. 'I'm not your daughter, remember.' Her tongue sought out his.

'There,' she said, 'I knew you wanted it really. Here's the envelope. I hope it helps you find out who killed him.'

'I don't know that it will do that,' Lannes said, 'but I think it may be important, all the same.'

'I'll see you again, won't I? Now you know how you feel?'

Lannes gave her his card.

'Ring me . . . if you've any trouble. Ring me especially if the Spaniard. . .'

'No other reason to ring you?' she said.

'What about your Wolfie?'

'Wolfie's sweet, but who knows how long he'll be here? Besides, I'm not what you might call exclusive. So?'

'So what?' Lannes said.

Lannes put the envelope in his breast pocket. He unpinned the rose from his buttonhole and tossed it to her.

Why did I do that? he thought, as he descended the stairs, but it was a rhetorical question, that is, one which answered iself. There was every reason why he shouldn't, but there was a compelling reason on the other side of the argument. He knew that and felt ashamed. Nevertheless, he said aloud, nevertheless.

XXVI

'The Alsatian was looking for you,' old Joseph said. 'Told me to ask you to see him soon as you arrived.'

'Fine,' Lannes said, and collected the two boxes of Ramon Allones that Fernand had given him on the Friday afternoon. That should put him in a good mood.

As usual Schnyder's desk was all but bare. Lannes laid down the cigars.

'Oh, good of you. What do I owe you?'

'I haven't paid for them yet. Here's the bill.'

He handed over the note Fernand had scribbled on a scrap of paper.

'The man who got them for you would prefer you to pay me, and I'll pass it on to him.'

'That's all right, but you'll have to wait till I've been to the bank.'

'There's no hurry. He's an old friend who can afford to wait.'

Schnyder opened one of the boxes, took out a cigar, clipped the end off, and lit it. For a moment he watched the blue-grey smoke rise, and sat back in his chair, contentment spreading over his face.

'That's better,' he said. 'These German ones were poor stuff and our own Fleur des Savanes aren't much better, even when you can get them. One for you?'

'No thanks,' Lannes said. 'I won't deprive you. Anyway, as you know, I prefer cigarettes.'

'Have you seen Schussmann recently?'

'He called in one day last week.'

'And?'

'The usual thing, routine visit, any problems with collaboration, that sort of thing, nothing of note.'

'How did he seem?'

'Again as usual, pleasant enough, he's not exactly the ravening Nazi beast, is he? Why do you ask?'

'He's been replaced, superseded. I'd a visit from his successor this morning. A Lieutenant Kordlinger.'

'Well,' Lannes said, 'it's no business of ours, is it, who the Boches assign to deal with us. Only hope the new chap's as easy and undemanding as Schussmann.'

'Quite so,' Schnyder said.

He drew on his cigar, got up and paced around the room.

'There's something I don't like,' he said. 'I got a whiff of a nasty smell. He asked me more than once, in different ways, if I knew of any French contacts Schussmann had outwith our department. Certainly not, I said, which happens to be true. But he kept probing. Something's up, that's obvious. It doesn't sound to me like the usual replacement of one officer by another. I got the impression that old Schussmann's blotted his copybook rather badly.'

'None of our business if he has,' Lannes said.

'I hope not. Then I started thinking. That spook you saw in the public garden – did he have anything to say about Schussmann? Mention him perhaps?'

'Villepreux – the BMA, he belongs to, by the way. Not a word.'

Bracal, he thought, knows about Félix and the Travaux Rurales, though not in detail. Schnyder doesn't as far as I know. Keep it that way.

'It was certain aspects of the old Chambolley case that interested him,' he said, conscious of Professor Labiche's envelope in his jacket pocket. 'Nothing about Schussmann.'

'But that case is dead, isn't it?'

'As I told him.'

'Puzzling then. You'll let me know if anything transpires. I wouldn't like to think the Boches were taking an interest in our department.'

'Can't think why they should be,' Lannes said.

*　　*　　*

But of course he could . . . 'Contacts outwith the department': well, there was certainly Léon – but clearly there was suspicion directed at the department itself, and this suspicion had led to Schussmann being replaced, perhaps. Well, that was no business of his, though he had liked him well enough. Damn these spooks and their tricks and plots. He collected his blackthorn and left the office. There was almost certainly no urgency, but the whiff of a nasty smell which Schnyder had detected alarmed him. He set off for the rue des Remparts.

There were no customers in the bookshop.

'Henri's upstairs as usual,' Léon said, and looked away.

'Schussmann,' Lannes said.

'What about him?'

Léon looked miserable, also guilty. Lannes had seen that expression too often, on too many suspects, to mistake it. He saw also that the boy was near breaking-point even before he had started what he would doubtless think of as an interrogation.

'Léon,' he said, 'I'm here as a friend, not a policeman.'

'Can you ever not be a policeman? How can I forget that's what you are?'

Lannes sighed. He felt ashamed. The boy was right. When was he ever not a policeman? Except surely at home, with Marguerite and the children. Yet even there his profession was a barrier. Could either Dominique or Alain be absolutely honest and open with him? Clothilde perhaps, but the boys? Even as he thought that, the memory of Yvette settling herself, naked, on his knees and demanding a kiss, came to him, excitingly and shamefully.

So he said, 'I don't know, Léon, but there are times when I try myself to forget I'm a policeman, as for instance when I gave you a warning and asked you to come to me if . . . '

'And I didn't because I couldn't,' Léon said before he could finish his sentence.

'All right, but now?'

'What's happened?'

'I don't know precisely,' Lannes said, 'but another German officer has been asking questions about Schussmann whom he seems to have replaced . . . Félix,' he said, and waited, his eyes fixed on the boy's face. 'Félix, you had really better tell. A man calling himself that came to see you, yes? And he threatened you? Yes?'

'How could I speak to you?' Léon said.

He buried his face in his hands. Lannes waited. There was no need to say anything more, not for the moment. He laid his hand on the boy's head.

'I couldn't even speak to Alain.'

Lannes got up and locked the door. Léon straightened up and pushed his hair back.

'You'd better read this,' he said, and took Schussmann's letter from his pocket.

'I think he refused the dishonourable course,' Lannes said.

'And the alternatives?'

'They might come to the same thing in the end. I suspect he realised that.'

Suicide or confession?, he thought. The speed with which he had been replaced suggested the former. A bullet in the head might be preferable to a concentration camp. On the other hand – damn these spooks – surely he might have agreed to collaborate, then played Félix false. Had he considered that course?

'I can guess what happened,' Lannes said. 'You don't need to spell it out.'

'He was a nice man, really, but I wouldn't have gone with him, if . . . '

'Félix,' Lannes said again.

'My mother, Aunt Miriam, he said if I didn't do as he asked, he would see that they were sent to an internment camp. They're good people, you know that. I couldn't say, go ahead, could I?'

'No, Léon. You couldn't. I understand.'

He suspected there was more the boy might have told him, but there was no point pressing, and even less point in saying that his aunt and mother were in danger as long as the war and Vichy lasted.

'Will he come back, do you think?'

'I trust not. You've done what he asked you to. It should be enough. It should be over. But if I'm wrong and he returns, this time, whatever he demands of you, you must let me know. Otherwise I can't help you or your mother and aunt. Understand?'

Léon nodded.

'Promise?'

'Promise.'

Someone rattled the door handle.

'Are you all right?'

'I think so.'

Lannes unlocked the door. A slim fair-haired boy smiled at him.

'You're Alain's father, aren't you?' he said. 'I'm a friend of his at school. Jérôme de Balastre.'

'Ah yes,' Lannes said, 'he may have spoken of you. You won't find him here however.'

'No, but it's Léon I've come to see.'

'Ah yes,' Lannes said again. 'Léon.'

He closed the door behind him. Jérôme kissed Léon on the cheek.

'I've a message from Alain,' he said. 'But what's wrong? You look terrible.'

Léon shook his head.

'Are you in trouble? Was it something Alain's father said?'

Again Léon made no reply.

'Tell me it's none of my business,' Jérôme said, 'if you like. I won't be offended. But, if I can, I would like to help. I'm fond of you, Léon. We haven't known each other long, but long enough for me to know that.'

'I would if I could, but there's nothing anyone can do.'

He felt a spurt of resentment. Nobody was going to haul Jérôme or his mother or stepfather off to an internment camp. No Félix was going to rape him and compel him to do something that was not only dishonourable, but cruel. For his deception of Schussmann, luring him into a trap, had been both these things, and now Schussmann was dead, by his own hand – that was clearly what Alain's father thought – and he was responsible. He wanted to tell it all to Jérôme, but he couldn't. Would Jérôme withdraw his friendship, despise him as he despised himself?

'What's Alain's message?' he said.

'He wants a meeting, this afternoon. Can you get away?'

'Henri never minds if I close the shop,' Léon said.

'Right then.'

'Remember,' Jérôme said, 'whatever it is, I'm with you, Léon. I'm on your side, contra mundum. I'm your friend, for always. People like us have quite enough enemies, even without counting the Boches. I'll call again for you later. Now I'm expected at home for lunch.'

XXVII

There was one customer in the tabac, a silver-haired elderly man hesitating over the purchase of a pipe. He was examining several, testing them for weight and balance, running his finger along the grain of the wood, doing everything but put them in his mouth. It was perhaps his biggest decision of the day, even of the week. Lannes was almost envious. Miriam signalled to him to go through to the back room, but it was fully ten minutes before she joined him.

'Did he buy one eventually?'

'At last; he took his time, but he's a good customer and a nice man, a retired doctor who had a good reputation for caring for his poor patients and not sending in a bill if he knew they couldn't afford to pay him. You look worried, Jean.'

He might have replied that she didn't look well herself. She had lost weight since she returned to the tabac after the deaths of her father and her husband, the old count. And she had aged; there were new lines on her face. It was hard to recognise the confident strapping woman who had sat in Henri's apartment above the shop and talked with such relish about the members of that household in the rue d'Aviau. Only a few months ago he had wanted to make love to her, and had been restrained by her good sense and his own need to keep his self-respect by being faithful to Marguerite. He knew she had felt the same way, and now he saw the shadow of the ghetto lying upon her, and she was on the point of appearing an old woman.

'Is it Alain?' she said, getting a bottle of marc and two glasses from the cupboard.

'No, though I'm always afraid he will do something rash. He's too spirited for the times we live in. No, I'm sorry, but it's Léon.'

'Léon,' she sat down heavily, and again he saw that dark shadow creep over her face.

'I would have liked to spare you,' he said, and went on to tell her the full story: Schussmann, Félix, the threats, the trap, and the consequences.

'I let him down,' he said. 'I should have taken it on myself to warn Schussmann off. But I was weak. I kept putting it off, and, when Léon said nothing to me, never came to tell me that the spook had approached him, I allowed myself to hope that nothing was happening. Not that I'm blaming Léon, you understand. The pressure put on him was dreadful. I'm not surprised he couldn't bring himself to speak of it.'

'And now?' she said.

'Now, I don't know.' He drank the marc and lit a cigarette. 'I really don't know. I hope the spook will leave him alone, I can't think that a similar opportunity to use him will arise. Nevertheless I can't be sure that he won't seek to make some other use of him. Once these chaps have their claws in someone, they don't withdraw them easily. So the threat is still there.'

'And not only from him,' she said. 'I've had that bastard Labiche in here again, crowing about his appointment to that circus set up to deal with the Jewish Question. I hadn't been aware that I was part of a question. Now I can't forget it. But poor Léon, to have felt he must keep this to himself, to take on the weight of responsibility.'

'Yes, poor boy indeed. He's been through hell, I'm afraid.'

'Do you think he told Alain?'

'No, I'm sure he didn't.'

'He thinks of him as his best friend, maybe even his only one. But you are probably right. He would have been ashamed to speak of it, and perhaps afraid.'

The shop-bell rang. Miriam got to her feet and went through to deal with the new customer. The bounce had gone out of her step. She moves like an old woman, Lannes thought. Alain would surely have been so indignant that he would have spoken to him. Surely? He leaned back in his chair and closed his eyes. Things were bad. They would get worse.

When Miriam returned, he said, 'All the same, I really think we should try to find a way to get you all out of Bordeaux.'

'Where could we go? And how? Anyway, why should I be driven

out of the city where I've lived all my life? I'm French, Jean, a citizen of the Republic. So are Léon and my sister, citizens.'

'We no longer live in the Republic,' he said. 'Only in the French State which is under German Occupation. But you would leave, wouldn't you, if I can contrive a way?'

'I don't know,' she said, 'I'm an obstinate bitch.'

XXVIII

Jérôme unhooked his arm from Léon's as they approached the Café des Arts, cours du Marne. They settled themselves at a table in the back of the room. The elderly waiter took their order for lemonades with a sniff. Léon thought, he'll be happy when the day comes that he's forbidden to serve me; but it was absurd. There was nothing in his appearance to suggest he was Jewish. If only there had been, Schussmann would never have approached him, would still be alive.

A poster on the wall across from the table advertised a production of 'La Dame aux Caméllias' starring Adrienne Jauzion. It was an old poster, a bit tattered at the edges and stained with smoke.

'Have you ever seen her?' Jérôme said. 'She can be wonderful, though my stepfather who knows a lot about the theatre says she's very affected, and never plays the character, always only herself. But I was crazy about her when I was fourteen, I thought her the most marvellous person on earth. Do you think that strange, Léon?'

Léon knew he was chattering in this way to distract him, and was grateful.

'Not at all,' he said. 'Well, I don't know. Actually I've come to realise I know so little about other people.'

'It's not unusual,' Jérôme said, 'for someone of my temperament – our temperament if I may say so. You know who I mean by Lucien Daudet? – Alphonse's son – you must have read the *Lettres de mon Moulin* – of course you have – and brother of Léon who writes for *L'Action Française*, which I don't expect you to care for – well, I don't myself, not really – but he is in charge of the literary pages, and they are brilliant, superb. Anyway, Lucien, despite having been one of Proust's lovers when they were boys or young men, devoted himself for years to the Empress Eugénie in her exile in England. He really adored her.'

'And Adrienne Jauzion is your Empress?'

'Well, she was and to some extent still is. She is really rather wonderful, so cold and superior – you feel she despises the world. I have only actually met her once, at a soirée – you must know that my grandfather's cousin, the Comte de St-Hilaire, who is also my godfather as it happens, not that it matters, has been her lover and protector for years. Anyway she extended her hand – in white lace gloves – to me, and made it clear that I was to kiss the tips of her fingers, which of course I did, obediently, and then she dismissed me – pouf , just like that – from her presence. I can tell you this, Léon. Alain would just think me silly, which perhaps I am, and Porthos would say I needed a kick up the arse, but it's one of the most exciting, even erotic, memories that I have. He's a bit crude, Porthos, as you may have remarked.'

'Alain's late,' Léon said.

'Privilege of the chief.'

Then the room brightened. Alain was with them, urgent as a dispatch-rider. He ordered a beer. The waiter looked at him searchingly, shrugged his shoulders. Alain waited till the beer was in front of him and the old man had retired behind the bar, before saying, 'I've got some bad news. Porthos – Philippe, I may as well call him again now – has ratted. He told me that what we were doing is futile, that the war and Occupation are going to last for years, and the sensible thing was to get on with preparing for a career. What do you think of that?'

'He's a bit of an ass, Porthos,' Jérôme said, 'I've always thought so.'

Two businessmen in dark suits came into the café and stood by the bar. They ordered a Ricard each. Alain drank half his beer in one long swallow, and, nursing his glass in his hands, fixed his gaze on them.

One said, 'This call for workers to go to Germany is going to mean a labour shortage here and rise in wages if many respond. Could you afford that, old man?'

'Not likely. I can barely afford to pay my staff as things are. Times are bad.'

'You're right there, and they're going to get worse.'

'I don't see the way ahead, I tell you that,' the second said, downing his Ricard, wiping his mouth with a white-spotted blue handkerchief. 'Same again?'

'Half of them are Communists, if you ask me.'

'Absolutely. I thought Vichy would mean discipline.'

'Fat chance.'

Alain fished out a packet of cigarettes, empty. Léon passed him one, and then to Jérôme, and they all lit up.

Alain said, 'Let's go for a walk.'

'Outside,' he said, 'people like that pair make me sick. Half of them are Communists if you ask me, when really they're probably decent working men wanting a decent wage for a day's work. Sometimes I loathe the French, and despise them. Maybe we deserve to be occupied by the Boches. I know that you're on the Right, Jérôme, because that's how you've been brought up, But really the rich stink. I'm sorry if that offends you.'

'I'm not so easily offended, not by you, anyway.'

They walked towards the river. Léon thought, Alain's like a coiled spring; then, but that's a literary expression, I don't even know exactly what a coiled spring is. He looked at his friend's profile, grim, set, determined, angry.

'Fortunately France is not the French,' Alain said. 'France is more than the French. France is an idea. The Republic is an idea. That's why it's worth saving.'

The sun sparkled on the water. A lorry full of German soldiers crossed the bridge. The men were singing what sounded like a hymn, though the words might glorify the Fuehrer rather than the Almighty, for all they knew. The sound drifted behind them.

'The bastards are happy,' Alain said, 'here in our city.'

He hoisted himself on the parapet and sat there swinging his legs.

'I could have punched Philippe,' he said. 'He made me so angry. But one reason for that was that actually he's right. What we are doing, what we've done so far, is futile. Oh it's something, we can agree on that, but it really amounts to nothing. Actually I didn't need him to lead me to that conclusion. I was down here on Sunday and I watched the river running so calmly to the sea, and I thought, I don't know anything useful, not really. I wouldn't know how to set about an act of sabotage for instance. So I have to learn, and there's only one place I can do that. London. London is where the real France is to be found today. So I'm going to find a way to get there. What about you, Léon? And you, Jérôme? Are you with me?'

'But of course,' Jérôme said, 'one for all and all for one – even if one – that ass Philippe – or Porthos, whichever – has chickened out.'

'Splendid. Léon?'

Léon hesitated a moment. He thought of his mother and aunt and the internment camp. Then he looked Alain full in the face and saw that he was very pale.

'How could I say no?' he said.

Alain leaped down from the wall, seized his friends by the hands and for a moment they danced in a wild circle.

'Liberty,' Alain cried.

'Equality,' Jérôme answered.

'Fraternity,' Léon shouted and felt tears prick his eyes; fraternity was what Alain and Jérôme offered him, and without it he was nothing, an empty husk.

'The next question,' Alain said, calling the dance to a halt, 'is how. How we get out of Bordeaux, how we find our way to London. It may take time, but we'll do it, I'm sure of that.'

He took Léon by the shoulders and hugged him, kissing him on either cheek, like a general bestowing a medal. Then he did the same to Jérôme.

'All for one and one for all.'

When Alain had left them, – 'because my grandmother's visiting and Maman will be offended if I'm not there – not that I want to listen to the old woman's moans and it'll be still worse if that pompous prick my Uncle Albert is there too' – Léon said to Jérôme, 'There's something I must tell you, you're the only person I can tell.'

'My dear, I'm flattered.'

'But not here,' – 'here' would always be a sacred spot, the place of commitment, the place where Alain had hugged and kissed him – 'somewhere quiet where we can sit down and not be in danger of being overheard.'

'The bookshop?'

'Not there either.'

Félix, he thought, Félix might already have heard the news about Schussmann, Félix might come to seek him out – like an ogre in a fairy tale.

'It's a lovely afternoon,' Jérôme said. 'We could go and sit in the public garden, it's not half an hour's walk.'

*   *   *

They stretched out on the grass. Jérôme had chattered, about this, that and nothing as they crossed the city, but now he fell silent. Children ran about playing while their mothers, weary of the privations of war and the difficulty of caring for their families in these grim times, took a welcome opportunity to rest, relax and even perhaps forget for a little that things were as they were. A boy of about ten was flying a kite. A peacock strolled across the lawn. It was a wonder nobody had yet carried it off for the pot. Jérôme chewed a blade of grass.

'There's no hurry,' he said.

Léon was very pale. There were dark circles under his eyes, pain and perplexity in his look. It was as if in a few days the pretty boy had become a careworn adult. And yet there was also something of the bewildered and unhappy child in him too.

'Did Alain ever mention a German officer who came quite often to the bookshop?' he said.

'I don't think so. If he did it made no impression on me.'

'Then I suppose he didn't. He was a nice man, a bit boring, even pathetic. Genuinely interested in French literature. He bought a couple of early editions of Gide.'

Jérôme smiled.

'All right,' he said, 'I can guess. His interest wasn't only in books. You don't need to spell it out. So?'

'So his attentions were noticed.'

Léon paused, looked Jérôme full in the face for the first time since they had settled themselves in the garden. The dam burst. The story flooded out. Félix's contempt, his threats, even – head hanging again – the rape, the humiliation and despair, the dinner with Schussmann, the misery of the Hotel Artemis, the shame, Schussmann's letter, the shame intensified, Alain's father. He kept nothing back, excused himself nothing, spoke of his fear and self-disgust.

'I never thought of myself as a Jew before the war,' he said. 'We don't practise, I thought of myself as French, as French as you are. But do you understand why just now when Alain said what he did, I hesitated to say "Yes" as immediately as you did? If it had been anyone but Alain, I would have said no. Do you despise me, Jérôme?'

'Despise you? If your story wasn't so terrible, I might be offended by such a suggestion. I think you're a hero.'

Léon was near tears again.

'That's ridiculous,' he said, 'but thank you.'

'It's not ridiculous. To have had this experience, to have suffered as you have, and to have kept it to yourself, and survived, that's heroic. I couldn't have done it.'

'But then you're not a Jew. That's something I have learned about myself: that I really am Jewish. We suffer and survive in silence. It's what we have learned over the centuries.'

Jérôme took hold of his hand and squeezed it.

'All for one and one for all,' he said.

'But you won't tell Alain, not any of it.'

'Not if you don't want me to.'

'I couldn't bear him to know. You're the only person I could bear to tell. I'm afraid it would disgust him. He doesn't even guess what I am, I'm sure of that, how I feel about him, how much I want him, even though I know it's impossible.'

'No, he's very innocent, Alain. Perhaps it's what we love in him.'

The peacock picked his way over the grass, his tail-feathers now resplendently spread.

'That bird thinks he's a German,' Jérôme said. 'He believes he owns the garden.'

'I feel better,' Léon said. 'I don't know why, but I feel better.'

'That's the beauty of confession. The Church has known that for centuries. There's no confessional in the synagogue, is there?'

'How should I know? I've never been in a synagogue in my life,' and for the first time in days, Léon found himself laughing, remembering how when he had suggested that Jérôme had seen him in the bank, he had said, 'I've never been in a bank in my life.'

'Alain's right,' Jérôme said, 'we have to get to London.'

'I know, but . . . '

'But?'

'My mother and my aunt.'

'Yes, of course. I think you have to speak to Alain's father about them.'

XXIX

The brown envelope lay on the desk, and Lannes couldn't understand why he didn't open it. More than once he felt around it, made as if to insert his thumb under the flap, only to lay it down again. He picked it up and ran his tongue round the edges, and replaced it on the desk. He lay back in his chair and lit a cigarette, got up and crossed the room to look out of the window, but if you had asked him what he saw he couldn't have told you. Was his reluctance occasioned by the fear that the contents of the envelope would reveal nothing of significance, or the suspicion that what was revealed was something he would prefer not to know? He couldn't find an answer to these questions.

It was a relief when a knock on the door came as a distraction and old Joseph entered to say that a young woman wanted to see him.

'To my mind she's a tart but someone's had a go at her,' he said. 'It wouldn't surprise me if she was asking for it, but there you are, it's a wicked world.'

Yvette had a black eye and a swollen mouth, and was trembling. Lannes took a bottle of Armagnac from the cupboard, poured out two glasses, gave her one, and said, 'Drink this and take your time.'

She winced as the spirit touched her lips. He put the brown

envelope away in the top left-hand drawer of his desk which he locked.

'It was that effing Spaniard,' she said, and took another sip of the brandy. 'He came back and I thought I knew what he wanted, well, you know what Spaniards are, and I was ready to oblige, because, why not? It's what I do, isn't it, and he was smiling and speaking sweet as honey. So I named a price, because he's not the sort I would give it to for nothing, not like the old gentleman, or' – she smiled – 'you yourself, superintendent, whenever you feel like it. But he said, still soft as a cream cheese, that it wasn't that he wanted, but to ask me again if I was sure the old gentleman hadn't given me anything to look after. "Or perhaps he hid it in your room. You won't mind if I take a look, will you. I'll even pay you to let me do so." "I'm not having you grub around among my knickers," I said, and then, because he was still looking all right, I thought, why the hell not, and told him that there had been an envelope but I had given it to you. That's when he went wild and began to clobber me, shouting out that I was a bitch. I screamed and Madame Mangeot came along the corridor, doubtless as fast as she could in her carpet slippers which she always wears on account of her bunions, and told him to bugger off. "This is a respectable house," she says, which it ain't, but I tell you I was that grateful to the old cow. She's not so bad really, not like her rat of a husband. I can tell you he wouldn't lift a finger to help anyone, and indeed when I'd tidied myself up and set off to come here, he was cowering behind his desk, pretending he'd seen and heard nothing. "Call yourself a man. . . " I said. I don't mind telling you I was scared when I stepped out into the street in case the Spaniard was hanging about. But he'd buggered off, doubtless because old Madame Mangeot had spoken of calling the police, which she wouldn't have done because they don't like having police in the hotel. So here I am, and what I want to know, is what the hell is it all about?'

She downed what remained of the brandy and held out her glass for more.

Lannes said, 'I can't tell you that, because I haven't opened the envelope myself yet.'

And now that you're here, he thought, I'm even less sure that I'm going to, because of the fear that what it contains would indeed be something I would rather not know about.

She took another mouthful of brandy and moved her tongue around in her mouth.

'The bastard's loosened a tooth too,' she said. 'So what do I do now? How do I know he won't come back?'

'He's got no reason to,' Lannes said. 'I don't think you need worry about him again. Not now that he knows I have the envelope. It was just temper that caused him to lose control. In any case I'll have him brought in and we'll make sure he doesn't bother you again.'

He went through to the inspectors' room, and told young René Martin to see the girl safely back to the Pension Bernadotte.

'I ought to warn you that she thinks you're quite a dish,' he said, and was amused to see René blush.

Then he turned to Moncerre and said, 'You've kept tabs on Sombra, haven't you? I want you to find him and bring him in. He's just beaten up that girl, and it won't distress me, for once, if you should find it necessary to rough him up. If you get him this evening, it won't do him any harm to spend the night in a cell. I'm off home.'

Back in his office, he took the brown envelope from the drawer and slipped it into his pocket. He put the brandy bottle back in the cupboard and was about to leave when old Joseph knocked at the door.

'This was left at the front desk for you,' he said, and handed him an envelope. It contained a single sheet of the cheap paper cafés supply to their customers.

'Do you really not want to know who your true father was, superintendent?'

At the desk he asked who had left the letter.

'Some street kid. Just handed it in and scarpered.'

'If he comes again, you'll detain him. That's an order.'

XXX

The Comte de St-Hilaire was a man of great distinction in Bordeaux, as his family had been for generations. His grandfather had been one of the founders of the exclusive Primrose Club and he himself had been its President. His vineyard in the Médoc produced a premier cru Claret. In the city itself he had a fine house in the Allée de Tournay which Stendhal had once called the most beautiful street in France. He had never engaged in politics, for he despised the Republic while indulging in an equally profound contempt for Action Français and the Royalists. He thought the famous Mayor of Bordeaux, Adrien Marquet, a vulgar fellow, and had an aristocrat's disdain for Fascism. No doubt, if compelled to choose, he would have opted for it rather than Communism, for at least the Fascists were unlikely to deprive him of his property, but he regarded both faiths as manifestations of the deplorable twentieth century. His family had been Huguenots in the time of the religious wars, but he himself had long ago discarded any remnants of religious belief. He was a Voltairean sceptic and viewed the Catholic Church as a deplorably superstitious survival. He owned racehorses and collected pretty women. In his youth he had enjoyed a formidable reputation as a seducer of his friends' wives – though in truth he had few friends, merely acquaintances with whom he was on easy conversational terms. For ten years now he had been recognised as the acknowledged lover and protector of Adrienne Jauzion, though she had come to bore him as almost everything did; and it amused him now to observe her toy with entering on an affair with that policeman who had been sent from Paris to command the Police Judiciaire. At the age of seventy he ignored the Occupation. It was something the French had brought on themselves by their folly and their contemptible politics. He placed no more trust in Marshal Pétain than in the God of his forefathers.

It amused him to read Mauriac's caustic novels about his native city, though he found the author's fervent Catholicism ridiculous. But so, to his mind, was almost everything. Life was something without reason, to which you had been condemned. The only thing was not to make a fool of yourself.

Jérôme was in awe of his godfather, dazzled by him also. He admired his massive indifference. Yet he had received occasional indications of what was almost tenderness. 'You may be a little idiot,' the Count had said once, 'but then most people are, and there are moments when you are not without intelligence.' And Jérôme, while in awe, also sensed that behind the imposing façade – itself as forbidding as the limestone of which the grand houses of the city were built – there was a disappointed romanticism, as if his godfather reproached himself for finding so little worth doing. And so he now nerved himself to call on him and present him with his problem. One thing was certain: the Count might tell him that what he proposed was foolish, but he would not demean himself by betraying him – not even to his mother and stepfather. So it was with a mixture of trepidation and hope that he presented himself at his godfather's door.

The butler showed him into a salon on the ground floor. The furniture was Louis Quinze, the paintings mostly ancestral portraits, though there was also a delicious Fragonard of nymphs bathing and a Courbet still-life of bread, fruit and a jug of wine. He didn't dare to take a seat but stood by the window, twisting his fingers and seeing nothing.

'My dear Jérôme, to what do I owe this unexpected pleasure?'

The count crossed the room with a firm step and long country-man's strides. He wore an English tweed suit and there was a monocle in his left eye. He overtopped Jérôme by several inches and as he leaned forward to greet him with a perfunctory kiss on the cheek, the scent of an expensive eau-de-Cologne mingled with the smoke from the cigar which he held in his right hand dangerously close to Jérôme's hair.

The butler re-appeared carrying a silver tray on which there was a claret jug and two glasses. He poured the wine and left the room without speaking.

'I don't know how to begin,' Jérôme said.

'You might sit down anyway.'

The count drew on his cigar and smiled.

'There's a fraudulent novelist, name of Malraux – you of course may admire him, dear boy – whom I once heard start a conversation with the question, "So, what do you think of the Apocalypse?" That was not an enticing opening.'

'I should think not,' Jérôme said. 'As for me, I don't even know what the Apocalypse is. Something to do with four horsemen, isn't it?'

'Famine, pestilence, war and death, quite appropriate for our wretched times indeed.'

'That's what I want to ask you about,' Jérôme said. 'The times we live in.'

'My dear boy,' – the count removed his monocle and, taking a square of chamois leather from his waistcoat pocket, began to polish the glass – 'why should you suppose that I have anything to say on the subject?'

Jérôme took a sip of claret to fortify himself, and found that his hand was shaking.

'Because it's intolerable,' he said, 'the times – the situation we're in – they're intolerable, for people of my age, that is . . . '

'And so?'

'That's it, you see. Vichy, the Occupation . . . it's intolerable . . . so, two friends and I' – he gulped and found himself unable to look his godfather in the face – 'we've decided, we want to get out, get to London, to join de Gaulle. There, I've said it. I wasn't sure I would be able to, but I have.'

He raised his eyes. To his surprise the count was smiling.

'And so you come to me?' he said. 'To share this confidence? I should be honoured.'

'You don't disapprove?'

'My approval or disapproval matters nothing. But I shall say this: if I was your age, I might feel as you do. These friends, would I know who they are, or rather who their parents are?'

'No, they're not of our class' – Jérôme felt himself blushing as he said this. 'One is a school friend, his father's a policeman. The other works in a bookshop. He's a Jew.'

'And I should care about that? If he's a Jew he may have enough brains for the three of you. You won't know this, Jérôme, but my father was a Dreyfusard. He was asked to resign from the Primrose Club, but refused, saying they might expel him if they chose but he wasn't going to resign. He told them that anti-Semitism was a sentiment unworthy of France. He had a high idea of France, if not of the French, rather like that mad general you want to join in London.'

'You think he's mad, Godfather?'

'He must be mad to suppose that any but a handful of the French retain a sense of honour. All they care about is their property. I speak of course as a man of property myself. I'm aware of the irony.'

The count replaced the monocle in his eye and picked up his glass.

'Your health,' he said. 'You'll hurt your mother, but you know that. It's the fate of mothers to be wounded by their sons. I take it you want my help. I'll think about it. Ways and means.'

He got rather stiffly to his feet. It was clear to Jérôme that the conversation – discussion? – was at an end. The count crossed the room and opened a drawer in a Buhl cabinet. He took out a small blue leather-covered case, and held it out to Jérôme.

'Open it,' he said. 'I was born in 1870, the year of our first German débâcle. I was forty-four when the last war broke out. I never saw service at the Front, but the English gave me that medal for the liaison work I did with them. That old fool Pétain distrusted the English even then, but they fought magnificently. We thought our war was the Apocalypse too. I had a good friend called Cameron, a colonel in a Scottish regiment. He was killed a week before the Armistice. He was a colonel but not yet thirty. I've never forgotten him. So I approve of your intention, Jérôme. I'll think about it. Meanwhile, you will please bring your friends to see me. We'll have lunch. A meal smooths over embarrassments. I'm proud of you. Your grandmother was the only woman I ever really loved. And lost, sadly lost, to my cousin who had been my closest friend.'

He moved forward to embrace Jérôme.

'Let yourself out,' he said. 'Don't trouble to disturb Jean-Pierre.'

Jérôme went dancing down the street. He wanted to sing at the top of his voice, but the dull stupor of the forbidding house-fronts deterred him.

XXXI

Lannes entered the apartment and heard his brother-in-law Albert holding forth. He could have done without that. The old woman, his mother-in-law, was bad enough, but Albert was intolerable. He had hoped he wouldn't be there. It was worse when Albert got to his feet to shake his hand, saying, 'I've been explaining to the boys why whole-hearted collaboration is in our national interest. And it's working smoothly. I'm sure you have found yourself that relations between the Germans and our police are excellent. Isn't that so?'

'We get along because we have to,' Lannes said.

He turned away to give his mother-in-law the obligatory peck on the cheek, and told her she was looking very well, happy in the thought that this observation would displease her.

'If you only knew how I suffer,' she said. 'But at least we have our Dominique safely home.'

'I was happy to do what I could to make that possible,' Albert said.

'And we're grateful to you,' Marguerite said. 'Aren't we, Jean?'

He gave a nod in reply. It was pointless to say that Albert had had nothing to do with Dominique's release from the prisoner-of-war camp. But he couldn't trust himself to say anything. Certainly he wasn't going to support the lie.

Madame Panard said, 'If only these wretched English would see sense, then the Germans would go home and things could be again as they were.'

'Unfortunately,' Albert said, 'Churchill is an obstinate drunkard blind to reality. And of course one must admit that the English have always been our enemies. Do you know why? It's because they are jealous of our superior civilisation and culture. They're a nation of shopkeepers, as Napoleon said, who know the price of everything and the value of nothing. That's why they ran away from Dunkirk and left us in the lurch. Fortunately we have the Marshal to protect us and give us this golden opportunity for national renewal.'

So it went on. Albert dominated the table when they went through to eat, talking with the authority he had assumed since the débâcle of the previous May.

'For instance,' he said, 'we are at last in a position to solve the Jewish problem.'

Alain made to speak, caught his father's eye, and, lowering his eyes, said nothing.

Lannes felt ashamed. Why should he tolerate this talk at his own table? Why should he feel obliged to urge his son to restrain himself? Undoubtedly Alain had been about to say, 'What problem is that, uncle?,' perhaps even to speak of his friendship with Léon and Miriam.

But what was the point of provoking an argument which would only distress Marguerite?

Madame Panard told them how she couldn't sleep at night, how she suffered from headaches and how her liver troubled her, even as she stuffed food into her mouth, and complained about the poor quality of wartime bread and the shortage of butter and sugar, both of which she needed for her health.

Lannes abstracted himself. Sometime the evening would come to an end. He wondered what Yvette was doing, and whether Moncerre had picked up the Spaniard, given him a going-over, and lodged him in a cell. Had Yvette invited young René Martin to her room and had he refused with an embarrassed blush? Picturing the girl lying back on her bed and smiling to him, he lost the thread of the conversation. He slipped his hand into his inside breast pocket and fingered the envelope which he was now almost sure he wasn't going to open. Not at least till he had heard what the Spaniard had to say, and perhaps not even then.

Alain's voice broke into his reverie.

'If the Marshal is our shield, uncle, who is our sword?'

'Sword, boy? We have no need of a sword. Things will arrange themselves without such nonsense. The war is over, you must understand that. It is now a question of using the opportunity we have been granted – by Providence, I dare to say – yes, by Providence, for unhappy beginnings may have happy outcomes – the opportunity to rid ourselves of the Jewish incubus and to suppress the Communists.'

'So you have no opinion of de Gaulle?' Alain said.

'But of course I have an opinion of de Gaulle, the same opinion that any man of sense and any patriotic Frenchman must have. He is a rebel and a traitor, properly condemned to death. That is my opinion of de Gaulle. Remember this, Alain: that in collusion with the English, he attacked the French Empire at Dakar where, I'm happy and proud to say, he was soundly defeated by loyal troops. Moreover he expressed his approval of the English destruction of our fleet at Mers-el-Kebir, where more than a thousand French sailors were killed.'

'I see,' Alain said. 'You make it all very clear, uncle.'

'I'm glad to hear you say so,' Albert said, deaf to Alain's irony.

It was a dreadful evening, but at last it was over. Albert and the old woman departed. Marguerite retired to bed. So, with some muttering, did the children. Lannes said he would sit up for a while; he had some thinking to do. He went through to the kitchen to smoke and drink marc. There were no good thoughts and even the marc offered little consolation. The ashtray was full and the bottle lowered by a couple of inches when the door opened and Dominique, wearing a dressing-gown over his pyjamas, joined him.

'I couldn't sleep either, Papa,' he said. 'Shall I make some coffee?'

'Please.'

'You don't much like Uncle Albert, do you?'

'Is it so obvious?'

'It's strange,' Dominique said, 'I agree with a lot of what he says, we do need a national renewal, I'm sure of that, but when he speaks of what I believe in, he makes it sound repulsive. Does that make sense, Papa?'

'Oh yes, it makes sense. Your uncle is a fool. You're not.'

'I've got something to tell you. I've been waiting for the right moment.'

And you think this is it? Lannes didn't speak the words that came to mind. I'm not going to like it, he thought, and I'm too tired.

'Yes?' he said.

'I've had a letter from my friend Maurice. Maurice de Grimaud. He asks to be remembered to you, by the way. He says you were very kind and helpful to him last year when his grandfather died. And in other ways too, he says, though he doesn't elaborate on them, whatever they were. Anyhow he has suggested I should come to Vichy where he says he can find me a position as a leader in the League of French Youth. That's where he is working himself. It's a great opportunity, he says, and rewarding work. What do you think, Papa?'

'Have you spoken of this to your mother?'

'Yes, naturally.'

Yes naturally, he would have spoken to Marguerite first. He was her boy. Lannes loved him, loved him dearly, but knew himself to be closer to the twins than to his eldest child. He couldn't say why. It wasn't because they thought differently about so much – the war itself, Vichy, religion. It was perhaps simply that both were aware that the connection between them was loose. In certain respects Dominique was the best of the three: the gentlest, a boy who had always shrunk from giving pain, from saying things which would distress those he was with. He was their eldest who sometimes seemed younger, because more trusting and innocent, than the twins.

'And what did she say?'

'She wasn't immediately happy, I have to admit that. But she said I must do what I thought was right. You must always do what you think right, she said.'

'So you've decided?'

'Not absolutely. I wanted your opinion too.'

Lannes lit a cigarette and picked up the bottle.

'Have a drink,' he said, 'get yourself a glass.'

'I won't, thank you. I don't really like alcohol, only the occasional glass of wine, and I had one at supper.'

'As you like,' Lannes said, and poured himself one. He held his glass in both hands, with the cigarette dangling from the corner of his mouth.

'The war's not over,' he said, 'I'm sure of that. Suppose Hitler attacks the Soviet Union, which I think he may, what then? Will Vichy last? As for the national revolution they speak of, I agree that there was much that was rotten in France, which is perhaps why we lost last year. But are the men in Vichy the people to put it right? I don't know. I'm an old Radical, remember, inasmuch as I am anything, and I believe in tolerance and the principles of the Revolution, our real revolution, especially equality and fraternity. There's much in Vichy that I detest – the persecution, which is not too strong a word, of the Jews, which your Uncle Albert approves of, for instance. So I don't know. You must make up your own mind.'

'I have really.'

'I thought so. You're an idealist, Dominique, as I'm not. Perhaps that's because I'm a policeman. It's not a trade that encourages one to think well of our fellow men.'

He drank his marc.

'But your mother's right, as she usually is. You must do what you think right. We must always try to do that.'

'There's so much that needs to be done,' Dominique said. 'For the Youth of France, and the future of the country. Maurice is enthusiastic about the work. You liked him, didn't you, Papa?'

'Yes, I liked him. He reminded me of you.'

'So you see.'

'I see. Wait a few days, that's all I ask. Turn it over in your mind, take account of my warning, and then do what you think is right.'

'I've been thinking, Papa. I really have, and I've decided.'

'Very well.'

He fingered the envelope in his pocket. He too had almost come to a decision.

'I may have to go to Vichy myself,' he said. 'To see Maurice's father. We might travel together.'

Marguerite was asleep when he joined her in bed. He laid his hand on her leg, but she didn't stir. He lay on his back, his mind racing. He should have spoken more firmly to Dominique, spelled out the fear with which the boy Maurice's invitation filled him. He should have said, bluntly, things are going to get worse in France before they get better . . . if they ever get better – and some day there may be a reckoning. It was that 'if', as much as his own weakness which had held him back. You don't want to find yourself on the wrong side. For there was indeed the other 'if': if Vichy survived, then Dominique might be right in choosing to engage in this enterprise. If good people held back, didn't that leave everything to people like Albert?

Sleep still evaded him. Marguerite was breathing easily. She shifted away from him and emitted a little sigh. He pictured Yvette lying back with her legs open. There was so much which you didn't control.

XXXII

'You can take the cuffs off him,' Lannes said.

Sombra's face was unmarked, but, when Lannes told him to sit down, he placed his hand on his kidneys and moved gingerly. The arrogance had left him. Moncerre had evidently done a thorough job on him, and would have enjoyed it.

'I don't like men who beat up women,' Lannes said. 'So you've nothing to complain of. You got what was coming to you.'

Sombra shook his head and gulped.

'What's all this about?' he said.

'That's my question, not yours,' Lannes said. 'Let's start from the beginning. Aristide Labiche. What did you want from him?'

Sombra made no reply.

'Come on,' Lannes said. 'You knew I was going to ask that question. You've had time to think of an answer. You called on him in the Pension Bernadotte, went down to the bar for a drink. Then a day or two later you visited the office of his brother, the advocate, and then Aristide was found murdered in the public garden. So you've some explaining to do.'

'I didn't kill him. You can't pin that on me.'

'Is that so? All right, perhaps you didn't kill him, though I've an open mind on the subject, but, believe me, I can pin it on you if I choose. I need his killer. You'll do as well as anyone.'

Sombra twisted the gold signet ring he wore on the little finger of his left hand.

'We were old acquaintances,' he said. 'I knew him in Spain. So when I learned he was in Bordeaux it was natural to have a drink with him. That's all. I know nothing about his death.'

'So you say, but you're the only suspect I have.'

Lannes took the brown envelope from his pocket and laid it on the desk.

'This is what you were looking for,' he said. 'It's what he left with Yvette. I haven't opened it, as you see. I don't know what it contains or who might be interested in that. Except you, of course. Look at it from my side, Sombra. You seek out Aristide, talk with him, and he gets frightened, so frightened that he entrusts the envelope to Yvette, for safe keeping. Then he's dead, and you return to search for it, and beat up young Yvette when she tells you she gave it to me. So it's important to you, or to whoever put you up to it. Is Sigi back in Bordeaux?'

Sombra shook his head again.

'Or perhaps it was your German friends who want the information. If the envelope contains what I think it does – evidence relating to Edmond de Grimaud's relationship to the girl Pilar – then I can see why they would want it, in order to put the squeeze on him. Perhaps you are playing a double game, Sombra? I don't think your friend Sigi would approve of that. Edmond's his protector, after all. Still nothing to say? Lost your tongue? You were talkative enough last time we had you in here. Claimed diplomatic immunity, didn't you, which was absurd.'

Still the Spaniard said nothing. Lannes looked him in the eyes. Sombra's were dark, liquid. He couldn't hold Lannes' gaze for long. He licked his lips.

'Can I have a glass of water?' he said. 'I think your bastard of an inspector has broken one of my ribs.'

'Too bad,' Lannes said. 'You broke one of Yvette's teeth.'

'I don't know who killed Aristide. Maybe his brother ordered it. I really don't know. It had nothing to do with me.'

'So you say,' Lannes said again. 'Tell me about the brother, the advocate. How well do you know him?'

'Not well. Why should I? Superintendent, please believe me, I know nothing, really nothing.'

'You're not a man it's easy to believe,' Lannes said.

He got up and crossed the room to look out of the window. He could sense Sombra shifting in his chair. To ease his bodily discomfort? Or his mental? Then he took a bottle of Armagnac and two glasses from the cupboard, poured out two drinks and passed one across the desk to the Spaniard, who hesitated before stretching out for the glass which, however, he downed in one swallow.

'You're small fry, Sombra,' Lannes said. 'Among other things you're a pimp. Is that your connection with the advocate? Have you procured little girls for him?'

'You accuse me of this now?'

'I can accuse you of several things. I don't like you, Sombra. I don't like your type. I have several different stories and you're in the centre of all of them. That's why I would advise you to speak. Because if you don't, if you choose to stay silent, then, believe me, you will be back in the cells and you won't be out for a long time. Of course that might be best for you. You may be safer there, even if I let Moncerre have another go at you. Think about it.'

'I know nothing about Aristide's death, I assure you. You must believe me.'

'Must I? Why should I?'

Lannes sighed. He had a sour taste in his mouth. He loathed this sort of thing. Sombra was a miserable rag of humanity, but he was nevertheless human. He was a murderer. Lannes had no doubt about that. Sombra and his mentor Sigi had killed Gaston Chambolley and Sombra had also killed that wretched clerk – what was his name? – Sigi's foster-brother who had tried to blackmail them after they had borrowed his car from which one of them – Sombra, he believed – had tried to shoot Lannes himself. Lannes had been forced to abandon that investigation, but not before he had frightened Sombra with the threat of the guillotine. But, rat though Sombra was, Lannes knew he had initiated nothing. He was an underling, a hitman, who merely carried out orders. The question was: whose orders?

'Tell you another story,' he said. He picked up the envelope and waved it in front of Sombra. 'There's an agent of one of the French Security Services who wants to have something on Edmond, wants to be in a position to damage him. He knows there are compromising papers relating either to his relationship with Pilar, a Spanish anarchist and spy, or to still more damaging connections with the Germans whom, despite the Armistice, the spook still regards as the enemy, and he believes that these are now in Aristide's possession. He knows about your reputation, which is not exactly a savoury one, and he commissions you to get in touch with Aristide and obtain the papers. You make his acquaintance and he promises to meet you again in a public place – for his safety, as he thinks – and enter into negotiations with you. I suppose he wants some sort of promise of safe conduct when he hands them over. But he has second thoughts, gets suspicious perhaps about your intentions, and you lose your temper and hit him on the head with your stick. Perhaps you hit him harder than you intended. No matter. He's dead. You pull his body into the bushes and make off in a panic. But you still have to get hold of the papers. I ruled you out, first, I don't mind admitting, because I said that this sort of killing wasn't your style. You prefer the garotte, don't you, Sombra. But I've changed my mind, you see, on account of your attack on Yvette. You lose your temper easily, and when you lose your temper, you lose your head. And now you don't know whether you should be more frightened of me or of the man who commissioned you, or even of Sigi and Edmond whom you have double-crossed. So you are playing dumb. How do you like that?'

'It's fanciful,' Sombra said. 'You've no evidence at all.'

'Evidence?' Lannes said. 'Let's not worry about evidence. I've enough, I assure you, to hold you on suspicion. In fact, after this conversation, I'm going to go straight to the examining judge to get authority to do just that. There's an alternative story of course: that it was the advocate Labiche, who knows you because you have obligingly provided him with the young flesh he likes, who commissions you to get the papers from Aristide. Why should he want them, you ask? Because though he denies that he met his brother since his return to Bordeaux, that's a lie, one of his many lies, and in fact they did meet and Aristide foolishly spoke of this document, which interests the advocate because he is anxious to get a hold on Edmond de Grimaud, for reasons which I know, even if you don't. So he commissions you to get them. The outcome's the same, whichever story we prefer. Either one puts you in deep shit. Actually I prefer this second one because I get the advocate too. As for you, Sombra, your only chance of getting out of the mess, is to come clean. You're not ready to do that yet? Fine, you're going to have long days and nights in the cells to think about it.'

*   *   *

He was pleased to be rid of his presence, of the whiff of corruption he exuded, but he knew he had got nowhere. Each of the scenarios he had sketched was plausible, but no more than that. He had no evidence to support any of them, and Sombra knew it. Worse, Bracal would know it too, and would be aware that even if any held water, Sombra had connections which might make it dangerous to take things further. Lift a stone and whatever lay under it might be something of which Bracal would prefer to remain ignorant. Lannes could picture him drumming his fingers on his desktop, stroking his chin, raising an eyebrow, every movement indicative of scepticism and impatience. Bracal might indeed have his own doubts about Vichy, but he wasn't – surely? – going to do anything which would have Vichy doubting him.

'We're getting nowhere,' he would say. 'Write the case off, file it as unsolved. Who'll care? The murdered man – his past seems a bit murky too. Nobody's calling for vengeance, certainly not his own brother, who is' – he might not say this, but the thought would be there – 'who is someone well in with Vichy, capable of causing us trouble.'

Like the Alsatian, Bracal would see no good reason to invite trouble. Quite the contrary. Push it all out of sight.

There was a knock on the door. Schnyder came in with a German officer.

'Allow me to introduce Lieutenant Kordlinger, superintendent,' he said. 'He has replaced Lieutenant Schussmann as the officer charged to liaise with us. We thought he should have a word with you, just to get acquainted, you understand. Always well to establish good relations quickly. You'll be glad to know he speaks excellent French.'

'Oh yes,' Kordlinger said, as Schnyder with a nod to Lannes left them alone. 'I'm quite a Francophile. I'm a Rhinelander, and indeed my mother's father was born a French citizen, in Lorraine well before the war of 1870. I'm delighted to meet you, Superintendent Lannes.'

Kordlinger was grey-haired – rather old for a lieutenant – lean, fine featured, with an aquiline nose. He wore pince-nez spectacles attached to his lapel by a black cord. His uniform was beautifully pressed – unlike poor Schussmann's – and his nails well manicured.

'My predecessor left a good report of you,' he said.

'I'm pleased to hear that, naturally.'

'Willing collaboration is so important.'

Lannes invited him to sit down and offered a cigarette.

'Thank you, no. It's a habit I have never cared for.'

'Each to each,' Lannes said, lighting one himself.

'Collaboration,' Kordlinger said again, 'so necessary if France is to take the place she should take in the New Order of Europe. I should like to know if any case that you may be engaged in has a relevance to us. I speak generally of course.'

'None at present that I'm aware of,' Lannes said.

'But you would inform me if that was so?'

'If that was what my superiors recommended, naturally.'

'Quite so. Hierarchy must be observed.'

No reply seemed necessary. Kordlinger removed his pince-nez and began to polish the glass.

'Yes,' he said, 'my predecessor, Lieutenant Schussmann – you got on well with him.'

'I had no complaints. I trust he had none either.'

'None at all. As I said, he made a good report of you. In certain respects, however – to be more exact, in one respect – it appears that Lieuenant Schussmann was too, shall we say, liberal in his interpretation of orders to collaborate. He behaved in a manner unworthy of the Wehrmacht, disgracefully indeed. You have heard nothing of this?'

'Nothing at all. You surprise me. May I offer you a drink, lieutenant?'

Lannes gestured to the bottle which he had not replaced in the cupboard.

'Thank you, no. Like the Fuehrer I detest alcohol. It is necessary to keep a clear head. Superintendent, it pains me to say what I am about to tell you, for it casts dishonour on the German army and the Reich. Schussmann should not have been entrusted with a position of responsibility. He was a degenerate, a homosexual, though naturally he tried to conceal this. He engaged in disgusting practices, with a French boy, perhaps several French boys, we cannot be certain. He exposed himself to blackmail. That is why at last he behaved honourably and shot himself when his criminal conduct came to light.'

'He shot himself? I had no idea. I'm shocked to learn this.'

'He had been under suspicion for some time, I believe. When threatened with exposure, he did as I say. Superintendent, you will understand that I tell you this – shameful though it is to the honour of the Reich – for one reason only. I must know who this boy is – or these boys if there was, as we believe, more than one. They – or he – cannot be allowed to remain free to attempt to corrupt more German officers. In Germany we send such despicable creatures to a punishment camp, which is where Schussmann would have gone if he hadn't escaped us.'

'But surely it is very unlikely that there are other officers open to such corruption?'

'One trusts not, but it is a risk that cannot be taken. The guilty – these degenerate boys – must be identified and arrested. That is what I require you to do. It is properly, as you will realise, a matter for the French police. If of course, for whatever reason, you fail to do as I ask, then I shall have to employ our own resources. I mean of course the Gestapo. Is that clear? I look forward, superintendent, to your willing collaboration, which will ensure the maintenance of good relations between my department of the Wehrmacht and the French police.'

* * *

As a child Lannes had played the game which the French call 'colin-maillard' and the English 'blind man's buff'. He had always disliked it when assigned the role of the blind man, and felt a fool. Now, not for the first time in his career in the police, he was landed with the part again, unable to see, stumbling round, reaching out to take hold of one of the other players and trying to identify him. Trying and failing. If Schussmann had already been under suspicion, had his visits to the bookshop in the rue des Remparts been noted? But if they had, then surely Léon would already have been identified and doubtless arrested? Or had Schussmann sought to protect him by leaving a suicide note in which he confessed to relations with a number of unnamed boys? That was possible; there had been a decency to him, even a sort of crazy gallantry – his letter to Léon had touched Lannes. But why leave any suicide note, any admission at all? Why not just shoot himself and leave these bastards to guess the reason? That too was possible . . . yet this Kordlinger had spoken with a certainty which suggested that they had indeed been keeping Schussmann under surveillance. And what of the role played by the spook who called himself Félix? Were the Germans on to him? None of it made sense.

And his own position? That wasn't comfortable either. Kordlinger had spoken politely, giving him to understand that he assumed their interests were the same. But his tone? Was that a bit different? Was there an undercurrent suggesting that Lannes was not entirely to be trusted?

He wasn't of course.

He looked out on the square. The sky had clouded over and a wind had risen, blowing hard in from the Atlantic. There was a flurry of rain and the passers-by had opened their umbrellas and were walking hurriedly.

One thing was clear. Léon was in danger and needed his protection. His first impulse was to go straight to the bookshop; his second, to do nothing of the kind. They might be watching him too.

There was a knock on the door. The Alsatian came in, smoking one of the Havanas Lannes had procured for him. He sat down without waiting for an invitation.

'I don't much like that chap,' he said. 'He's not going to be as easy to deal with as poor Schussmann. Is there anything in his story, do you think?'

'How should I know? I don't even know if he told you the same story he told me.'

'I was surprised when he told me Schussmann was a queer. Did you know that?'

'Can't say it had occurred to me either,' Lannes said. 'None of our business, was it, anyway?'

'Seems it is now. Kordlinger came straight from you back to me, insists we must find this boy friend, make an arrest and hand him over to them – an assault on the honour of the German army, or some such nonsense.'

'Not our business,' Lannes said again.

'I wish it wasn't,' Schnyder drew on his cigar, 'but things will be uncomfortable for us – to say the least – if we ignore the request. I say, request, but it's really an order, and one we can't ignore. I don't like it any better than you do, Jean, but we exist on sufferance, we both know that. So you'll make inquiries, please. Have a word with what's his name of the Vice Squad. We have to come up with something.'

'If you say so.'

'I do. I'm afraid I really do.'

The Alsatian strolled off, saying he had a lunch engagement. With La Jauzion perhaps? Well, he was welcome to her. He wasn't really concerned. For him Kordlinger's demand was an inconvenience, no more than that. The idea of handing over a boy of whom he knew nothing to the Gestapo didn't trouble him. No doubt he would rather it wasn't necessary – he was a decent enough sort after all – but for him it would be merely another of the pieces of the price exacted by defeat, the Occupation, and the requirement to collaborate. In the name of the Higher Good, individuals were expendable; unfortunate, but there it was. Lannes swore, savagely, as he had scarcely sworn since his days in the trenches a quarter of a century ago. He took his hat and trench-coat and left the office.

He had no destination in mind. It was enough for the moment to walk in the wind and rain which was filling the gutters with yellowish water. He leaned heavily on his blackthorn, his hip painful. They surely hadn't yet identified Léon, that was one thing. Or had they and were they putting him to the test himself? Should he speak to Bracal? Could he trust him? And find some way of getting in touch with the spook who called himself Félix? He after all was responsible for Léon's plight. Bracal might have a means of making this possible – he was a bit of a dark horse.

It was still the lunch hour, but the streets were almost deserted, emptied by this sudden summer squall which was still hurling the rain down. The vile weather was a sort of relief, or at least suited his mood. He didn't know where he was heading. The city seemed like a maze in which he was trapped in the centre with no idea of how to find his way out.

XXXIII

When the bookshop door opened Léon had a moment of apprehension. But it was an ordinary customer, a middle-aged lady who had been there before and who apologised for her presence because, she said, 'I'm not really looking for a book today, just taking refuge from the weather.'

'Yes, it's dreadful, isn't it?' Léon said. 'Can I give you a cup of coffee perhaps?'

'That would be very kind.'

While he filled the pot, put it on the stove and waited for the water to boil, she browsed the shelves in the manner of someone who is merely killing time.

'You're Léon, aren't you?' she said when he passed her a cup.

'Yes,' he said.

'It's all right,' she said. 'You don't need to look anxious. I'm an old friend of Henri.'

'He's upstairs. Shall I fetch him, or tell him that you're here?'

'No, don't do that. There's no need to disturb him.'

'As you wish.'

She drank her coffee and dabbed her lips with a lace-fringed handkerchief.

'These are terrible times, aren't they?' she said. 'They say truth is the first casualty of war and the same seems to be true of the Occupation. One finds oneself telling lies, even quite unnecessary ones. For instance, I am not only taking refuge from the weather, as I said, though I suppose that I might have done so in any case. But really I came here to speak to you. Oh dear, that sounds dreadful, as if I was going to tell you off. But it's not that at all . . . '

Léon waited. He looked beyond her to the street where the rain was still pelting down.

'It's so difficult,' she said. 'I'm sure you're a nice boy.'

Well, there was nothing he could say to that, was there?

She opened her handbag, took out a bunch of papers and laid them on the desk before Léon. They were copies of the Cross of Lorraine which he had duplicated.

'I found these in Jérôme's room when I was tidying it,' she said.

'Oh, you're Jérôme's mother?'

'Of course. Didn't I say so? He's my only child, we're very close and he has always told me everything . . . '

'I see.'

Everything? He thought – not my story, surely, I couldn't bear that.

'Do you? Then you understand why I've come here. Jérôme's not like other boys, I know that. Perhaps it's my fault. He's soft, easily influenced, led astray. But what you are doing, the three of you, for I know about Alain Lannes' involvement too – Jérôme adores him and will do whatever he suggests – what you are doing is dangerous. Perhaps you don't understand that. But it must stop before you are all in serious trouble. I've come to ask you to do this. There's no point in speaking to Alain, he's wild and headstrong, but nevertheless, from my point of view, you are still children, all three of you, and perhaps you don't understand what this can lead to. The Occupation, whatever we think of it, is going to last for years, there's no doubt of that, to my mind. So I'm urging you, Léon, to give it up, give up what you are doing which may seem like a game to you . . . '

Léon thought: Félix, Schussmann, the Hotel Artemis.

'It's not a game,' he said. 'Have some more coffee.'

He lit a cigarette and found that his hand was shaking.

'You're wrong to think Jérôme's soft,' he said. 'Perhaps I shouldn't speak to you like this . . . '

She dressed him as a girl when he was a little boy and perhaps she would still like to do so.

'He's sympathetic,' he said, 'but he's not soft.'

He told her about the incident at the swimming pool.

'So you see he's brave.'

'What does that matter?' she said. 'Don't you understand? If you go on like this, you will get yourselves killed. For nothing. For an idea. Trying to change what you can't change . . . '

I'm a Jew, Léon thought, I certainly can't change that. But he didn't speak the words that came to mind; it would have been as if he was claiming some special privilege. And in any case she might reply, 'So you're a Jew – that's your problem – it's got nothing to do with Jérôme.' She would be right of course, and yet she would also be mistaken. Jérôme had made it his problem too.

Instead he refilled her cup and said, 'For us the position is intolerable. So what else can we do?'

'You can do nothing, like the rest of us.'

She began to weep. Léon was sorry for her and embarrassed.

'We're careful,' he said. 'I promise you.'

'Careful!' she said.

Léon thought, my mother would say exactly the same thing if she knew what we were doing. So, I'm sure, would Aunt Miriam. Alain's mother too, even though I know almost nothing about her. And his father. But this doesn't mean we're wrong. It's a matter of generations perhaps.

He looked up. The rain had stopped as suddenly as the storm had broken, and the sun was shining.

Madame de Balastre dried her tears.

'I've said what I came to say. I can't prevent you from carrying on with this madness – for that is indeed what it is, Léon, madness – but I beg you not to involve Jérôme in it any further. I've implored him to stop, but he speaks of loyalty to you and Alain. There,' she said, 'please do as I ask. And destroy these' – she pointed to the pile of Léon's drawings of the Cross of Lorraine.

When she left he waited for a few minutes, then fixed the notice, 'Closed for Lunch' to the door and stepped into the street, looking first both left and right as had become his habit since the day Félix had been waiting for him there. He started to walk, briskly, with no destination in mind; it was simply that inactivity was intolerable. But then everything except the hours spent with Alain and Jérôme was now intolerable, had been since that evening in the Hotel Artemis, since before then indeed, since that day Félix forced himself on him. And now Jérôme had in a sense betrayed him. To his mother admittedly, only to his mother. He wouldn't tell Alain – that would be to betray him in turn. People were re-emerging into the sunlight. Waiters at the Café Régent in the Place Gambetta were straightening the chairs which they had tilted up when the rain started. He went into the café and ordered a beer – a demi – and, when he took out his wallet to pay, found that, without thinking, he had folded one of his Cross of Lorraine posters in his pocket. He went through to the toilet and pinned it up where Alain had posted their first manifesto. That was no longer there. Of course it wasn't. The management had removed it as they would remove his poster as soon as it was noticed. His gesture was an empty one – except that it made him feel better.

Only a little better.

Jérôme's mother didn't realise what she had demanded of him. Jérôme could drop out as she urged. Alain too if he chose. Their life would go on as before, and the worst they might feel would be a certain shame. His position was different. He was an outcast, a Jew, and compromised whether he acted or not. If only Schussmann had never found his way to the bookshop. If only Gaston who had loved him and understood him and made him laugh was still alive. If only they could all go back eighteen months and wipe out everything that had happened since. If only he wasn't so afraid . . .

His steps had taken him into Mériadeck, the Jewish district. A girl, about his age, with a black eye, smiled at him. He shook his head, and she said, 'Another time, darling.' He walked on, then stopped and looked back. She was leaning against the wall and the beckoning smile was still fixed on her face. If I was normal, he thought, I would have accepted her invitation. He found himself in front of a tailor's shop. His great-uncle Léopold, he realised. He turned the door handle and went in.

The old man was sitting cross-legged on the table, sewing. He didn't recognise Léon. It was at least five or six years, maybe more, since he had been here, and he had been only a child then.

'What do you want, young man? A suit made?'

'I don't know what I want,' Léon said.

'Then you're in good company in today's world.'

'I'm Rebecca's boy,' he said, 'your great-nephew, Léon.'

'Well, well, well, quite grown-up, I see. And what brings you to see old Léopold?'

'I don't know. I just found myself here.'

As if it's where I belong, he thought.

'Make yourself useful then. Make some tea while I finish this. Then we'll talk. That's what you want to do, isn't it? Talk to the old Jew.'

Léon did as he was bid. The half-light of the shop was comforting. The place smelled of dust, cloth, tobacco and the ginger-coloured cat that came and brushed against his legs, purring when he leaned down and scratched it behind the ear. The kettle boiled. He made the tea.

'There's a lemon and sugar in the cupboard,' the tailor said.

'So?' he said, as Léon handed him a mug, 'Rebecca and Miriam married out, but you've come back.'

'I don't know,' Léon said again.

'Because you're in trouble you come to the old Jew.'

'I didn't think of myself as a Jew, not till recently,' Léon said. 'Now I can't avoid realising that's what I am.'

'Tell.'

He obeyed. It all spilled out, from Gaston onwards and Alain's father.

'That policeman? Coincidence, he's been here to ask me about another matter, the murder of an old customer of mine,' old Léopold said. 'As policemen go, not a bad man. So? What then?'

Schussmann, Félix, the Hotel Artemis, Jérôme and Alain, Jérôme's mother: Léon held nothing back, except the rape – he couldn't speak of that as he had to Jérôme, only Jérôme – and his friends' names. He had indeed been about to reveal them but the old tailor raised his hand and said, 'Tell me nothing that isn't necessary. I don't want to know who they are. If I'm ignorant, I can't betray them.'

'What should I do?' Léon said.

'You ask me that? How can I give you an answer? I'm eighty-three. You're what? Twenty?'

'Eighteen.'

'Eighteen, are you? When I was your age I believed in God. Then I believed in Marx and the Revolution. Now I have only one certainty which is that I shall soon be dead. There was a girl came to me with questions like yours. A Spanish girl. She was married to your employer, Monsieur Chambolley. Did you know he had had a wife?'

Léon nodded his head.

'I knew, but he never speaks of her.'

'No? She wanted advice, just like you. I told her to go home and cook her husband's dinner. Instead she went to Spain where she was murdered. People don't want advice. They want to be told that what they want to do is right. So: what do you want to do, Léon? You want to escape to England with your friends. Yes? So what do I say? It's madness and you will probably be killed. Is that what you want to hear? Of course it isn't. You want me to say, go ahead and be a hero. Yes?'

'And if I stay here?'

'Then you are in trouble, in danger and will probably be killed in any case.'

'You're encouraging!' Léon said, and smiled for the first time that day. 'If I go to England I'm deserting my mother and Aunt Miriam.'

The old Jew took a pinch of snuff and sneezed. Sunlight streaked through the dusty window.

'And if you remain here in Bordeaux, which is already a prison, you can protect them?' he said. 'You, a mere boy, a Jew, a homosexual as you tell me, can protect two middle-aged Jewish women from whatever threatens them? That's good, that's really good.'

'So you advise me to escape to England with my friends?'

'Who am I to advise anything? You will do what you want. If I say, don't fall in love, love is dangerous, keep out of other men's beds, or women's, would you pay any attention? Of course you wouldn't. So advice is futile. All I can say is, this or that is likely to be the consequence of what you choose. You must live with the consequence. Or die of course. So I am no help, am I?'

The ginger cat stretched up with his front paws against Léon's leg. Then he leaped onto this lap and thrust his face into Léon's, purring demandingly. Léon stroked his head and ran his hand along the line of the cat's back.

'What's his name?' he said.

'All my other cats have had names. Not this one. I call him simply "Cat". Do you know why? It is to remind me that for the men of power in the world I have survived into, I have no name myself. For the Nazis, I am no longer Léopold Kurz the tailor, I am merely a Jew, another Jew. So Cat is only a cat. We are all now only what the label says we are. In Germany we wear the yellow star. That will come here in France too. And I read that in Germany people who are like you in another respect are branded with a pink triangle. So there you are, Léon, a yellow star on one lapel of your jacket and a pink triangle on the other. You think you should stay in France? There: that is merely a question, not advice, you understand.'

XXXIV

Moncerre said, 'So how was it, kid. Did you take what she was offering?'

Young René Martin blushed, but was saved from having to answer immediately because Fernand that moment brought a platter of crudités and charcuterie.

A burst of laughter came from the table in the middle of the room where eight German officers had reached the brandy stage.

'You mustn't be shy, kid,' Moncerre said. 'Keep yourself pure for a wife and you'll have no choice but to find one. And then you're trapped. I speak from experience. So, chief, you got nowhere with that bastard. Do you want me to have another go at him? It would be a pleasure.'

Lannes said, 'We're going to have to release him.'

Arriving at the office that morning, he had been summoned by Bracal. There had been representations, he was told.

'What puzzles me,' he said now, 'is who knew that you had picked him up.'

'Who did the representations – I like that word – come from?' Moncerre said.

'Bracal wouldn't say. Just gave me to understand that they came from a level he couldn't ignore. Said he was sorry.'

'Big of him.'

'I think he may have been. In any case, he gave me instructions. Aristide's case is to be closed down, written off as unsolved. That's official, he said, it's not my decision, you understand. To be fair to him, I don't think he's altogether pleased. On the other hand, if people at the top demand the investigation be abandoned, there's a nasty stink of rotten fish.'

One of the German officers shouted for more brandy.

'Just leave the bottle,' he told the waiter.

Fernand leaned over to remove Lannes' plate.

'It's not the good brandy,' he said, 'whatever the label. Rot-gut into which I pour a drop of molasses. They like it sweet.'

'So this is an end of case lunch,' Moncerre said. He picked up the bottle of claret and poured out three glasses. 'We might as well get drunk, chief, and you, young René, should return to your bit of fluff.'

'She's actually quite a nice girl,' René said.

'Worse and worse.'

Fernand returned with dishes of lamb's kidneys and fried potatoes.

'By the way,' he said, 'I've another present from Cuba. Will your man want more?'

'He doesn't do much work. He might as well smoke,' Lannes said.

'I'm not happy,' Moncerre said. 'I really had my teeth into that bloody Spaniard.'

'He says you broke one of his ribs.'

'I bleeding well hope I did. One has to get some satisfaction from a cock-up like this. Sorry, chief, I'm not implying you cocked it up. But you have to admit we've been well and truly fucked.'

'Well and truly.'

'Again. Yet again'

Song – a marching-song by the sound of it – rose from the German table.

'This is intolerable,' Lannes said. 'I'm off. I've a couple of calls to make. Moncerre, if you intend to get drunk, I'd advise you to do your drinking somewhere else. Where there are no Boches.'

*　　*　　*

It was his duty to inform Adrienne Jauzion that the investigation of her father's murder was being abandoned. Judging by her previous indifference, she probably wouldn't care. Nevertheless it had to be done. He was right. Her response was icy. Could she really, he wondered, be so utterly unconcerned? His face must have revealed his feelings, for she said, 'You are not entitled to judge me, super-intendent, since you know nothing of what put a distance between me and my father. Things happen in families that are not to be broadcast to the world. It's a matter of honour and shame.' And so she dismissed him.

No such official requirement took him to the cours de Verdun and Aristide's old mistress. But he had liked her and she had been obliging enough to identify the body. So it was a matter of courtesy.

She was in the same chair, again with a glass of port wine on the little table beside her, and the white cockatoo in its cage, as if she hadn't stirred since his previous visit. She dabbed her eyes with a handkerchief and said, 'Silly of me to weep when I hadn't seen the old boy for years till he was laid out as a corpse, and it's nothing to me whether you find the brute who killed him. What's the murder of an old professor in today's mad world? Give me a cigarette, superintendent, if you please. My doctor forbids me to smoke, but at my age, what does it matter? And Aristide and I would always light up after we'd made love. That's good. I really can't think why I have deprived myself of such an innocent pleasure for so long.'

'I've wondered,' Lannes said, 'about two things. He returned to

Bordeaux three months ago and you said he didn't come to see you. Why was that? Wouldn't it have been natural to call on you, seeing how long you had lived together, especially since you gave me to understand you parted quite amicably?'

'Perhaps it would, but he didn't. I've wondered about this too, and, to tell you the truth, it's made me sad. I never missed him when he left, but, since he was killed, I don't know why it is, but the thought that he had been in the city without choosing to visit me, has been painful. I've told myself he may have thought me dead, but he might at least have taken the trouble to find out, and if he had he would have found me still in this apartment where we lived for so long. It was selfish of him, I think. But there it is, it's silly to cry over spilt milk. I suppose he simply didn't care, the old bastard. What was the other thing?'

'The daughter,' Lannes said. 'You gave me to understand you knew nothing about her, but I can't believe you didn't know she is Adrienne Jauzion.'

The old woman laughed, a wheezing short-breathed laugh that ended in a fit of coughing. She held out her glass to Lannes who re-filled it.

'Of course I knew,' she said. 'The truth is, I was always jealous of her, of the idea of her, that is, for naturally I have never met her. But he was so proud of her that I didn't even want her to have a share in his death. Was that wicked of me, do you think, to want to keep him to myself even after he was dead?'

'If it makes you feel better,' Lannes said, 'she doesn't give a damn for him, dead or alive.'

'Why should that make me feel better?'

'I don't know,' Lannes said. 'I've been ordered to release the man who may have killed him. And, if it's any comfort to you, I suspect Aristide may not have come to see you because he knew himself to be in danger and was afraid.'

The cockatoo began to dance on its perch, shifting from one foot to the other. It cackled happily, then in a muttering voice, said, 'Poor boy, pretty boy, poor boy.'

XXXV

'On n'est pas sérieux quand on a dix-sept ans.' Clothilde's friend, Marie-Louise, daughter of a fashionable dentist, was fond of quoting this line of Rimbaud's. It was for her the justification of her attitude to life, even under the Occupation. 'There's nothing we can do about it,' she would say, 'so let's enjoy our youth while we can.'

'We're eighteen now,' Clothilde said. 'So perhaps we have to be more serious.'

She had taken her father's warning about Manu to heart. Perhaps it was indeed wrong to associate with Germans, even with a nice boy like him.

'So we're eighteen,' Marie-Louise said. 'That needn't prevent us from going to the swimming pool. I made a sort of arrangement with Alain's friend Philippe. I think he rather fancies me. When I suggested the pool, he said, all right even though he added that he only likes swimming in the sea. So that must mean something, don't you think?'

Marie-Louise was small, dark, bouncy, and eager for experience.

'And do you fancy him?' Clothilde said.

'Not a lot really, but it's nice to be fancied, don't you think? Mind you, I'd rather it was Alain.'

'Alain? He thinks of nothing but rugby and politics.'

'Goodness, how sad, I'm not interested in either. So Philippe will have to do for now.'

He was there before them, sitting by the edge of the pool. He had changed into his swimsuit but hadn't entered the water.

He said, 'You're late. I would have given you up if I hadn't met a friend here.'

'I'm always late,' Marie-Louise said. 'That way, I'm not kept waiting myself. I hate having to wait, you see. Where's your friend?'

'Oh he's in the pool. He swims like an otter. Actually I was a bit nervous coming to the pool, because the last time I was here, I was thrown out.'

'Why was that? Did you start a fight? I hope that was why,' Marie-Louise said. 'I like to think of you fighting.'

'Nothing so dramatic. Alain had brought along Jérôme and another friend who turned out to be a Jew. So we were all asked to leave, and there was almost a scene till I got them to see sense and go quietly. But it was embarrassing.'

'It's not a good idea to have Jewish friends,' Marie-Louise said. 'Alain should have more sense. You should speak to him, Clothilde.'

'Oh, Alain goes his own way,' Clothilde said. 'He's as obstinate as a pig.'

'Actually, I thought the Jew boy was a bit of a twerp,' Philippe said. 'But then I don't care for Jews. You never know where you are with them and I can't think of them as French. Not proper French.'

A blond boy swam to the edge of the pool. He put his hands on the edge and sprang out, shaking the water from his hair. He stood up, the sun sparkling on his wet bronzed skin. He wore only a black slip which emphasised, rather than concealed, his sex. For a moment he remained still, commanding admiration. Then he ran his hands over the upper part of his body and strolled towards them.

'This is Michel,' Philippe said, and introduced the girls.

'Which one's yours?' Michel said.

'This one,' Philippe said, laying his hand on Marie-Louise's shoulder.

'Ripping,' Michel said, and settled himself beside Clothilde. He gave her a brlliant smile and looked on the point of making a pronouncement, but all he said was, 'It's lovely in. You're a fool to stay out, Philippe.'

'Only like swimming in the sea.'

'What about you?' Michel said to Clothilde.

'Oh I love it.'

'Come on then,' he said bounding to his feet and holding out his hand.

They swam two lengths, then came to rest at the far end of the pool. He put his arm round Clothilde.

'You're jolly good. Not many girls swim as well as you.'

He pressed her close to him.

'Why haven't I met you before? Where have you been all my life?'

It was a line from a movie. She was sure of that, though she couldn't remember which film she had heard it in. But the right reply came straight to her lips.

'I don't know, do I?' she said.

'You're gorgeous.'

He flicked his tongue from side to side.

'I'd really like to kiss you.'

'Well, you can't,' she said. 'Not here.'

'Somewhere else then.'

'Perhaps. Some time. I don't know. Anyway I never kiss boys the first time I meet them.'

I've never kissed a boy, she thought, not really kissed, the way they did on the screen. I don't know what's happening.

'Then we must meet a second time,' he said. 'You really are gorgeous. Do you know that?'

'Stop it,' she said, as she felt his hand press against her bottom. 'People will see us. What will they think?'

'Don't care,' he said, still fondling her.

'Well, I do. I'm a well-brought-up girl.'

'That's part of what makes you irresistible.'

'I'm not one of your tarts. Do you have tarts?'

'That would be telling.'

He put his mouth close to her ear and whispered, 'Let's slip away.'

When she didn't immediately reply, she felt his tongue licking her cheek.

'Please,' he said. 'I want to be alone with you. Really. I really do.'

'All right then.'

They climbed out. He held her hand as they returned to the others.

'We're going to leave you two love-birds to each other,' he said.

'That was quick, even for you, Michel,' Philippe said.

'Don't be silly,' Michel said, and led Clothilde to the changing-rooms.

'See you outside, five minutes.'

Her hands trembled as she buttoned her blouse. Is this it?, she thought, how could I have supposed I fancied Manu? She took more than the five minutes he had given her to look as she wanted to look.

Michel was waiting for her. He was leaning against a wall, with one leg drawn up behind him, his foot resting on the stone. He wore white linen trousers and a blue shirt. He had combed his hair which was rather long, touching his shirt collar. He didn't move as she approached and then took the cigarette from his mouth and placed it between her lips.

'It's awfully erotic sharing a cigarette with a lovely girl,' he said.

He took hold of her hand again.

'Tell me all about yourself.'

'Nothing to tell. Not really. Tell me about you.'

'Nothing to tell. Actually I have seen you before, at a Legion meeting. You were with your brother. I don't mind saying I fancied you at first sight.'

'I thought you hadn't even noticed me,' she said. 'What did Philippe mean when he said that was quick even for you?'

'He's an idiot. Don't pay any attention to what he says. Not ever.'

'Does that mean he knows you too well?'

'I like to think nobody knows me.'

'He meant you have lots of girls, didn't he?'

The sun shone. They walked close together, hip against hip. It was even more like a movie. An old woman dressed in black and wearing a wide-brimmed black straw hat, rounded like a priest's, shook her head.

'She disapproves,' Clothilde giggled. 'She thinks I'm fast.'

'She's jealous.'

'She's forgotten what it is to be young, poor woman.'

They came to a garden. Clothilde who had lived all her life in Bordeaux, couldn't have said where they were. In a litle clearing fringed by azaleas and oleander bushes they lay down on the grass. Michel drew her head to him and kissed her on the lips. He lay on top of her and put his hands either side of her head and kissed her again. His tongue sought out hers. She responded, but when she felt his hand stray under her skirt, said 'No' softly, and, to her relief and disappointment, he obeyed. For a long time they lay there, no need or desire for words.

Later he took her by the hand and raised her to her feet. They kissed again. I'll never forget this, she thought. They walked back toward the centre of the town. He asked if he might see her home. Not yet, she said, not today, I need to think. Another time? Oh I hope so.

Finding themselves in the Place de l'Ancienne Comédie, by her favourite café, she said, 'Let's have an ice-cream.'

They found a table. There were three German officers at the next one. For a moment she thought one of them was Manu. But of course it wasn't, though she had sat at this same table with him.

'Tell me about yourself,' she said again, 'I want to know.'

'My parents are dead. I live with my grandfather. He used to be a professor. And you?'

Two boys passed.

'Look,' she said, 'there's Jérôme, he's one of my brother's friends.'

'I know him myself. We're both members of the Légion des Jeunes d'Aquitaine. Actually I don't like him much. That's to say he gets on my nerves. He's a pansy and always hanging around me.'

'Poor Jérôme,' she said.

Lucky me, she thought.

'When can I see you again?'

'Soon,' she said, 'soon.'

'Tomorrow?'

'Tomorrow, yes.'

'We might go to a movie.'

XXXVI

'So it's you again.'

Jules laid aside the glass he was polishing and the towel, and stretched across the zinc counter to shake Lannes' hand.

'Did you ever find out who killed that poor bugger, Monsieur Chambolley?'

'I found them, yes.'

'So are they behind bars?'

Lannes shook his head.

'Oh it's like that, is it?'

'It's like that.'

Jules drew him a beer. 'On the house,' he said. 'So what brings you here today? No trouble, I hope. They'll have told you in Vice that I keep a respectable establishment.'

'Not exactly how they put it, but they've no complaints. Get many Germans in, do you?'

Jules tugged at his moustache. Then he took a bottle of Armagnac from the shelf behind the bar and picked up two glasses which he held upside down by the stem, called on the waiter to take over, stepped round the counter, and without a word, led Lannes to the back of the bar and through a door marked 'Private'.

He settled himself at the table, gestured to the other chair, and began to fill his pipe. Only when he had got it lit and taken two puffs, after which he pressed the tobacco down again with a small metal stubber, did he say, 'I'm not sure I like your question.'

'It's simple enough,' Lannes said.

'Simple questions can have awkward answers.'

He poured out two glasses and pushed one across the table to Lannes.

'I respect my customers,' he said. 'It's a long time ago that I learned when to ask questions of them and when to keep silent.'

'I see you've changed the name of the bar,' Lannes said.

'I'm a careful man. Got to be. "The Wet Flag" now – not very clever to have an English name these days, is it?'

'Not very clever, no. Why was it English in the first place? I've often wondered.'

'Sailors,' Jules said. 'My uncle had the place before me. It was his notion.'

He drew on his pipe, and sat back, stout, bald-headed, obdurate.

'Vice have no problem with me. They'll have told you that. I keep my nose clean.'

'Fairly clean.'

Lannes smiled.

'It's no concern of mine what sort of house this is,' he said. 'I told you that before when I came inquiring about the Chambolley case, and I'm happy to tell you now that there was no connection between his murder and your bar. I know what sort of place it is, but I accept that you are careful, and long as Vice is happy, then as I say it's none of my business. On the other hand I do you the credit of supposing that you have the sense to realise it's in your interest to be – what shall we say? – obliging, and answer my questions. So again, do you get many Germans in here?'

Jules stroked his moustache again and then pulled at the wart on his right cheek.

'What do you expect me to do? Tell them they're barred? Superintendent, in my experience, the Boches are like other people, like anyone else. They have their inclinations and tastes just as we have. So, if they find their way here, well, to my mind, their money's as good as a Frenchman's.'

'Quite so,' Lannes said. 'I'm not disputing that, though the day may come when you find others who will.'

'May come is right. If you want my opinion that day doesn't look like arriving soon. And in the meanwhile, what do you expect me to do? Tell any Boche who puts his head round the door to fuck off? That would be bright, wouldn't it? So I just take their money and keep my thoughts to myself.'

'I don't expect anything of you.'

Lannes produced the photograph of Schussmann which he had had the Alsatian obtain for him and pushed it across the table.

'What about this chap?'

Jules glanced at it, briefly, then, for the first time, looked away.

'I need to know a bit more,' he said. 'I've got my principles.'

'You have? Can you afford them in your line? Anyway, you've answered my question.'

'I've said nothing.'

'You've said enough. So he came here. Good. Regularly?'

'Not regularly, no.'

'To pick up a boy?'

'Couldn't rightly say.'

'Come off it,' Lannes said. 'Don't ask me to believe that. I've too much respect for you, Jules. For your intelligence anyway. A Boche officer comes here and you expect me to believe you don't keep your eye on him, that you aren't made a bit anxious by his presence. It would be a relief, wouldn't it, if all he did was make a pick-up? Business as usual, you might say. Nothing to worry about.'

'Look,' Jules said, 'I make it my business to keep out of the shit.'

'Very wise.'

Lannes fingered his glass.

'The thing is, the chap's dead. Shot.'

Jules knocked back his brandy and poured himself another glass. He drew on his pipe again and this time looked Lannes in the eye.

'One Boche fewer,' he said. 'Do you expect me to go into mourning? Or you think I should help you pin it on one of the boys? No chance. I'm a good Frenchman, whatever else I may be, and if I knew who did for him, I'd shake him by the hand, even if he seemed a decent enough sort of chap for a Boche. Quiet too, spoke decent enough French.'

'I need to speak with the boy. Don't pretend there isn't one.'

'No chance,' Jules said again.

'Which means you know who he is. But there's one thing you don't know. There's no hand for you to shake. Schussmann' – he tapped the photograph which lay on the table between them – 'wasn't murdered. He shot himself. Trouble is, the Gestapo are interested. If I can't come up with the right story, you'll have them here. Does that change your mind?'

Jules fiddled with the wart again, twisting it between thumb and forefinger.

'Shit.'

'That's what we'll all be in if I can't head them off. So I must speak to the boy.'

'Why should I trust you, superintendent?'

'Because you have no choice and because if I wasn't trustworthy, I'd have already suggested to them they should look here. They want the boy who compromised the honour of the Germany army – don't laugh – that's how they put it. I want to make sure they don't get hold of him. But I assure you that if I can't satisfy them, they'll find their way here sooner or later. There aren't so many places like yours in Bordeaux, are there? So, if he's one of those I saw in the bar, just fetch him now, and, if he isn't, tell me where I can find him.'

Jules closed his eyes and didn't move for a long time. Then he sighed and heaved himself upright. His trousers sagged behind and his feet were flat. He left the door a few inches open. Lannes lit a cigarette. He wondered if it might have been wiser simply to have confirmed that Schussmann had frequented the bar and to tell Jules to order the boy to make himself scarce. But – he didn't know why – he had to see him for himself.

'I've done nothing.'

He had been abstracted, hadn't noticed the boy come in. Jules stood behind him, feeling that wart again. Lannes flicked his head to indicate that he should leave them alone. The big man hesitated, looking at Lannes as if appealing to him to be gentle with the boy, then took a couple of steps backward and closed the door behind him.

The boy shifted from one foot to another. Lannes told him to sit down. He was a slim boy with olive skin, deep brown eyes, long lashes and black curls tight to his head. He wore a white singlet and black trousers wide at the ankles. His fingers were long and thin and when he sat down they flew to his mouth as if his lips might betray him. Different hair, Lannes thought, nevertheless he looked a little like Léon. His hands left off fluttering like a moth and he made as if to speak, then didn't. Lannes pushed Schussmann's photograph towards him.

'What's your name?'

'Karim.'

164

'Karim?'

'My father's an Arab but my mother's French. I'm a French citizen. My papers are in order. Do you want to see them?'

Lannes picked up the photograph and turned it towards the boy. Then he laid it on the table just in front of him.

'Where did you take him?'

'Who says I took him anywhere?'

'Where did you take him?'

'All right then. I took him home.'

'Home? Your home?'

'Yeah, where else?'

'And your parents?'

'Dad's in prison. Mum, sure, she calls me names – dirty little boy, filthy Arab queer – but she takes the money I bring in. We've got to live, haven't we? And I need money to spend on my girl. I'm out of a job, so there's nothing left but renting. What's all this about then? Jules says you're not Vice.'

'He's dead.'

'Who?'

'Schussmann.'

'That his name? It's nothing to do with me, honest.'

'I know it's not. He shot himself. Suicide.'

'Stupid sod. What'd he do that for?'

'It's a complicated story.'

Lannes told it from the beginning, omitting only Léon's name.

'If it wasn't me,' he said, 'it would be the Gestapo here.'

The boy's upper lip quivered. His eyes filled with tears and he turned his head towards the door as if calculating the odds on making a run for it.

'You going to hand me over to them? But I'd nothing to do with it.'

Lannes went through to the bar, asked for a glass, brought it back and poured Karim a drink from the bottle Jules had left on the table. He gave himself one too.

'Drink this,' he said, handing it to the boy. 'You're not listening. I said, "If it wasn't me, it would be the Gestapo." And if they start asking questions here . . . So you mustn't be here. Understand?

You mustn't be in Bordeaux. You don't understand? I'll spell it out. I've got to come up with a story to satisfy the Boches. They discovered Schussmann was a queer. That's why he killed himself. They want the boys who corrupted the honour of the German army – that's how they put it. So I've got to give them an answer, names and description. They won't be satisfied otherwise. Meanwhile I'll get you away. Understand now?'

'What about the other boy, the one that was used to set him up?'

'I'll see to him too. Meanwhile go home. Don't come back here. Meet me tomorrow afternoon, 4 o'clock. The Buffet in the Gare St-Jean. All right?'

'Why are you doing this?' Karim said. 'Are you . . . ?'

'No,' Lannes said, 'let's just say, I don't like the Gestapo. Or the Boches.'

On the way out, he gestured to Jules to follow him onto the street.

'We've a couple of days before I have to come up with my story. The Boches will want to check up on it, I'm afraid. So you can expect a visit. Probably not the Gestapo, a mildly less noxious bunch. Tell them Schussmann came here more than once, sat in the corner drinking and eying up the boys. One evening he left with a boy. Not one you know, never been here before. Give them a description, a bit like Karim – in case someone else saw them – but not exact. Then tell them that one night, but you can't remember precisely, there was another German officer in here. When Schussmann saw him he left in a hurry. Meanwhile I'll have got Karim out of Bordeaux. And don't say I've landed you in the shit. You were there already.'

As he left the bar he thought, it's my first act of resistance. And then: Yvette and Karim, how many kids were there like that in Bordeaux?

XXXVII

Léon now spent little time in the bookshop. He hadn't been able to think of it as a refuge since the evening Félix walked in, not that he had had the word 'refuge' in his mind before then. But that's what it had been, and now it wasn't. Henri didn't mind if he closed the shop; he was vaguer than ever and even more often tipsy. Léon was sorry for him, grateful too of course, and felt that by his absences he was in a sense deserting him; it was another burden of guilt. Yet every time the door opened he felt a stab of fear. It was no better at home. Ever since that night he returned late from the Hotel Artemis, he was oppressed by his mother's anxiety on his behalf. She knew there was something very wrong, and didn't dare to ask what it was. So they existed in uneasy and nervous silence. Often it seemed she couldn't bear to be in the same room as him, then, would find herself saying, 'What's going to become of you, Léon?' There was no possible answer. It would be like that in Jewish homes all over Bordeaux, all over France. You could never wake happy in the morning. It was no better when he called on his Aunt Miriam. The way she looked at him was full of painful knowledge. Once, she said, 'Alain's father . . . ' and then broke off. It was enough, it was more than enough. So he spent hours walking the streets, or he would go to the railway station and gaze longingly on departing trains. Only visiting the old Jew, his great-uncle Léopold, was of any comfort, precisely because he offered none. Léon responded to his bleak refusal of hope.

He hadn't seen Alain for days, not since that last magical moment when, hand-in-hand with him and Jérôme, they had danced by the river. But yesterday there had been a note from Jérôme, pushed under the bookshop door, and so today he had put on the suit he used to wear in the bank.

Alain arrived at the bookshop first. He looked pale and out of sorts. There was a moment of embarrassment between them, Léon couldn't think why. Then it occurred to him: this is the moment of commitment, that's what Jérôme has arranged for us, and we are both nervous.

Alain said, 'I've just had a row with my brother. He intends to go to Vichy. It's intolerable. I was so angry, I nearly told him we were heading for London.'

When Jérôme came in and smiled, the mood lightened. They all three embraced, musketeers again.

'We're going to have lunch with my godfather,' Jérôme said. 'He's promised to help us.'

The butler showed them into a salon. Léon was conscious of the poor quality of his suit, and abashed by the room, the paintings and the furniture.

'It's like something out of Balzac,' he said to Alain. 'And I've never encountered a butler before.'

'Me neither, but courage.'

The count entered, embraced Jérôme and extended his hand, first to Léon and then to Alain. He wore a light-grey flannel suit, double-breasted, with an orchid in his buttonhole. His gaze was penetrating. Léon thought, this is madness, I don't belong here.

Lunch was served by the butler and a footman. They ate asparagus – Léon watched Jérôme to see how to deal properly with it – followed by langoustines, also a problem for him, and gigot of lamb with new potatoes. There was a salad and Roquefort cheese. No evidence of rationing. They drank a very dry Graves with the fish and a bottle of the St-Hilaire claret with the lamb. When coffee was served – real pre-war coffee – the servants withdrew. Throughout the meal the count directed the conversation. He spoke of literature and history. He asked no personal questions, apart from enquiring about their taste in books.

Now he lit a cigar, after offering the box to the boys. Only Jérôme took one. Alain said he preferred cigarettes.

'Jérôme has told me that the three of you want to get to England, to join General de Gaulle,' the count said. 'I approve your ambition, but sadly . . . ' He paused and smiled. 'Sadly I am not a magician. I can't therefore help you to do that. I am sorry to disappoint you. To attempt to reach London from Bordeaux – well, it would have been possible in the days around the Armistice, before the arrival of the Occupying Army, but now, without connections which I no longer possess, it would be foolhardy. You would most probably be taken and shot. That would be undesirable. However, it's not, as they say, the end of the world, for I can set you on your way.'

'What do you mean?' Alain said.

'We have an empire in North Africa.'

'But North Africa is Vichy.'

'Quite so – but how reliably Vichy? An interesting question. I have friends there whose allegiance to Vichy is – shall we say? – at best provisional. Some of them are Royalists, which is foolish, others Gaullists, which is dangerous. Certainly you will find people there who are waiting only for the war to turn – as it must, though the fools in Vichy do not understand this. I take it your papers are all in order? Very well.'

He rang the bell for the butler, and, when he appeared said, 'Jean-Pierre, will you please go to the desk in my study. In the top right-hand drawer, you will find a large white envelope. Please bring it to me.'

The boys looked at each other, none daring to speak. The count leaned back in his chair. When the butler returned with the envelope, the count restored his monocle to his eye, and laid the envelope before him.

'You are all certain?' he said. 'Have you spoken of your intentions to your parents? No? Your mother, Jérôme, will find it hard to forgive me. I have here three Ausweis – that is, the pass which permits you to travel from the Occupied to the Unoccupied Zone. You need not ask how I came by them. It's enough to know that I retain a modest degree of influence. There are rail tickets for Marseilles and then air tickets and a booking which will enable you to fly to Algiers. You should have no trouble at the airport. Flights are regular and generally reliable. If you are questioned, which is unlikely, you are going to stay for the summer with my cousin, General Mercillon. He will confirm this, if asked. I have seen to that. He is a loyal officer at present – that is to say, a dutiful one – but his inclinations are not towards Vichy. Like many patriotic Frenchmen he is biding his time, training the troops under his command, committed to renewing the war when the hour is ripe.

Once in North Africa he will, at my request, put you in touch with others who think as you do. The flight booking is for this day week. There is also a hotel booking for you, in my name, in Marseilles. The bill will be sent here. This is the most I can do for you. Please do not thank me. Think instead that I do this, not only for you, but for France. I wish I was your age. I think that is all.'

He handed the envelope to Alain whom he had recognised as the leader.

'What you tell your parents, whether you tell your parents, these are matters on which I cannot advise you. One other thing,' he said, laying his hand on Alain's shoulder, 'I would be grateful if you would tell your father – oh yes, I know who he is – that it would give me great pleasure if he would be kind enough to pay me a visit. My request is not, I must say to put your mind at rest, related to your departure. Now, be off with you, and good luck. No, no more, I detest prolonged farewells as I detest being thanked.'

XXXVIII

Fernand was one of the people Lannes trusted. There weren't many: Marguerite of course – even if they now found it so difficult to communicate and their marriage often seemed a hollow shell, they were bound together, for better, for worse; Henri, certainly; Moncerre and young René, because they were his team and had shared successes and failures; Miriam, because he respected her and was comfortable in her presence especially now that his desire had faded; Jacques Maso also. But he had known Fernand since childhood, since they had played truant from school together and stolen apples. In summer holidays Fernand had come with him to his grandfather's farm in the Landes where they had shot duck at first light and in the evening. Consequently when they were alone, they usually spoke in the Landais dialect, which Lannes' grand-parents had always spoken with him and which Fernand had been happy to learn on his visits. It was another bond between them. Later, as adolescents, the pair of them had set off together in pursuit of girls. Now in middle age the irony with which Fernand addressed life was comforting. Nothing surprised him, very little impressed him.

It was still the cool of the morning, with swifts and martins flying high, and the brasserie was not yet open. He rang the bell. Jacques, the young waiter who was Fernand's illegitimate son – one of several indeed, for Fernand, who had never married, had always been a skirt-chaser – admitted him. The tables were bare. An old woman was polishing the tiled floor. At this hour the restaurant was like a theatre before the curtain goes up. Jacques said he would fetch Fernand who was busy in the kitchen. Lannes took a seat at a corner table. Fernand appeared, his blue shirt unbuttoned almost to the waist and a gold medallion dangling. They shook hands. Fernand told Jacques to bring them coffee.

'And a nip of marc,' he added. 'So?'

'So.'

They didn't say more till Jacques had brought his father's order.

'He's quite a good boy,' Fernand said, 'but he says the trade isn't for him. He's decided he wants to join the police.'

'Tell him on no account,' Lannes said.

'Have already.'

'It was bad enough before the war. Now . . . '

Lannes spread his hands and turned his thumbs down.

'We don't know where we are,' he said.

'Must be difficult. How are your boys, Jean?'

'It's difficult for them too. It's difficult for everyone and it's worst for the young. They know they've been betrayed and that's all they know. Or so I think sometimes.'

It was restful. The old woman finished her polishing and disappeared. In a little they would start to lay the tables, but for the moment it was quiet except for voices coming from the kitchen, and Lannes felt some of the tension leave his body.

He said: 'We're both trapped in collaboration, aren't we? You feed the Boches and I take orders from them. Neither of us likes it, but . . . '

'What do you expect me to do? Show the bastards the door or poison them?'

'The chap whose job was to liaise with me shot himself.'

'That's one fewer, but it'll be a long occupation if we have to rely on them topping themselves, one after the other.'

'Resistance?' Lannes said.

'You must be joking.'

'Yes, I'm joking. He wasn't a bad chap really – unlike his successor who's by way of being a bastard – but he was a bloody fool. A queer, pederast really, and one of our spooks set him up. He couldn't face doing what was demanded of him – I suppose he was a German patriot in his way. Now the Gestapo want his boy-friends.'

'And you've been told to deliver them?'

Fernand smiled. There was mischief in his smile. There had always been mischief in his smile.

'I've got to give them something,' Lannes said. 'My boss seems quite happy with it.'

Fernand whistled, got up, and crossed to the bar. He was a big man but he moved lightly. He hummed a little dancing tune as he collected the bottle of marc, brought it back to the table and refilled their glasses.

'Vichy and collaboration,' he said, 'do we drink to them or call them a bad joke?'

'We don't drink to them.'

'And so?'

'Better days?'

'That'll do. I've always had a taste for the improbable.'

They clinked glasses.

'There are two boys,' Lannes said. 'I want to get them out of Bordeaux. If I can do that, get them safely away, then I can give their names to the Boches. But they have to be out if it. They wouldn't last twelve hours if the Gestapo got hold of them.'

'Which of us would? And a couple of fairies, no chance.'

'It's even worse,' Lannes said. 'One's a Jew, the other's half-Arab. I wondered, your smuggler friend? Spain? Could he get them over the border? Do you trust him?'

'If he's paid well enough. But Spain? I don't know. A farm in the mountains, perhaps.'

'How much?'

Fernand laid his hand on Lannes' arm.

'I'll take care of that. Don't worry. It'll be Boche money. The prices are higher on my German menu.'

'Really?'

'Not exactly, because one or two might have the sense to compare that with the French one, but when they buy champagne or brandy, I tell them they are getting a special bottle at a special price. Bloody special it is too. Rooking the Boches is my only form of resistance, and one that pays me well. However, if it's cheating the Boches of them, getting these kids out will be another pleasure. It'll take a few days to set up. Are the kids safe for the time being? If not, send them over here. They can work in the kitchen and doss down in the attic. It's time we began to fight back, even if we are not actually doing any fighting. Besides, to be cynical, it's in my interest too. The day may come when it will be good to have evidence of putting a spoke or two in the Boche wheel. . .'

The claim to cynicism didn't surprise Lannes. It was in character for Fernand to cover a good deed with such a cloak.

*   *   *

He went from the brasserie to the rue des Remparts. The bookshop was closed, and it was several minutes before Henri answered his ring. He was bleary-eyed and unshaven and his breath was sour with last night's white wine. He stumbled as he turned away and Lannes thrust out his hand to prevent him from falling over. Henri led him up the stairs to the apartment, holding tight on to the rail and swaying. He was panting heavily when he reached the top.

'Léon seems to have deserted me,' he said. 'I haven't seen him for two days. You haven't come to tell me something's wrong? I worry about him. I worry about everything and I wake in the night even when I have gone to bed drunk.'

He sank back on to his couch. He was sweating freely and mopped his face with a handkerchief.

'I'm going to pieces,' he said. 'Breaking up. I'm ashamed of myself, and then, I think, what does it matter? Is Léon in trouble? In danger? Do you know?'

Lannes went through to the kitchen and made coffee. Henri had to hold the cup in both hands to get it to his lips.

'What a mess I've made of things,' Henri said.

'What a mess France has made of things.'

'Do you know, Jean, it's strange, as long as Gaston was alive and needed me to support him, I could be strong, but now . . . there's nothing to live for. I think of him more often than of Pilar. She seems so long ago. We were happy for a little though. If it wasn't for Léon I would close the shop. Where is he? Do you know? Perhaps he's ill.'

What could Lannes say? That the boy wasn't ill, but ashamed and afraid? And that he had reason for the fear, though not for the shame? But where was he? Perhaps Alain would know.

Henri said, 'Would you mind taking Toto out? I can't face the streets. Léon usually does it these days, but since he's not here . . . '

'Of course.'

He clipped the lead on the little bulldog, and locked the shop door behind him. When he returned, Henri had fallen asleep, His mouth was open and he was snoring. It was half-past eleven. Already it seemed like a long day. His cheerful mood of the morning had darkened. He scanned the bookshelves, and took a volume of *Le Vicomte de Bragelonne*, and settled to lose himself in it. Kordlinger might be seeking him out to ask what progress he had made. He was better off here. He came to the passage in which d'Artagnan's old servant Planchet said: 'Monsieur, I am one of these good sorts of men whom God has breathed life into for a certain time in order that they may find everything good throughout their sojourn on this earth.'

And so: 'D'Artagnan sat down by the window, and, Planchet's philosophy seeming solid to him, reflected on it . . . '

To find everything good throughout one's sojourn on this earth . . . Dumas himself had been a happy man, despite all that assailed him. It was his generosity of spirit which Lannes found both comforting and invigorating, his sense of honour which saw him approve the ability of a man to cling to what was left of even his most severely damaged qualities. For more than three hours Lannes, reading while Henri continued to sleep, escaped from the urgency of his anxieties.

*　　*　　*

The boy was leaning against the wall outside the station. A cigarette dangled from his lips, screen gangster-style. He looked a stylised picture of boredom; he had learned how to present himself, open for trade, though no doubt it came naturally to him. When he saw Lannes, he straightened up, but didn't remove the cigarette, and waited for Lannes to approach him. Instead Lannes walked past him and into the station. He went to the bookstall and stood for a couple of minutes pretending to examine the titles on display. A couple of times he lifted his head and scanned the concourse. He crossed over to the buffet, which was full of German soldiers. They carried kitbags and looked cheerful; he supposed they were going home on leave. He ordered an Armagnac and leaned with his back against the bar. Then he went through to the toilets and washed his hands, glancing up at the mirror in front of him. He left the buffet and walked out of the station. Karim hadn't moved. Lannes turned right towards the river. When he had gone fifty metres, he paused and turned round. The street was deserted. He jerked his head. Karim detached himself from the wall. Lannes resumed his walk. He turned right at the first corner and waited. In a minute the boy joined him.

'All right?' Lannes said.

The boy smiled.

'Why not? I've been on this game before, you know. Customers are often shy.'

For a moment Lannes felt resentment – the boy had regained his self-possession and now seemed more assured than he was himself. It was as if this was indeed a pick-up and Karim in control, while Lannes was like the respectable middle-aged man embarking with mingled eagerness and shame on what he had long desired but feared to do. Which was ridiculous. He was on edge. There was no reason to think he was being shadowed, but he couldn't shake off the suspicion that Kordlinger didn't trust him. He told himself it was only because he was taking a first step into the unknown, the first small step that was transforming him from a policeman per-forming, however reluctantly, what he was required to perform, into a man leading a double life, collaborating as he was ordered to collaborate, and at the same time engaging in subversion and resistance. He had made his choice and he couldn't deny that it frightened him. What would become of Marguerite and Clothilde if . . . He led the boy into a little bar.

The proprietor came forward and shook his hand.

'Superintendent, a pleasure . . . '

'And for me, Gustave. How's the family? All well?'

'As can be. Even Paul. You taught him a lesson.'

Lannes had arrested Gustave's son a couple of years before the war for a botched burglary, given him a good talking-to, and dismissed him without a charge.

'Mind you,' Gustave said, 'he couldn't be climbing over any roofs now, even if he hadn't learned his lesson. He got a bullet in his knee in the first week of the war and will be lame, they say, for the rest of his days.'

'Sorry to hear that. Maybe it would have been better if I had sent him where he deserved to go.'

'No, you showed him the road he was on. What can I get you?'

'An Armagnac, if you please, and for you?'

He turned to Karim who asked for a lemonade.

'Can I use your back room? There are things I have to put this young fellow straight on.'

'As you did Paul? Certainly.'

*   *   *

Karim leaned back in his chair. He ran his fingers up and down the glass in front of him.

'I still don't get it,' he said. 'When you looked at me as you came out of the station, I thought, maybe he really does want to have me and just has a taste for elaborate games,'

'Don't be impertinent,' Lannes said.

Moncerre would have given him a blow on the chops and knocked him off his chair. He would say, 'It's the only language types like that understand.'

Lannes said, 'You've got your nerve back, haven't you? Which isn't very bright. Or is it all an act? At least you kept our appointment.'

'Didn't have much choice, did I?' The tone was sullen now. 'I've heard what the cops do to boys like me.'

'Some cops,' Lannes said. 'Let me spell it out. Again. If I don't satisfy the Boche, Jules' bar and the two or three others like it in Bordeaux are going to be flooded with the Gestapo. Jules and the boys and any customers will be taken in for questioning. Questioning's a polite way of putting it. How long do you think you would last in the Gestapo's hands? An hour? More like five minutes, I would say, and you'd be squealing like a pig having its throat cut. Only you wouldn't enjoy the luxury of a quick death like the pig.'

All at once Karim looked the way he had when Jules ushered him into his back room, perplexed and frightened.

'I'm spelling it out, Karim,' Lannes said. 'So you understand your position, understand it fully. You took Schussmann home with you, let him do whatever the poor sod wanted, and took his money. I don't care what he paid or whether it was in francs or Reichsmarks.'

'Francs,' Karim said in a voice that was now scarcely more than a whisper.

'You've got yourself in trouble, deep trouble. Nobody else is responsible, but I've made arrangements to get you out of it. With luck, that is. This is what you do.'

He gave him directions to Fernand's brasserie.

'Go there straight away. Tell nobody. Not even your mother. Understand? But give me her address and when you've been got out of Bordeaux, I'll see her myself.'

'She won't care what happens to me – except that I won't be bringing any money in.'

'I'm sure that's not true.'

'You don't know her.'

When he had got the address and sent Karim off to Fernand's, with instructions that he was to present himself as the new kitchen assistant, Lannes' thoughts turned to Léon. Perhaps Miriam knew where he was. Or Alain?

XXXIX

Alain woke early before the sun had broken through morning mist. He got out of bed, careful not to wake Dominique. He picked up his clothes and, dressed only in his underpants, went through to the bathroom. He flapped cold water on his face, brushed his teeth, and, dropping to the floor, did twenty-five press-ups. Then, from a wide stance, he touched his right toes with his left hand, his left ones with his right, repeating each exercise twenty times. He ran his hands over his body and was happy to find that he hadn't raised a sweat. He dressed in a white singlet and blue cotton trousers and went barefoot through to the kitchen where his father was already up, sitting over his coffee, with half a dozen cigarette stubs in the ashtray. He poured himself coffee from the pot and sat down facing Lannes. For a moment they sat in silence, companionable silence. Alain thought, 'I've got to tell him,' but still hesitated.

Lannes said, 'Have you seen Léon recently?'

'Why, yes, of course, we're good friends as you know and . . . why do you ask? Is he in trouble of some sort?'

'Henri's worried about him. He has taken to being out of the shop.'

'I expect he gets bored. There aren't many customers now, he says.'

'Do you know where his mother lives?'

'No idea. Miriam would know of course.'

'Yes of course.'

Each had something to tell the other. Neither could find the words to speak. Across the courtyard a baby began to cry. Alain pushed away the lock of hair that fell over his left eye. Lannes lit another cigarette and smiled at the boy.

'I like these early mornings,' he said. 'You're well muscled now.'

'I have to be for rugby, but . . . '

'But?'

'Nothing. Who's the Comte de St-Hilaire?'

'What a strange question. Why do you want to know?'

Alain twisted his finger in his hair.

'My friend Jérôme took me to see him. He's his godfather, and some sort of cousin. Léon came with us. He asked me to say he would be pleased if you were to pay him a visit. I don't know why.'

'Go on. There's something else, isn't there?'

Alain hesitated, got up, crossed to the window, and leaned there with his arms on the sill. His legs were long and straight. He's almost grown up, Lannes thought.

'You have to go on,' he said.

Alain turned, very slowly and lifting his chin looked his father in the face.

'That's just it,' he said, 'going on. We – the three of us – it's intolerable here, the Occupation. For years perhaps. And Vichy. And I don't know what. So . . . '

It all spilled out in a rush of words: de Gaulle, Free France, London, North Africa, what the Comte de St-Hilaire had arranged, and finally, 'You must see, Papa, it's what we want to do and what we have to do, need to do, really. You can't disapprove, you think as I do, about things, don't you?'

Lannes said, 'It's what I was afraid of.'

'Afraid?'

'Yes, Alain, afraid. All fathers are afraid for their children, and the more spirited the children are, the sharper the fear . . . '

He thought, Alain's the brightest, I've always known that, and it makes him vulnerable because he sees himself as a winner always, but he also has the biggest dark side of any in the family, which he keeps so well concealed most of the time that people can know him, think they know him well, and never be aware of it. But I've always known it was there. I've seen it on the rugby field where he has moments of meanness, and he's the only one of us who might kill or die for an idea. Which is why Marguerite doesn't understand him, why she is impatient with him as she isn't with the others and calls him selfish. I've always known he could go off the rails, and though what he is proposing to do isn't that, I don't know where it will lead him. I admire him and am afraid for him and I'm envious of him because I wish I had the courage to break away myself instead of which I'm bound to this wheel of duty and responsibility . . . And then in his whirl of confusion he thought, but, despite the danger he is running into, and will be in whatever use they put him to, he may yet be safer than if he stayed here fretting in Bordeaux, where he might get involved in something that was stupid as well as dangerous. Which is how eventually I shall put it to his mother.

Alain said, 'I didn't know if I could tell you. I thought of just leaving a note. And then I knew I had to speak. It would have been cowardly not to. But you won't tell Maman, will you, not till I've gone.'

'No, I won't,' Lannes said, knowing this was treachery. But speaking would be treachery too.

He embraced Alain, hugging him close and then kissing him on both cheeks.

'I'm afraid for you, that can't be avoided, but I admire you too. We must always try to do what seems right and feels necessary. Now I must go to work.'

'Thank you, Papa. I promise I'll . . . '

'Don't promise anything. It's better that way.'

As he descended the stairs he thought, it's a solution for Léon too, but what of Miriam and his mother? And what can the Comte de St-Hilaire want of me?

It was a beautiful June morning. The sun shone, leaves on the trees sparkled after night rain. There was a song in his heart that he couldn't account for. He must tell Fernand that there would be only one boy to get out of Bordeaux. Then he understood why he was happy: he had never felt so close to Alain. It's crazy, he thought, I'm a beat-up policeman with a lousy job, in hock to the Nazis in our beautiful occupied city in our lovely humiliated France, and my boy has just confided that he's embarking on a ship that may sink at any moment for a voyage that may lead him to destruction, and I'm happy. It makes no sense, except that it makes a lot of sense. I'm so proud of him and so afraid for him.

*   *   *

The Alsatian was wearing what looked like a new suit: double-breasted, dove-grey with a thin pale pinstripe. His shirt was cream-coloured, his tie maroon, and there was a white carnation in his button-hole. His black shoes were highly polished.

'I'm bidden to lunch with our new Prefect,' he said. 'We are, apparently, to discuss ways in which we may advance the national revolution. Our first preoccupation, I'm informed, must be the means of preparing for the New European Order.'

'Good luck to you,' Lannes said.

'Oh, I don't take it seriously, as you may imagine. But it's necessary to go through the motions. Talking of which, Kordlinger has been badgering me. He wants to be kept informed about the course of your investigations.'

'And you told him that was a matter for the French police?'

'Not precisely. There's no point antagonising the man. And unfortunately he is by no means a fool, not your bull-necked Prussian with a block of wood for a head.'

He perched on the corner of Lannes' desk, and swung his foot.

'So have you anything for him? We really don't want to stir him up.'

'Enquiries are proceeding. You can dress it up in bureaucratic guff if you like, but the only conclusion I've come to so far is that Schussmann was even more of a bloody fool than I had supposed. I don't suppose you want to tell him that, however.'

'Don't think it would serve.'

He clipped the end of a cigar and lit it with a match.

'We're going to have to give him something,' he said. 'Someone actually.'

And it doesn't matter to you what happens to whichever boy we select as victim, Lannes thought.

'It's not so easy,' he said. 'Still, you can tell him I'm devoting my time to it and hope to have something for him in a couple of days. Meanwhile you might ask him if I could be given a copy of Schussmann's suicide note. I'm assuming there was one. And a diary, if he kept one'

'He'll never agree to that.'

'Tell him co-operation's a two-way street.'

Schnyder smiled.

'I'm glad to see you still keep your sense of humour, Jean.'

'What else is left to us?' Lannes said.

German proverb, he thought: when the Devil is hungry, he eats flies.

* * *

He left the office, with no purpose in mind. It was simply that he found the place oppressive, and in any case there was nothing for him there but paperwork, none of it of any importance. It was better in the streets where the Bordelais went about their business with an appearance of unconcern, so thoroughly had most of them now accustomed themselves to the Occupation. What else was there for them to do? It wasn't even as if real life was in suspension. On the contrary, real life is whatever it is here and now. Lannes knew well how easily men could reconcile themselves to life behind bars. Those who rebelled against prison were the exceptions. Even first-time offenders, let alone old lags, made a routine for themselves in a matter of weeks, sometimes even days. Life goes on wherever you find yourself. He thought of Yvette, stretched out invitingly on her bed; how else should she be expected to behave? He went into the Rugby Bar to telephone the Comte de St-Hilaire's residence and made an appointment for that afternoon. Then he called Fernand to check that Karim had presented himself and to say that other arrangements had been made for the other boy. He drank a glass of beer and thought about Alain and why he had made no effort to dissuade him, as he had put the case against going to Vichy to Dominique. Was it because he believed that, against all appearances, Hitler would yet lose the war that Dominique's course seemed more dangerous? And yet it was Alain who risked being killed.

* * *

When the Comte de St-Hilaire joined him in the salon where the butler had asked him to wait, Lannes, like Léon there before him, was conscious of the shabbiness of his suit, also of the exhaustion which was the result of the empty wandering hours since he had left the office. St-Hilaire extended his hand, asked him to sit down, and then waited without speaking while the butler brought in wine and poured each a glass.

'My son said you wanted to see me. He also told me what you are doing for him and his friends.'

'And does that displease you?'

'Say rather that it alarms me.'

'Yes, of course it must. You will understand it was my godson who approached me and told me that he and his friends were determined to find a way to join the Free French. I have to say that I didn't try to dissuade him, and not only because I approved his determination. I took it on myself to make arrangements because I was in a position to ensure that the first steps at least should be safe, or as safe as anything can be now, and because I feared that any action they might take themselves would be as dangerous as it was rash. How does one deal with the impetuosity of youth and the ignorance of innocents? Have you come to reprove me?'

Despite the question, there was a flinty arrogance in his tone.

'I can't do that,' Lannes said, 'because I approve the intention.' He sipped his wine. 'Nevertheless I have to say that I am afraid for them.'

'Naturally.'

'On the other hand . . . '

'Yes?'

'On the other hand, I have been afraid ever since the débâcle that Alain would engage in some act of resistance here in Bordeaux, and that this would probably end badly. And I should add that while I scarcely know your godson, there are reasons why it is desirable that the other boy Léon should be out of Bordeaux. Finally, since it seems that all three are determined to join de Gaulle, I can only be grateful to you for having made arrangements which, it seems, involve as little risk as may be possible. But it wasn't, I think, about this matter that you wished to speak to me.'

St-Hilaire did not reply immediately. He took his monocle from his eye and polished it.

'I do this,' he said, 'when I need to think. It wasn't on a whim that I asked your son to ask you to come to see me, but now that you're here . . . '

He paused again, and Lannes was surprised to find this aristocrat who seemed so sure of himself – as why not in these surroundings? – apparently at a loss, what had seemed to him just a moment ago to be flinty arrogance now splintered.

'I understand that you have been charged with the investigation into the killing of Professor Labiche.'

'I was, but I should tell you that the case has been closed, marked unsolved. That is, you will understand, my superiors' decision.'

'But you yourself..?'

'To my mind no murder should be dismissed in this manner.'

It would be impertinent to say, 'you have some information?' The thought irritated Lannes. It offended his sense of equality to suppose that a rich man like St-Hilaire should be treated differently from any other who came forward with information, and yet that was how it was.

'Aristide was an old friend of mine,' St-Hilaire said. 'You may be aware that I am also a friend of his daughter, the actress Adrienne Jauzion.'

He replaced his monocle and met Lannes' eyes.

'I hadn't thought to find this embarrassing,' he said. 'I am not accustomed to embarrassment. Our relationship is not what you may suppose. We have never been lovers. I regard her as a daughter. She has never had lovers except on the stage. You have spoken to her, and it may be that you have understood this. How shall I put it? She is in need – always – of admiration, but the bedroom door is closed.'

There was pain in his voice. Lannes thought, we're two men who no longer understand why the world is as it is, and we don't like it being what we don't understand.

'Aristide, however . . . ' the count said.

He rose and drew a curtain against the afternoon sun.

'He was an idealist, an unworldly man. He called on me when he returned to Bordeaux, and I urged Adrienne to make peace with him. Since you have talked with her, you will know that she declined to do so. She may have spoken of his politics. That was not the cause of their estrangement. She cares nothing for politics. It was his failure as a father which oppressed her. You will know his brother, the advocate, I suppose. Yes? Well then, I don't doubt that you have heard stories about him and his tastes? You have? That was how Aristide failed his daughter. When she was eleven. She tells me that she is sure you judged her harshly, because she could not speak to you of these things.When he saw her on his return he spoke of his intention to make amends. But what amends were possible? It was ridiculous. She found it even offensive when he spoke of exposing his brother. But what could that serve? It would make her an object of pity and of course scandal, even if she was herself as innocent as the victim of an outrageous act must be innocent. She pleaded with him to do nothing. And then he was dead. Now you tell me the case is closed. Perhaps that is for the best.'

Lannes was amazed by St-Hilaire's audacity. If he hadn't told him the case had been filed away, would he have spoken as he did? But if that had not been his intention, why summon him here?

'The death was of course accidental,' St-Hilaire said, 'the result of a moment of anger and panic, long stored-up anger, outrage and sudden panic. He had acquiesced in the silence, and now, when it could mean nothing, was determined, for his own satisfaction, his own idea of justice, to bring it into the open. You understand? I am sure you do. I may add that it is by her request that I speak to you in this way. So now, in my turn, I ask you if you will think it necessary to speak to her again.'

Lannes placed his glass on the table beside his chair.

'As I have already said, my superiors have decreed that the case is closed. I have no evidence that would cause me to ask them to reconsider this decision.'

'Poor Aristide,' the count said, 'he was a good man but a weak one who failed in everything he attempted. It was characteristic that he should have been so disgracefully weak at the time of what we need not hesitate to call the crime, and, so many years later, have thought it possible to make amends. As for the brother . . . '

'As for the brother,' Lannes said, 'he is now, in our present circumstances, a man of influence, even power, well thought of in Vichy.'

'By the moral architects of our national revolution,' St-Hilaire said, and Lannes responded to the wintry irony of his words.

'*Quelques crimes toujours précèdent les grands crimes,*' the count said, and Lannes recognised the quotation.

'Madame Jauzion is a remarkable actress,' he said. 'Her performance at our two meetings was flawless. Pray give her my compliments. I am surprised to have been told that she fails in Racine, and especially in *Phèdre* which you quote – so appositely, if I may say so.'

The count said, 'I am pleased we understand each other, and that you also approve of the steps I have taken with regard to your son and his friends. Boys of spirit. I envied their ardour. I shall show you out myself . . . '

He said this as if doing Lannes an honour.

'As for *Phèdre*, I suppose that you can play tragedy only if you open yourself to what is tragic and do not prefer to shut such knowledge away and live in denial. Which is itself tragic, for denial renders you incomplete. Or so it appears to me. Nevertheless my affection for her is sincere.'

In the hall, he stopped by the door and took a heavy walking-stick with a silver knob from a stand.

'This was Aristide's,' he said, 'but you will have no need of it, will you?'

XL

'So that's how it seems it was,' Lannes said.

'Jesus Christ,' Moncerre said, 'and Jesus Christ again. He had a nerve. You believed him, didn't you?'

'Yes, I believed him.'

'How could he be sure you wouldn't act on it?'

'I've wondered about that of course.'

What he couldn't say to Moncerre: he treated me like a man of honour, not a policeman. It was a form of flattery, and I succumbed as he knew I would.

'Fucking aristo,' Moncerre said.

Lannes thought of the count's smile when he went out of his way to show him what was undoubtedly the murder weapon –

their blunt instrument – the late nineteenth-century dandy's cane with the silver knob which had belonged to the professor and which his daughter in her fury had picked up to stave his head in. It was remarkable and ridiculous. Some crimes always precede the great crimes. Had the count learned, he wondered, of Lannes' detestation of the advocate Labiche? He thought of Adrienne aged eleven and her uncle, and her father's pusillanimity. If it had been Clothilde . . .

'There's still a puzzle,' he said now. 'Assuming, as I'm sure we should, that I've just been told the truth about the killing, why was pressure put on Bracal to close down the case and order us to release Sombra? It doesn't make sense. That pressure didn't come from St-Hilaire, I'm sure of that.'

'It's obvious,' Moncerre said, 'whoever stepped in thought that Sombra had done it when the professor wouldn't hand over whatever was demanded of him, and was afraid he would break under questioning. Just because he made a balls-up of it doesn't mean "whoever" wasn't afraid – and with reason.'

'You may be right.'

'Makes sense anyway. Not that it matters, does it? We're fucked either way.'

Lannes wondered if Moncerre despised him for having in effect given his promise of silence to the count.

'We couldn't have proved anything,' he said. 'There was no evidence. Certainly she had the presence of mind to remove his papers, but I have no doubt that these have now been burned. So all she would have had to do was to deny everything.'

The 'bull-terrier' grinned.

'You don't need to make excuses, boss. Not to me. I don't give a damn, you know. But I would have enjoyed having another go at that effing Spaniard. That's the truth. He may be innocent of this one, but if ever I saw a man who was asking for it, it's that bastard. One day he'll be ours. And that effing advocate too. So what now?'

'What now? Nothing,' Lannes said. 'There's nothing to be done now.'

Moncerre said, 'Have you heard, a Boche sailor was stabbed near the Porte du Palais last night?'

'That's nothing for us either,' Lannes said. 'That's for the gendarmerie, or for their own police.'

'It was probably a quarrel over a girl, nothing more than that,' Moncerre said. 'No business of ours anyway, as you say. Pity whoever did it made a botch of the job though.'

*   *   *

The sky was a deep summer-blue with a breeze from the Atlantic making the leaves on the plane trees tremble. It was a day like a Charles Trenet record, inviting you to be idle and happy. Lannes walked without purpose. It was again enough to be out of the office and alone. Even the ache in his hip was still. He sat outside a little bar in the rue du Vieil Temple and ordered a beer. He couldn't account for his mood, for his freedom from anxiety, his unaccustomed contentment. The words, 'it's a moment out of time,' came to him.

Léon appeared, leading Toto, hesitated a moment when he saw him, and responded when Lannes raised his hand.

'Henri thought you'd deserted him,' Lannes said.

The boy flushed and sat down.

'No,' he said, 'not that.'

The waiter approached and Léon asked for a lemonade.

'Alain has spoken to me,' Lannes said.

'And?'

'Perhaps it's for the best.'

Léon said, 'It's strange. What we are doing, it's right, I'm sure of that. So why do I feel I'm running away?'

'Have you told your mother?'

'I can't.'

'Or your Aunt Miriam? No? I'll see to that, when you've gone. There's nothing you can do to protect them, you must know that. So there is no reason to feel guilty.'

'But I do.'

'Oh, I understand that. One never needs a reason to feel guilty. I trust you to look after Alain. He's headstrong and rash, needs restraint.'

For a little they sat in silence. Then Lannes said, 'I have the impression you know yourself better than Alain knows himself. You've had reason to learn what and who you are as he hasn't. That's why I ask you to look after him. And the other boy?'

'Jérôme looks soft. But he isn't.'

'Good. I'm glad to hear that.'

It was strange. He had felt sympathy for Léon, pity too. Now he found that he respected him.

He said, 'Only one thing. Say good-bye properly to Henri. Don't just slip away without a word. You'll find he understands you.'

Léon drank his lemonade, and said, 'I'd better get Toto back. Henri worries if I have him out for long in case he over-exerts himself. Not that he ever would, he's a lazy old thing. Do you remember, you once told me to forget that you are a policeman.' He smiled. 'I think I've just managed to.'

*　　*　　*

Lannes remained outside the little bar for a long time, enjoying sunshine and idleness. In two days Léon would have gone, Karim also, and he could speak to Kordlinger. It wouldn't be easy. Kordlinger might suspect he had been playing a double game, bringing him information only when it could be of no use. There would be a black mark against his name, branded unreliable. Well, things would get worse. At least he had put in the application for an 'ausweis' which would permit him to go to Vichy to meet Edmond de Grimaud. There should be no difficulty about that. Edmond had readily agreed to authorise his journey. And Dominique already had his 'ausweis' and was eager, even impatient, to join Maurice and take up the position secured for him as an officer in the Chantiers de Jeunesse. So he would have one son in Vichy, the other with the Free French; an insurance policy for the family? That wasn't really a welcome thought. But which thoughts were welcome now? And what would Marguerite say when she learned of Alain's departure? If only they could speak to each other as they used to do.

Clothilde was alone in the apartment when he returned. She was bare-legged in a summer dress, with sandals on her feet. Her face glowed.

'You're looking very smart, darling. Are you off somewhere?'

'Just to the cinema.'

'With your German?'

'Manu? No, Papa, that's over. I took your advice. Anyway his unit's been recalled. Just with Dominique and a friend of his from the legion.'

And it's the friend, he thought, who accounts for the excitement you are trying to suppress.

'Good,' he said. 'Perhaps you'll bring him back afterwards?'

'Depends on how long the movie lasts. The curfew, you know.'

'Yes, of course, the curfew. Where's your mother?'

'She went to see Granny. Apparently she's got a pain. I must fly or I'll be late.'

She gave him a quick hug and a kiss on the cheek.

'Don't worry, Papa. I'm happy.'

'I can see that.'

'You worry too much. You know you do. And it's pointless.'

It was strange to be in the apartment alone with the sunlight slanting in and falling on the bowl of pink roses on the table. It felt wrong. He couldn't settle to read, but found nothing else to do. Pointless to worry? How could he not? He put a record on the gramophone: Ravel's Bolero. Quite the wrong music, with its insistent gathering tension; but he couldn't bring himself to take it off and play something else. He lay back in a chair and closed his eyes. The music stopped and there was only the whirring as the turntable went round and round. He fell asleep.

When he woke he heard Marguerite busy in the kitchen.

'You look terrible,' she said.

'I always do when I wake from an afternoon sleep. You know that.'

'You didn't used to. How I wish you weren't a policeman. I've always felt like that, but it's worse now. It's not only that you are always exhausted, it's because I'm convinced you have come to hate the job itself.'

He felt closer to her than he had for months, but all he could reply was: 'How would we live if I wasn't?'

She looked away, lowering her eyes.

'I would feel that I was running away,' he said.

'And why not?'

'The war and the Occupation won't last for ever.'

'Won't they?'

'I'm sure they won't. How was your mother?'

'It's her liver, she says, but I think it's mostly boredom and bad temper. And she complains about rationing and worries about money.'

'Don't we all? It's a lovely afternoon. Come for a walk, eat an ice-cream in a café? We haven't done that for a long time.'

He took her hand as they strolled to the Place de l'Ancienne Comédie, and thought that this was how they had walked through the streets before they were married and indeed in the early years of marriage, when she was still only a wife and not a mother. Was it the thought of Clothilde's face, glowing with happiness as it had been that afternoon, which awoke this feeling of tenderness in him? He was ashamed to remember that only a couple of hours previously he had been imagining Yvette lying naked on her bed. He squeezed his wife's hand and found the pressure returned.

He ordered an ice-cream each and a citron pressé for Marguerite and a marc for himself. Their silence in the sunlight was companionable, without strain. They spoke first of Dominique.

'You'll miss him,' he said. 'So will I of course,' he added, as if his first words suggested indifference.

'Of course we will, but he is so eager to do good, and he says this work is so worthwhile, that it would have been selfish to try to persuade him to stay at home. Birds must fly from the nest, I do realise that, Jean.'

'Who's Clothilde's new boy? Have you met him?'

'Oh yes, he's charming, quite charming, a well-brought-up boy from a good family, I'm sure. I told you that young German was merely a passing phase.'

'Well, it seems you were right there.'

'Of course I was. I do know our children, Jean. As for this boy – he's called Michel – he is good looking, which isn't so important, and has lovely manners.'

'Very different from me then,' he said.

'Oh I don't know,' she smiled. 'Nothing wrong with your manners, not when we were young anyway. Even Mother approved of you then.'

'Not so as I noticed,' he said, and returned her smile.

'You don't need to worry about Clothilde. I know she irritates me and I'm sometimes short with her, but she's a sensible child really, and as for this boy, when you think of how she is deprived of so much that she should enjoy at her age, I can only be happy to see her engaged in what is probably only a flirtation. It's Alain who causes me concern. I never know what he is thinking or what he wants and he is so intense that I am really afraid he will do something stupid. I know you think he's perfect, Jean, just because he plays rugby and reads books, but I am so anxious for him, and not only because he never speaks to me about his feelings, unlike Dominique who tells me everything.'

It occurred to him that this might be the moment, when for the first time in so long they were really talking to each other, to tell her of Alain's intentions. But he had promised him not to speak of his plans till he had gone.

'We have to trust our children, all of them, to do what they think best,' he said.

'That's weak, Jean. Alain's too young and immature to know what is good for him.'

XLI

Lannes kept well back from the platform as the train pulled out, ten minutes late in leaving. Alain had slipped out of the house, early, as he quite often did, before his mother was awake. He met Léon and Jérôme as arranged in Gustave's Bar near the station. It had been Lannes' suggestion, and he joined the boys there. They were nervous, all four. Only Jérôme managed to assume an air of gaiety and make jokes.

'There's no need to be anxious,' he said, 'my godfather's plans never go wrong' – an assurance that failed to reassure Lannes; he felt his stomach tightening. Gustave brought them coffee and croissants as if it was an ordinary morning. Lannes ran over words of advice in his mind, but couldn't bring himself to utter them. He sensed they were eager for him to go, to leave them on their own with their adventure; he was the odd one out. They had no need of him.

Léon said, 'You will see to my aunt, won't you? And . . . '

'Of course I will. She'll be relieved, I think, that you are getting away, and, as I've said, there is nothing you could do to protect her if you remained here. Your mother too will be happy to think you are safe. They'll both know that you are acting for the best.'

'I feel guilty nevertheless,' Léon said. 'I did speak to Henri, as you told me to. That was bad enough. He wept.'

'He's fond of you. What about your parents, Jérôme?'

'My godfather's invited them to lunch, and I gave him a note for my mother. It's all right. He'll see that she doesn't try to interfere, to do anything to stop us in Marseilles. We can trust him.'

Alain was very pale. He had thought about this moment for so long, been so eager for it, and now the adventure he had imagined was all but underway, and for the first time he wondered if he would ever see his mother and father, sister and brother again. That at least was what Lannes read in his son's eye, and his thought was confirmed when Alain stretched across the table, took hold of his hand, and pressed it hard.

'You mustn't worry,' he said.

'Of course not,' Lannes said. 'I have every confidence in you.'

If only that was true. He did indeed have confidence in his son, but disclaiming worry, anxiety, fear, that was a lie, and Alain knew it as surely as he did himself.

In a fortnight it would be a year to the day since the first motorised column of German troops had crossed the bridge over the Garonne and rolled up the cours Victor Hugo while the Bordelais had stood watching, powerless, mystified, silent and ashamed. Now, for the three boys . . .

'It's strange,' Jérôme said. 'I really feel as if we were off on our holidays.'

'Gustave,' Lannes said, 'bring us a bottle of champagne, please.'

The cork popped. Glasses were poured. It was a moment of solemnity.

'All for one and one for all,' Alain said.

Jérôme raised his glass and clicked it against the others.

'To the Liberation!' he said.

Léon drank with them, but remained silent. Lannes thought, he can scarcely contain his excitement, and yet he is ashamed, as the others aren't, to be abandoning his family to their uncertain future here in Bordeaux.

'It's time you were off,' he said.

He embraced them all, clasped Alain tight to his breast and kissed him on both cheeks, like a general who had just pinned the Croix de Guerre on his uniform.

They set off for the station. As they entered it, Léon turned and looked at the Hotel Artemis across the street.

*   *   *

Lannes followed at a distance, keeping in the background. When at last the train pulled out, and the smoke from the engine drifted away, he felt desolate. His son was off to fight for France, and he was trapped here in Bordeaux. Tomorrow the boys would be in Algiers, and he had to account to Kordlinger for his inability to satisfy his demands. Meanwhile he would play truant, keep clear of the office till he was sure the boys had arrived in Algiers, just in case he had an unannounced visit from Kordlinger.

He was surprised to find Henri downstairs in the bookshop, sitting at the desk which for months had been occupied by Léon. More surprising still, Henri was sober. He had shaved and was wearing a suit and a collar and tie.

'Yes,' Henri smiled. 'I've been letting myself go, I know that. It's Léon who has shamed me into pulling myself together.'

'It's good to see you looking yourself,' Lannes said. 'All the same, would you object to locking up so that we can talk upstairs, over coffee perhaps?'

Henri still moved uncertainly.

'I don't know if it can last,' he said. 'My sobriety, I mean. But, as I say, it is Léon's example that has shamed me into making an effort. If he can risk his life in this way, then I can at least try to stay off the booze, during the day anyway. It's good to see you, Jean.

The boys will be all right, won't they? Léon told me what was arranged. I'm afraid for them, I have to admit that.'

'One can't not be. We live in fear. We're condemned to live in fear. But I had already had to make plans to get Léon out of Bordeaux.'

He told Henri about Schussmann and the attentions he had paid to Léon, about the spook Félix, and Schussmann's suicide, and Kordlinger's demand.

'Poor boy,' Henri said. 'To bear that weight while I sat drinking myself silly up here, and to say nothing about it. Terrible, but I'm grateful to you for telling me, and all the more relieved that he has got away.'

Lannes had told him all he knew, not all he suspected. But there was no need to burden Henri with that.

'It's possible,' he said, 'that this chap, Félix, the spook, may come in search of Léon. You'll let me know if he does.'

'But it's not likely, is it? With the German dead.'

'No, it's not likely.'

'And that poor Aristide – are you any closer to finding his killer?'

'I know who killed him,' Lannes said. 'But there's nothing to be done about that. It really doesn't matter.'

Which was true, even if he hadn't given his word to St-Hilaire.

'There are many reasons to kill, Henri,' he said, 'but, outside the class of professional criminals who for the most part kill only to escape arrest or on rare occasions because they have been hired to do the job, you may be surprised how often the motive is respectability – the need felt to protect it, I mean. Take Schussmann. He killed himself because he was afraid – at least I suppose that was the reason, and I can hardly blame him for being afraid. But he refused to collaborate with Félix because to do so would have cost him his self-respect. I don't think it was patriotism or anything like that. From my observation and from what Léon said about him, he was a decent enough chap, certainly no Nazi and not even much of a soldier. Respectability and fear are brothers.'

*　　*　　*

'You knew he planned this and you said nothing. You didn't try to stop him or tell me about it.'

'What would you have done if I had?'

Marguerite started to cry. Lannes was sorry for her. He should have taken her in his arms and offered comfort. He did nothing.

'I can't forgive you,' she said. 'I shall never be able to forgive you. He will get himself killed and it will be your fault.'

What was there to say? He has done what he thinks is right. Pointless. He thought: you haven't tried to stop Dominique from going to Vichy. That may be more dangerous in the long run. You don't understand how things are. You don't understand why Alain has to do what he is doing. You don't understand because you don't know him as I do, and because you care nothing for anything outside the family. He didn't tell you what he planned to do because he knew that you wouldn't try to understand him, that you would just tell him not to be silly. You don't know what the world is like because you don't care to know.

He said none of what ran bitterly in his mind. And really he had no right to reproach her. Weren't there mothers all over France who shut their eyes to the war, the humiliation of defeat and Occupation, and enclosed themselves in the little world of home and family? What else should they do? And yet her determination to exclude the reality by which they were as a country and a people oppressed exasperated him, not only because he couldn't behave in the same way but because there was selfishness in this wilful blindness. All the same she was entitled to speak to him as she had. He had deceived her, and they both knew he would do so again. The fabric of their marriage was torn. Trust once lost is never fully recovered. He had seen too many examples of marriages and relationships in which the light has been extinguished. They would patch things up, after a fashion, find a way to come to some form of accommodation, because it was necessary to do so, and life would be intolerable otherwise, but they would both know that things could never be again as they had been. His secrecy, his deceit, and her words 'I shall never be able to forgive you', could not be forgotten. His own mother used to say, 'time is the great healer.' It wasn't always true. There are wounds that never close but continue to suppurate.

He got to his feet

'Alain has done what he believes is right. That's how we've brought him up. We should be proud of him. Now I must go out, back to work.'

'That's right,' she said. 'Run away. As usual. Take refuge in your work, like a coward. Or go and get drunk with that loathsome bull-terrier of yours. I don't care what you do. I'll never care again, do you hear? My mother was right about you, she always said I had made a mistake marrying you.'

He picked up his stick. On the stairs he found he was trembling and leaned for a moment against the wall to steady himself. He could hear her sobbing, or thought he could, but there was nothing to say or do about it. He had no comfort to offer and she would refuse it if he had.

XLII

'Well, he's safe up in the mountains,' Fernand said, 'the farmer's a cousin of a cousin. Christ knows what he'll make of the little bastard – I don't suppose he even knows that milk comes from cows. He's a right one – I'm glad enough to be rid of him – he propositioned my Jacques, you know.'

'And what did Jacques do?'

'Smacked him in the kisser.'

'How did Karim take that?'

'Do him credit. He laughed and said, "Have it your own way, anyway I really prefer girls myself too, just thought I'd try it on." Maybe he's not such a bad kid, even Jacques says that, though he was mighty offended at the time. Anyway he's safe for now.'

'Thank you. I'm grateful. I felt a responsibility to the boy. I don't think he's had much of a chance. Maybe he'll learn to go straight now.'

As ever, even a short conversation with Fernand left Lannes feeling more cheerful. He made his way to the address Karim had given him. It was a mean street no more than a hundred metres from 'The Wet Flag', or 'Chez Jules' as the bar was now called.

There was no concierge. The building stank of poverty. He climbed the stairs to the third floor. There was a smell of something cooking in stale fat and the stairs hadn't been swept for days. He knocked and the door was opened by a woman dressed in a housecoat with a pattern of faded flowers. She had curlers in her hair, a couple of them working themselves free, and her crimson lipstick extended beyond her mouth to smear her left cheek. A cigarette dangled from the corner of her mouth and her feet were bare.

'What's he done now?' she said.

'What do you mean?'

'What do I mean? Do you think I don't recognise a cop when I see one? I wasn't born yesterday.'

'May I come in?'

'Don't suppose I can stop you.'

She stepped aside and as he passed her he realised that she was wearing nothing under the housecoat. The room was warm and damp, the air stale and smelling of unwashed garments, and there were cobwebs across the window. The table was covered with dirty cups and glasses. An empty bottle of Rhum St Jacques stood beside a pack of playing cards and a plate of half-eaten macaroni.

'Go ahead. Finish your meal,' he said, but when he looked at the macaroni he saw that a fly buzzed around it and a cigarette had been stubbed out among the tubes.

'So what's he done?' she said again. 'I know he's up to something, the little bastard. He hasn't been home for three days.'

'Is Karim your only son?'

'One's enough. More than enough, I often think. You don't happen to have a drink on you?'

Lannes shook his head.

'He hasn't done anything that need worry you,' he said.

'That's new,' she said. 'So what do you want?'

She picked up the empty bottle and sighed.

'I'm needing badly,' she said. 'How old do you think I am? I'm thirty-five and I look fifty and I can't talk without a drink.'

'All right then, I'll fetch you one.'

'Rum,' she said. 'Rum's what I drink.'

When he returned with a bottle from the 'alimentation', she

was sitting at the table with her head in her hands and groaning. He poured her a glass which she downed in one swallow; then shuddered and held it out for a refill.

Lannes moved a pile of dirty clothes from a chair and sat down opposite her.

'He brought a German officer here,' he said.

'One!' she said. 'If it was only one. I have to give up my bed' – she gestured to the other door in the room – 'so the Boches can stick it up his arse.'

Lannes found it hard to picture Schussmann, who had seemed fastidious to him, in this squalor. He produced his photograph and laid it before her. 'This one?'

'Him,' she lifted the glass again. 'That one was a laugh. He took one look at me coming out of the bedroom with sleep in my eyes, threw some francs on the table and was off down the stairs like a rat making for its hole. We had a good laugh over that one. Never made easier dough, Karim said. But the others. One of them wanted us both at once. "Not on your nelly," I said, "first one, then the other." "All right, call me Hermann," he said. Where's Karim, why are you here?'

The couple of large tots of rum were already thickening her speech, but her voice was stronger. Lannes tapped the photograph of Schussmann,

'This one's dead, shot himself when they found out he was queer, and the Boches want the boys he went with.'

'And you're here to do their dirty work, clapping the cuffs on my Karim. Bastard. Well, you're out of luck. Like I say, I haven't seen him for days. So you can get out, Mr Policeman, you can fucking well get out.'

Lannes said, 'Calm down. You've got it wrong. I came to tell you he's safe, out of Bordeaux, where the Boches won't find him. You've nothing to worry about.'

'What do you mean? Nothing? How am I to live without my boy? Where's the money to come from? They pay him more than they pay me. That's the Boches for you, filthy swine.'

She gave herself another rum and lit the cigarette which had gone out.

'You'll manage,' Lannes said. 'I just wanted to let you know he's safe.'

'Bastard,' she said again.

'That's all right. I wasn't looking for thanks. If anyone comes asking about him, you've no idea where he is.'

'Well, I haven't, have I?'

On the stairs he passed a bald German sergeant.

'She'll be pleased to see you,' he said. 'She's a lovely old woman, all ready to go.'

I shouldn't have said that, he thought. I shouldn't mock her. How else is she to get by, and perhaps she really cares for the boy? Why didn't he tell me Schussmann had run away, in a panic or disgust? Maybe he was ashamed.

*　　*　　*

Dominique and Clothilde were playing cards. She had been crying and her eyes were red-rimmed.

'Where's your mother?'

'She's gone to bed,' Dominique said. 'She says she has a headache, but I think it's more than that. There's something wrong, isn't there? It's about Alain, isn't it?'

'Where is he?' Clothilde said. 'We're all worried. He hasn't been arrested, has he?'

'No, of course not. It's nothing like that. You don't need to worry, darling. Your mother hasn't said anything, not even to you, Dominique?'

'All I know is that she's unhappy.'

'And angry,' Clothilde said. 'With you, Papa. I know that. What's happening?'

'Yes,' Lannes said, 'she's angry with me. There are things we don't think alike about. It happens. It'll pass.'

'We're not children,' Clothilde said.

'No, you're not. It might be easier if you were. Still children, I mean. It would be a lot easier.'

'You're unhappy too, Papa. And anxious. Why don't you go through to her and make up?'

'No,' Dominique said, 'don't do that, not now. Do it later. I looked in a little while ago and she's asleep. But you must talk to each other. I know that. You really must, whatever's wrong. Oh, I forgot, there's a letter for you. It was delivered by hand. Here it is. Rather grand, with a crest on the envelope.'

He slit it open, a single sheet, from St-Hilaire.

'I have had a telegram from my cousin, the General. The birds have landed safely. All is well. I made my peace with Jérôme's mother. I am grateful to you for your understanding concerning the other matter we talked about.'

Assurance of distinguished sentiments and all that.

Lannes said, 'I can tell you now. Your brother is in Algiers. He flew there yesterday with two friends. They have arrived safely.'

'I don't understand,' Clothilde said.

'I do,' Dominique said. 'You knew and you didn't stop him. And you kept it from Maman. It's terrible.'

'But why Algiers?' Clothilde said.

'Tell her, Papa. Tell her. You must tell her.'

'You know Alain's opinions,' Lannes said. 'You know how deeply he feels about the Armistice and the Occupation, how indignant he is. Well, North Africa is the first step for him and his friends towards joining de Gaulle and the Free French. And, Dominique, you are correct. I didn't stop him. I didn't try to stop him. He knew it was dangerous, there was no need to tell him that. I said merely that he must do what he thought was right, just as I said that to you when you declared your intention of going to Vichy and taking up the position offered to you there. Which, as you will remember I told you, is not without danger too. You are both doing what you believe to be right, and I'm proud of both of you. There's no difference.'

There was a silence. It lasted perhaps a couple of minutes. Clothilde dabbed her eyes with her handkerchief. Then Dominique said: 'But there is. There is a difference. I discussed the invitation Maurice sent me with Maman. I discussed it fully with her as well as with you. Alain kept his plan secret from her, and you – her husband – colluded with him in this secrecy, this deceit. That was wrong, monstrous. Do you think she will ever forgive you?'

Lannes lit a cigarette and found that his hands were trembling.

'I don't know that she will,' he said.

'Poor Maman, to be deceived and betrayed,' Dominique said.

'Poor Papa,' Clothilde said, 'to think you had to deceive and betray her. And Alain, he might have said good-bye. I am his twin after all. And he didn't even ask me to look after No Neck. I will of course, but, all the same . . . I don't understand it . . . '

'I don't understand how you and Alain could cause her so much pain,' Dominique said.

'No, I don't suppose you can,' Lannes said, 'but that's how it was. That's how it is.'

XLIII

He had barely slept. Twice, as he lay staring into the dark, Marguerite had cried out, but she did not wake, and, to his relief, did not stir when he slipped out of bed. It was scarcely dawn. He left the house like a guilty man escaping the scene of the crime. In the Place du Marché, stalls were being set up and goods laid out. The familiar bustle could not disguise the paucity of what was available. The first bars were open and the traders were drinking their ersatz coffee, many enriching it – and making it palatable – with the addition of a nip of marc, brandy or rum. The mood was sombre, conversation restricted to grumbles. It would be like that every morning now. Lannes called for a double dash of marc in his coffee. He took his cup to the door of the café. It was still cool but the sun was pushing its way through the mist that rose from the Garonne. It was going to be a hot day again. He thought of Alain waking in Algiers and feeling the exhilaration of the African dawn. He wondered how he and the other boys would pass the day, when and how they would take their first steps towards the Gaullists.

Miriam was rolling up the iron shutter of the tabac as he approached. She greeted him with a smile. Maybe it was an effort, but she looked almost cheerful.

'It's the morning,' she said, 'such a beautiful morning, it tempts you to forget that things are as they are. All the more reason to live for the moment, take such small pleasures as come one's way.'

She made coffee. They brought out two chairs to sit in the sunlight.

'I've been expecting you,' she said. 'Léon left me a note. Actually he left it with my uncle, old Léopold Kurz, who sent it round last night.'

'The old tailor?' he said. 'I didn't know he was your uncle.'

'So I have to thank you.'

'I did nothing,' he said. 'The boys arranged it themselves, or rather . . . '

'Yes, I know, the Comte de St-Hilaire. What a thing it is to have influential relations. But you've protected Léon and you did nothing to stop them as you might have done. You'll miss Alain.'

'Yes,' he said, 'but it's for the best.'

'I hope so. I'm sure it is.'

He was tempted to speak to her about Marguerite – her anger, disapproval, resentment – but family matters were family matters.

'I had a note from St-Hilaire yesterday. They've arrived safely in Algiers.'

'And now?'

'We can only hope. I've lost the ability to pray. If I ever had it.'

He threw his cigarette into the gutter.

*   *   *

'You're an early bird,' old Joseph said. 'Out catching worms?'

'No such luck,' Lannes said, 'worms all gone to earth.'

Joseph acknowledged the pleasantry – it was an old exchange between them – with a wheezy chuckle, his bronchitis bad again.

'That young judge – what's his name – Bracal is it? – wants to see you. "Ask the superintendent to have the courtesy to call on me" – soft soap – and there's a note for you too. Another street-boy, I tried to hold him as you asked me, but he slipped away and scampered off before I could get a grip on him. Sorry.'

The same thing again – 'Surely you want to know who your real father was?' It made no sense. If the writer of the letter wanted to disturb him, he would have to do more than repeating himself.

Bracal was spruce, Lannes conscious of his own unshaven face and weariness.

The judge asked him to sit down, and smiled.

'What I'm about to say is strictly none of my business. So I shouldn't say it. Which is why I'm going to. Even for a judge, there is pleasure in acting improperly on occasion. It may even be a duty sometimes in present circumstances. I had dinner with the new Prefect last night. He's an enthusiast for Collaboration, as you may have heard. Very zealous. There are advantages. He hears things. Some of them unwelcome. This business of the German liaison officer who shot himself now. As I say, it's no concern of mine, but it is, I gather, of yours, and the word is that his replacement – can't remember his name . . . '

'Kordlinger,' Lannes said.

'Yes, Kordlinger, thinks you're dragging your heels. I tell you only because I have formed a respect for you, superintendent. So can you satisfy him?'

It was unexpected. Lannes hesitated, lit a cigarette to give himself time to think. Sunlight streamed in, falling on Bracal's face. He picked up a pair of dark glasses, toyed with them and replaced them on the desk. Had it occurred to him that putting them on would make him seem less trustworthy? Was he sincere in that expression of respect? When Lannes made no immediate reply, Bracal rolled his signet ring round and said, 'I'm younger than you, superintendent, and I'm aware that there is rarely complete confidence between the judiciary and the PJ. It's regrettable but understandable. Nevertheless it's desirable and, I hope, in your interest, that on this occasion, we should speak frankly. So, again, can you satisfy this Kordlinger?'

Lannes said, 'I'll take you at your word. To speak frankly, the answer is "No." Schussmann was a fool, a decent enough chap actually, but a fool and unbelievably rash. Perhaps simply because he was lonely and unhappy. There are two or three bars in Bordeaux, as there are in every city, where men of his inclinations can usually find what they want. You'll be aware of this; it's no secret. The Vice Squad knows about them of course, but, as long as they are reasonably well conducted, they let them be. Rightly in my opinion. As you know, in these matters, there is illegality only where minors are concerned or public decency offended, this being something which depends on circumstances. Schussmann took to frequenting at least one of these bars, possibly others. He is not, I should say, the only member of the Occupying forces to do so. That won't surprise you. Homosexual activity is illegal in Nazi Germany, but the German disposition towards it is well known. As to Schussmann, I have identified only one boy he picked up in one of these bars. The boy has – unfortunately or otherwise – disappeared, perhaps left Bordeaux. No doubt he learned of Schussmann's suicide and panicked. There's a suggestion that on another occasion Schussmann left the bar hurriedly when he recognised another German officer there. If this is so, it may be that this officer reported him to his superiors and so precipitated his suicide. That's for the Boches themselves to decide. I doubt if this will satisfy Kordlinger.'

Bracal smiled again.

'I share your doubts. You are sure that the boy in question has indeed gone missing. Left Bordeaux, I think you said.'

'I believe my information to be reliable. I have also spoken with the boy's mother.'

'A reliable witness.'

'Reliable perhaps. Reputable no. A prostitute herself.'

'But you are sure the boy has gone?'

'As sure as I can be.'

'Good.'

Bracal played his little finger-drumming game and said, 'A sordid little story. I like the idea that one of his colleagues should have betrayed his secret. But will that suggestion hold up?'

'Probably not,' Lannes said. 'Though it might muddy the waters.'

'I have the impression that you have another story for me.'

'Yes,' Lannes said. 'just as sordid, and nastier.'

'Even nastier? Perhaps we should fortify ourselves.'

He fetched a bottle of cognac from a cupboard and poured them each a glass.

'You probably prefer Armagnac, but my home country is the Charente. Your health, superintendent. Please carry on.'

There is an English expression from the hunting-field: to throw your heart over a hedge. It means to take a jump blind and boldly without thought of what lies on the other side. Lannes had never of course heard of it, but this is what he now did.

'There's a bookshop,' he said, 'in the rue des Remparts. The owner is an old friend of mine. Last year he took on a young assistant, a good-looking boy. Lieutenant Schussmann was a cultivated man, with an interest in literature. I believe he may have been a schoolmaster before the war. No matter. He found his way to the bookshop and made a habit of calling in there. He took a fancy to the boy. He might have been more careful if he had known that the boy was Jewish – or perhaps not, I don't know. His attentions were remarked, but not necessarily, so far as I have been able to ascertain, by his colleagues.'

He paused and took a sip of the brandy. It was very good brandy. He looked up at Bracal who continued to smile.

'Travaux Rurales,' he said. 'The spook who called on you and made an appointment with me. You won't have forgotten him. You may even know his name. I don't. Félix, he called himself. He approached the boy and instructed him to encourage Schussmann, lead him on. Naturally the boy was reluctant. And afraid. But he is, as I say, Jewish, and he has a mother – he's her only child – and an aunt who is, I'm prepared to tell you, a friend of mine. It is not a good time to be Jewish, as I don't need to remind you. Threats were made. Félix terrified and humiliated the boy. I won't go into that. You may imagine the worst. It was indeed the worst which happened. So the boy did as he was told, unwillingly. An assignation was made in a cheap hotel where they are accustomed to this sort of thing. Félix interrupted them, catching Schussmann in the act. His intention was, as you will have realised, blackmail. Schussmann was to be turned, to supply information about – I don't know exactly what Félix had in mind. But instead of submitting he shot himself. You might say he took the honourable way out. You might also say that Félix was acting as a patriot, in the interests of France, if not necessarily of Vichy. Again I don't know. Do you think I should tell this story to Kordlinger?'

'It's a remarkable story,' Bracal said. 'Or at least remarkably interesting. And the boy? I don't suppose you are in a position to hand him over to the Germans and satisfy Kordlinger? No? Where is he now?'

'I believe he is no longer in metropolitan France.'

He looked Bracal in the eyes. For a long moment they held each other's gaze.

'Good,' Bracal said. 'Satisfactory. For the boy, but not for you. It doesn't help solve your problem with Kordlinger, does it?'

'Not at all. Perhaps I should give him Félix.'

'Not a good idea.'

'He's a bastard.'

'But a French one. And a patriot. One who may have stepped out of line, acting on his own initiative, since Travaux Rurales, like the Deuxième Bureau and the other branches of these services are – officially – committed to collaboration, just as I am and you in the PJ are. Isn't that so?'

'Certainly. That is our duty – officially.'

'So what will you say to Kordlinger?'

'What can I say? I am merely a slack inefficient French cop who is embarrassed to have made a balls-up of the investigation.'

'Don't push your incompetence beyond the limits of his credulity. That's all. I'm pleased to have had this conversation. It's cleared the air, hasn't it? Brought us to an understanding. One other thing. I understand that you are about to make a visit to Vichy. I would be grateful if you would present my compliments to a friend of mine.'

He picked up a card and scribbled a name and address.

'You'll find him here. He will be expecting you. He also works for the TR, but I believe you will find him more sympathetic than you found Félix.'

'I'll be happy to oblige you, even though I don't care for spooks. By the way, since we have had this conversation . . . '

'But we haven't. There will be absolutely no record of it, and my memory is terrible.'

'Nevertheless,' Lannes said, 'the Spaniard Sombra. The order to release him?'

'Ah yes, that disreputable fellow. Was he by any chance guilty of the crime for which you had arrested him?'

'No, but . . . '

'Quite. You wonder who leaned on me? That's how you would put it, isn't it?'

He inspected his fingernails and then smiled.

'Strangely I find my memory working quite well again for the moment. You will have heard of the BMA?'

'A man calling himself Villepreux approached me some weeks ago.'

'There you are then,' Bracal said, 'though of course I don't recall that name. Thank you for coming to see me, superintendent. It has been a delightful and instructive conversation, don't you think? I'm happy to find that we understand each other.'

XLIV

Kordlinger's boots were as highly polished as those of a Great War general thirty kilometres behind the Front. It was afternoon but his face shone as bright as his boots and it looked as if he had only just shaved. He gave off a whiff of eau-de-Cologne. His nose twitched when Lannes lit a cigarette.

'So,' he said, 'what have you discovered? Are these degenerate boys under arrest?'

'There are difficulties,' Lannes said. 'I am anxious of course to collaborate with you, as I have been instructed to do. Naturally I recognise that it's in the interest of the PJ to have good relations with you as the Occupying power. This has been made very clear by my superiors. Nevertheless . . . '

He blew out smoke, held his cigarette between thumb and his first two fingers, and sighed, waiting for Kordlinger to speak. He let the silence stretch out, then smiled at Kordlinger as if inviting his confidence. When the German made no reply, he said, 'I am quite happy to lay my cards on the table, but let me say first I fully appreciate your concern. You have expressed it very clearly. There is however a difficulty – I speak as a policeman, you understand, not, if I may put it like this, as a politician. You understand? As a police-man, an official of the French State, I am constrained by the law.

That is the position – is it not? – of officials in Germany too, and of policemen in the Reich? We are bound by the law, must not over-step its limits. I deal with crime, that is, with acts defined as criminal by our code of law, commonly styled the Code Napoléon. Now I respect your position. I understand your desire to have any who had sexual relations with Lieutenant Schussmann apprehended, but . . . '

'But?'

'There have been no such criminal acts. Homosexual practices are not illegal in France, unless public decency is outraged or minors have been corrupted. You may think this deplorable, since I am aware that the law is different in Germany – Article 175 – isn't it? – of your criminal code covers the question, or so I believe. I might agree with you, but my opinions, whatever they are, must be irrelevant. You understand my predicament?'

'I understand only that you are being obstructive, and appear to have forgotten the relationship in which you find yourself with regard to the forces of the Reich.'

'I am sorry to hear you say so, being well aware of the require-ment to collaborate, and of my superiors' orders that I should do so. However, I have some information which may be useful to you. It seems likely that Lieutenant Schussmann killed himself either because he was being blackmailed or because he feared exposure. These are two possibilities.'

'Superintendent, pray don't insult me by stating what would be obvious even to a blind man.'

Lannes paused. He wondered how clever Kordlinger was, what he could get away with, how close he dared edge towards the truth.

'Schussmann was not careful,' he said. 'Indeed he was rash. He frequented certain bars, places which are not illegal, where people of his tendency gather and recognise each other. I may say he was not the only member of the Occupying forces to do so. It is possible that he may have learned, suspected or feared that he was being spied upon by one of his colleagues, even perhaps an agent of the military police. My investigation leads me to believe that this was so. He may therefore have panicked, being well aware that the Wehrmacht does not tolerate such depravity.'

'This is mere speculation,' Kordlinger said. 'Meanwhile I insist that such establishments must be closed,' Kordlinger said.

'That would be a matter for the Prefecture, not for the PJ.'

'Very well, I shall speak to the Prefect. It is of course within my power, as a representative of the Occupation, to act unilaterally in such matters. Nevertheless I am content to leave it in the Prefect's hands. Meanwhile you have not only failed to arrest any of these degenerates, as I requested, but it appears that you have not even identified them.'

Lannes spread his hands, conscious that he was behaving like a Frenchman in a stage farce.

'Lieutenant Schussmann frequented these bars, but my investigations have established that he was careful to this extent, in that he always left alone. No doubt he may have made assignations to meet elsewhere, but I have found no evidence that he did so. I am sorry to disappoint you.'

Kordlinger clenched his fist and banged it on Lannes' desk. It was not an impressive gesture, not one, Lannes thought, that came naturally to him. Kordlinger too was playing a part and one in which he was less comfortable than he would have wished. No doubt he was afraid of his superiors.

'I am sorry,' Lannes said again. 'My investigation might have been more fruitful' – he hesitated – 'more fruitful if it had been possible to accede to my request, which Commissaire Schnyder will have relayed to you, that any diary or private papers which Lieutenant Schussmann kept should be made available to me.'

Kordlinger got to his feet.

'There were no such papers,' he said. 'None at all. Only some embers in a fireplace. Schussmann died as he had lived, guarding the secret of his degeneracy. Superintendent, you have failed me. I was advised to put my trust in you and you have betrayed it. Rest assured, you have not heard the last of this matter. Heil Hitler!'

Not heard the last of it? That was only too probably true. He hadn't played the scene as he had intended. But he had avoided giving anything more than a hint of the involvement of the spooks – which hint Kordlinger hadn't picked up on. Apart from that, would it have been any better if he had named Karim – or at least indicated that he knew a boy whom Schussmann had picked up but that the boy had gone to ground or slipped out of Bordeaux? He had meant to give him that much. Then it had stuck in his gorge. Kordlinger hadn't even asked for the name of the bars. Because he knew them already? Because there had indeed been a German officer or NCO, or even someone from the Gestapo, spying on Schussmann? But if that had been the case, wouldn't they have identified Léon and arrested him? Or had Kordlinger's intention been to put him to the test?

One thing was clear. He was a marked man himself, from now on. Bracal had warned him not to push the impression of his incompetence beyond the limits of Kordlinger's credulity. Was that what he had done? Or worse, had he simply shown himself to be defiant, determined to obstruct Kordlinger? He had been stupid, had let himself be carried away. And why? Because he had been enjoying himself, taking pleasure in this little act of resistance. Yes, he had been a fool. He couldn't deny it.

He sat for a long time smoking and thinking. Then he called Moncerre in and went over the meeting with him.

'You might just as well have punched him in the face,' Moncerre said.

'That's how it looks to you?'

'Can't look any other way. You've made a pig's arse of it. You don't think the Alsatian will defend you, do you? Not bloody likely.'

'Things are as they must be,' Lannes said.

'And that's consolation?'

'Not a lot. You know that queer bar, used to be called 'The Wet Flag' now 'Chez Jules'? I can't approach it myself, not again. And it's safer if you don't either, not now. So I want you to get hold of one of your snouts and have him take a message to Jules. Tell him the dead German – he'll know who's meant – was never in his bar. He doesn't recognise his photograph, sorry. And I never came to interview him either.'

'And you think that'll help you.'

'Not a lot. Not at all really. But it's the best line to follow. You'll understand why.'

'So collaboration's off the menu. The Alsatian won't like that either.'

'He doesn't have to.'

'And we're resisting?'

'That's up to you, my old bull-terrier.'

'Jesus Christ.'

XLV

For most of the train journey to Vichy Dominique kept his eyes on his book, while Lannes looked out of the window. There was constraint between them. Marguerite had kissed Dominique with tears in her eyes, and spoken lovingly to him. She had said nothing to Lannes, turning her head aside and looking downwards when he moved to embrace her, so that his lips had done no more than brush her cheek. It's as I feared, he thought, she'll never forgive me, or not for a long time, no matter how things turn out. He felt sad and resentful at the same time; she might have made an effort to understand. But that wasn't quite true. She understood one thing only too well: that he had put loyalty to Alain above loyalty to her.

German field-police had boarded the train at Bordeaux, checking that the passengers had an 'ausweis'. As Lannes presented his, it was as if he himself, the policeman, was now a suspect. He wondered if Alain and Léon and Jérôme had each felt his heart race while their documents were being examined. But probably the glance given their papers had been as cursory and perfunctory as the one given his and Dominique's now. There was no reason why it shouldn't have been.

It was a long journey. They had to change twice, at Brive la Gaillarde and Clermont-Ferrand. The hour between trains at Brive gave them time to eat lunch in the station buffet, an omelette for each, a quarter-litre of white wine for Lannes and a bottle of Châteldon mineral water for Dominique. The company which produced it was owned by Pierre Laval, who had masterminded the dissolution of the Third Republic and the naming of the Marshal as Head of State. He had been Pétain's first Prime Minister before being ejected the previous December in a coup organised by the Catholic Right. It was as a successful businessman and Republican politician that Laval had persuaded the national railways – the SNCF – to grant him a monopoly of the supply of mineral water for its restaurants and station buffets. Lannes spoke of this to Dominique who made no reply.

'At least we're relieved of a German presence,' Lannes said. Dominique merely nodded. The rest of the meal passed in silence.

Maurice de Grimaud was waiting for them on the platform at Vichy. He shook hands with Lannes and embraced Dominique.

'It's so good to see you,' he said. 'I've really been looking forward so much to your arrival and to working with you.'

He explained that for the moment he had arranged that Dominique should share his room.

'You've no idea how hard it is to find accommodation here,' he said. 'The town's simply packed, it's exhilarating. I hope you didn't find difficulty, sir, in obtaining a hotel room?'

It was obvious that Dominique was eager to be off with his friend. He submitted to Lannes' embrace and to the suggestion that they should meet the following evening before Lannes returned to Bordeaux the next morning.

Maurice said, 'I understand you are meeting my father for lunch tomorrow. He asked me to confirm that with you.'

The boys set off, chattering, Dominique evidently relieved to be free of his father.

As for Lannes himself, what was left to him but the opportunity to do nothing, to walk the streets of the spa town on a beautiful summer evening? It was all a sort of make-believe. He could pretend that he was on holiday, carefree, just as all the functionaries gathered here could pretend that they constituted the government of France. No doubt they were fully occupied, drafting minutes and papers, in the manner of functionaries, and plotting against each other, in the manner of functionaries; but it amounted to nothing. Which was not to say that Vichy hadn't, in the eleven months of its existence, passed innumerable laws and issued count-less decrees. Oh yes, it was a busy little world, no matter how futile. 'Achtung,' the Boches snapped, and Vichy sprang to attention.

Lannes settled himself on the terrace of a café and ordered a beer. The terrace was crowded, as it would have been before the war, but with this difference. Many of its clients were young – younger than Lannes anyway – and some were in uniform. In the days of peace the clientèle would mostly have been in Vichy to take the waters, sick people or rich ones who had been persuaded by their expensive doctors that their health required a sojourn in the spa town.

A girl at the next table laughed. She was leaning back in her chair, her glossy black hair resting on her shoulders. The movement of laughter had pulled her skirt up to reveal a stretch of thigh. Her companion – husband? lover? – reached forward to tug the skirt down. The morality of the National Revolution? Not so: his hand rested there, pressing on her thigh. She swung forward, bringing her elbows down on the table and cupping her chin in her hands. They gazed into each other's eyes. The man – scarcely more than a boy – took one of her hands and raised it to his lips. He wore the blue uniform of the Service de l'Ordre Légionairre. He was telling her how he and his mates had 'turfed' a Jewess out of her apartment and taken it over. 'So we can go there,' he said. The girl crossed her legs, trapping his hand between them. 'That's good,' she said, and her forefinger played lightly on his mouth.

Lannes thought of them as he lay in his hotel bed. It was a hot night and he could not sleep. They would be making love now, happily, perhaps in the bed which belonged to the evicted woman. And where would she have found to rest? The girl had been lovely, and the boy, with his smooth skin and laughing eyes, nice-looking. Were they naturally vicious, or were they infected by the mood of the times? Neither thought was agreeable.

*   *   *

It still felt like holiday in the morning. The sky was blue, with only a few little wispy clouds, and a gentle breeze blew from the mountains. A troop of schoolchildren passed chattering as he took his coffee on the terrace of a café next door to his hotel. It was strange to see no German uniforms in the streets. When he went to be shaved, the barber was eager to talk about football. 'I'm a rugby man myself,' Lannes said, 'from the south-west,' and wondered if he would ever watch Alain play again. He had half an hour before his appointment with Bracal's friend; nothing to do but stroll, as aimlessly as visitors to the spa must often have strolled on summer mornings to fill in time before they were due to take the waters or have their next appointment with their doctor. He admired the flower-stalls in the square in front of the monument to the fallen in his war, and thought how they would have delighted Marguerite. Vichy was really charming, he had to admit. There was a light-opera feel to the town; it was as if the air was filled with music by Offenbach.

The office occupied by Travaux Rurales was, suitably, above a branch of the Crédit Agricole, and the secretary at the desk was a burly young man who looked as if he would be at home behind a plough. And why not, in this town where everything seemed to Lannes to belong to the theatre, where the Marshal was playing at being a Head of State and where one day the curtain would descend, bringing an end to the make-believe?

Naturally he had to wait; it would not do for someone playing the role of a zealous official to receive him on time, destroying the illusion that he was overburdened with work. Lannes was content to play his part too and sat and smoked three or four cigarettes while the fan suspended from the ceiling turned slowly. The burly young man stamped papers and sighed. Then he got up and disappeared, leaving Lannes alone. Eventually he returned and said, 'He can see you now.'

'Ah, my friend Bracal's friend.'

Lannes was surprised to find that the man greeting him looked no more than thirty. He was short, thick-set with a broad face dominated by a huge nose. He had bounded from his desk to shake Lannes' hand, with none of the lassitude Lannes already associated with Vichy. The handshake was vigorous, even crushing, and there was a sparkle in his brown eyes. His accent was of the Midi and his smile was welcoming.

'Bracal tells me I can speak to you frankly, and that I may expect frankness in return. Good. That's what I like to hear. How are things in Bordeaux?'

'Not good, and getting worse.'

Lannes sat in the chair on the other side of the desk. There were only two chairs in the room which was scarcely furnished. A green metal filing-cabinet seemed an incongruous article under the huge Second Empire chandelier.

'You can call me Vincent. I should explain, this is an outpost, manned only by myself and Georges who received you. Our head-quarters, as you may know, are in Marseilles, largely because the boss's mother used to teach school there and so he knows the city. Bracal says you know something of our work.'

'What I've seen of it hasn't impressed me,' Lannes said. 'A man who called himself Félix. I'm a policeman. I don't like spooks.'

'Nevertheless, you've come here as our mutual friend Bracal suggested you should. Why?'

Lannes thought, he's testing me. I must remember that he is probably cleverer than he looks. He lit a cigarette, and said, 'Curiosity.'

'Good answer. Bracal's spoken about you. He thinks we may think alike.'

'I don't know what you think.'

'Of course you don't. So I'll speak frankly. We're a small organisation, full-time staff not more than twenty-five, perhaps twenty-seven. Not a lot, eh? Not for the work we have to do. So we need to recruit agents, mostly people to keep us informed – we've a couple of hundred already, a few more than that maybe – it's not my department, keeping count. What's their job? Keeping us up to date about, for instance, German activities in the Occupied Zone. There you are! I haven't surprised you, have I? Of course,' he gestured at the portrait on the wall behind him, 'we're loyal to the Marshal, couldn't be otherwise, could it? Not if we are to survive. And the Marshal has committed France to a policy of collaboration. How do we reconcile this with our activities?'

'How do you?'

'We take this line. The old man says what he has to say. But is what he says what he thinks? Nobody knows. Some of us make guesses. They may be informed guesses, but again they may not? Who do you think will win the war?'

'There's not much fighting, is there?' Lannes smiled for the first time, amused by the abrupt change of direction. 'Germany seems to be victorious.'

'Seems? Good word. I've read your dossier of course.'

'Of course.'

'Médaille Militaire and all that.'

'A long time ago and in another war.'

'Which we won. One up, one down, eh?'

'Two down,' Lannes said, '1870.'

'Which we recovered from, to win the return match.'

'Which we recovered from. Eventually.'

'Good,' Vincent said, 'I think we understand each other. You're in trouble with the Boches, Bracal tells me.'

'If he says so.'

'Oh, he does, I assure you he does.'

'If I am, it's thanks to your friend Félix. I didn't care for his methods. And he made a mess of things. I suppose – from what I know of his ways – because he frightened his quarry, who was, as it happens, an honourable man and took what he considered to be the honourable way out. Or perhaps he was just afraid. I don't know. Either way, your precious Félix bungled things, and has caused a deal of trouble.'

'He can be a bit crude. Nevertheless. Chap called Kordlinger, isn't it? You can't satisfy him? Funny thing. His grandmother was French, born French anyway.'

'So he told me, or at least said his grandfather was born a French citizen.'

'Quite right. So he was. Grandma too, but she was also Jewish. Bet he didn't tell you that?'

Lannes said, 'I don't suppose it's something he would broadcast. Is it true?'

'Oh yes, it's not something I would lie to you about. No point in lying unless it's necessary. Don't you agree?'

'How do you know?'

'Cousin of his, distant cousin, works for us. Jew himself.'

'Here in Vichy?'

'Well, Marseilles actually. It's not as unusual as you may suppose. Not everyone here is entirely in favour of the anti-Jewish legislation.

Makes no sense to me, personally, and, as for you, I have you down as a good Republican, That right?'

'As much as I'm anything.'

'Good,' Vincent's smile broadened. 'Very good. No time for enthusiasm myself. Does a lot of damage, enthusiasm. Félix's trouble, you know. He was a good man in his way – I mean, at his work, I'm not talking about his character, another business altogether, but . . . enthusiastic. Too much so for us. Bit of a loose cannon, as the saying goes. So we've had to sideline him, office job, can't do much harm shuffling paper. So, again: what do you say? Happy to keep us informed, are you? Good, Bracal'll fix it. Good man, Bracal, speaks very highly of you. Enjoy your lunch with de Grimaud, Oh yes, I know about that. He's one of those we keep tabs on. Interesting chap, don't you think? Likely to jump the wrong way, however. That's my opinion, personal one, you know.'

XLVI

The Hôtel des Ambassadeurs seemed exactly as it had been when Lannes met Edmond de Grimaud there the previous year. The tables in the foyer were again fully occupied. Waiters floated about with silver trays held aloft. There were flowers in pots – roses, hydrangeas, carnations, freesias – and an air of comfort and unhurried elegance. But then nobody, Lannes thought, hurried in Vichy. At the back of the room four old people were playing bridge; perhaps they were the same four he had seen on his previous visit; it was as if they hadn't moved in the intervening months. A bald man, with the ribbon of the Légion d'Honneur in his lapel, was dealing the cards with slow deliberation. Lannes thought he recognised him: a minister in several of the Cabinets of the Third Republic, now marking time here in Vichy? He paused in the middle of his dealing to pick up the cigar that was smoking in an ashtray, and kept it clenched in the middle of his mouth as he dealt out the last cards and arranged his hand.

Lannes went through to the bar where, in contrast to the foyer, only a few tables were occupied.

The young barman greeted him as if he was a familiar and respected customer. Lannes remembered how he had looked on him with resentment on his last visit, when Dominique had been a prisoner of war and he had wondered how this young man had contrived to escape military service.

'I have a message from Monsieur de Grimaud, sir. He apologises for being delayed and says he will be with you as soon as possible. Meanwhile he has instructed me to open a bottle of champagne for you.'

'I'd rather have a pastis,' Lannes said.

'I'm sorry, sir, but we are no longer permitted to serve it, not since the prohibition of aniseed-based liquors.'

He twisted the wire off a bottle of Perrier-Jouet, deftly popped the cork, poured Lannes a glass and replaced the bottle in the ice-bucket, with a napkin wrapped round its neck.

Particles of dust floated in the sunlight which streamed through the windows of the bar.

'We can still get pastis in Bordeaux,' Lannes said.

'Then you are fortunate, sir.'

'Nice to be fortunate in one respect.'

'Indeed yes.'

The barman smiled, as if inviting Lannes to join him in the pretence that all was for the best, or at least to agree that irony was their only possible defence against the reality of the way things were.

'You may be interested to know that Monsieur Laval agrees with you about pastis,' he said, 'but the management forbids me to keep a bottle even for him. We still have bottles of course, but they're under lock and key, until . . . '

He smiled again, engagingly.

'Until . . . ?'

'Who knows? Perhaps one day they will be liberated. Meanwhile, there's no pastis even for Monsieur Laval.'

'Well, he's in the shit, isn't he, since they kicked him out last December. Put him under house arrest, didn't they?'

'Till his German friends stepped in, to countermand the order. As for that one, he may be in the shit, as you put it, for now, but he'll rise again, you can be sure of that. His type always does. Meanwhile when he comes here on his rare visits to the town, he tells me how happy he is to be out of power and watching his Charolais cattle in the meadows. I don't believe him of course. He's a deep one.'

'You speak very frankly,' Lannes said.

'And why not, sir? This is Vichy where we all say what we think even though we don't always think what we say.'

Lannes smiled in his turn and took his glass over to a table by the window. The barman followed with the ice-bucket and a stand to place it in.

'I trust you will enjoy your visit, sir. It's very good wine, you know, always the best for Monsieur de Grimaud.'

'I expect you're right.'

'Thank you, sir.'

Lannes was content to wait. It certainly was good wine, much better than the bottle Gustave had produced the morning the boys took the train out of Bordeaux. As the barman had said, nothing but the best for Monsieur de Grimaud. Lannes felt for the brown envelope in his inside pocket.

'My dear superintendent . . . '

Edmond de Grimaud approached him with hand outstretched. Lannes hesitated a moment before accepting it.

'I trust Pierre has been looking after you.'

'Certainly.'

De Grimaud settled himself at the table, accepted the glass which the barman handed him.

'Your health, superintendent.'

Lannes nodded but did not lift his glass. He was uncomfortably aware of de Grimaud's elegance, the well-cut navy-blue suit, the cream-coloured silk shirt, the neatly knotted bow-tie, the highly polished black shoes, the whiff of bay rum from his sleek hair.

'Let me say how delighted I am to see you again, and add that Maurice is equally, perhaps even more, delighted, that your Dominique has come to join him in the excellent work he is doing. They had dinner with me last night. Your son is a charming boy and I am so pleased to have been able to be of some assistance in arranging for his repatriation. It is not good for young people to be held in prisoner-of-war camps. I only wish we could get them all home. We are of course working on that; it is one of the prime objects of our policy of collaboration, as you will know. As for my Maurice, the work he is doing has been the making of him. He is no longer the troubled adolescent you knew in Bordeaux. The transformation has indeed been remarkable. Meanwhile, if you permit, we shall eat here in the bar. I've been summoned un-expectedly to a meeting this afternoon with the Marshal and Admiral Darlan. Pierre, would you be kind enough to bring us some smoked salmon? I am so sorry, superintendent, I had looked forward to a long leisurely lunch, and it is possible to eat well here.'

Lannes took the envelope from his pocket and pushed it across the table.

'These are Aristide Labiche's papers,' he said. 'As you see, I haven't opened the envelope to examine them.'

De Grimaud made no move to pick it up. It lay on the table like an accusation.

'I think this clears me of my debt,' Lannes said. 'Of course it may be of no significance, I can't tell, but since your nephew Sigi's man, Sombra, went to some lengths to get hold of it . . . '

'But not to the length of murder?'

'Not this time.'

'That poor Aristide,' de Grimaud said. 'I knew him when he was a journalist in Paris. Such a clever man, such a fool. Have you discovered who did kill him?'

'The case is closed. And as for poor Aristide . . . ' He put his finger on the envelope . . . 'I would rather say, "poor Pilar . . . ".'

'Such a lovely girl,' de Grimaud said. 'I'm grateful to you, of course. As you say, this envelope' – he stretched forward, picked it up, and put it in his pocket – 'assuming it contains what I expect it to contain, then indeed, we are, as the Americans say, "quits". You have had no more trouble with his deplorable brother, the advocate Labiche, I trust?'

'It depends what you mean by trouble,' Lannes said. 'What's his connection with Sombra?'

De Grimaud raised an eyebrow.

'His connection with Señor Sombra? I wasn't aware that there was one.'

'Sombra called at his offices, at least twice, to let him know, I believe, that Aristide was in Bordeaux. It seems possible – I put it no more strongly – that if he had found this envelope, he would have delivered it to the advocate, perhaps to have the contents copied or photographed, before handing it on to you or, rather, your nephew Sigi. There's nothing in Sombra's dossier which suggests he is trustworthy. He has done time for blackmail and he's the sort who would sell his grandmother if the price was right.'

De Grimaud raised his chin and stroked it. He took a cigar from a dull-red Morocco leather case, clipped the end off with a silver guillotine, held a match to it to warm the tobacco, lit it, and blew out smoke. Pierre the barman approached and refilled their glasses. In the far corner of the bar a young man with dark curly hair settled himself at the piano and began to play a Strauss waltz.

'Is there more?' de Grimaud said.

'Speculation only. The advocate has a reputation. You know of course that he shares your brother the count's tastes, but is more daring and demanding than the count.'

'My unfortunate brother,' de Grimaud said. 'He's an idiot, of course. My father bullied him and so he never became a man.'

'You made use of this knowledge to threaten the advocate on my behalf and cause him to back off when he was trying to ruin me. I'm grateful to you, it goes without saying. Now, besides being a blackmailer, thief and hired killer, Sombra's a pimp,' Lannes said. 'He's also a very frightened man. Well, if you play as many sides as he does, you've a lot to be frightened of. We had him in custody – you'll know this – suspected of killing Aristide. I was ordered to release him. Someone leaned on the examining magistrate. I don't think that was you?'

'It wasn't.'

'So who was it?'

De Grimaud frowned, made no reply, drew on his cigar, waited for Lannes to continue.

'And why?' Lannes said.

'I have no idea. Evidently you have. So?'

Lannes said, 'We don't think alike, Monsieur de Grimaud. There's no point making a secret of that, or pretending that we do. Moreover, since we are speaking frankly – or, at least I am, for you have said very little – I have no doubt about the circumstances of my shooting outside the Hotel Splendide. There's no need to go into that. We have since come to some sort of understanding. You have done me a service for which I am grateful, and which I have repaid by securing that envelope for you. As you said we are quits. That was the word you used, wasn't it? So I owe you nothing now. Nevertheless I'll say this. Since you didn't arrange for Sombra to be released, someone else did, and this must be someone who has found a use for him. And that use may be against you. In short, I put it to you that Sombra has been turned. You are a man – I have reason to know – who has enemies, perhaps in Bordeaux, as, for instance, the advocate Labiche – or perhaps here in Vichy, people who take an interest in your dealings with Germany before the war. There, I've said it. You'll have an idea yourself who these people might be. I've no doubt of that. The question is: who would Sombra have given that envelope to, if he had managed to get hold of it? To you by way of your nephew Sigi? To the advocate Labiche? Or to this someone else?'

De Grimaud got to his feet.

'You have given me much to think about. This time it is I who am in your debt, superintendent. I won't forget it, I assure you. As I may have said before, I have developed a regard for you – whatever our differences. I am delighted that our sons are friends, and you may rest assured that I shall keep my eye on your Dominique and see that he comes to no harm.'

Again he extended his hand, and this time Lannes took it without hesitation. De Grimaud paused on his way out to speak to the barman. The pianist played an American tune that Lannes recognised but couldn't put words to. Alain would know, he thought, Clothilde also.

Pierre came over to refill his glass again.

'I apologise again for not being able to serve you pastis,' he said.

'Nevertheless this is very good champagne. Monsieur de Grimaud is indeed one of our most valued customers. A man of considerable influence, I believe.'

'I'm sure you're right, Pierre,' Lannes said. 'In your profession you know these things, don't you?'

'As in yours, sir.'

'In mine?'

'I heard how Monsieur de Grimaud addressed you.'

'Yes, of course. But I have no standing here in Vichy.'

'Do you still wish the smoked salmon, sir?'

'Why not? After all, I suppose you will put it on Monsieur de Grimaud's bill.'

He wondered if he had behaved rashly. Would de Grimaud realise that his words about men in Vichy who might take an interest in his dealings pre-war with Germany suggested that he himself had been approached by one of them? Almost certainly; he was no fool. Strangely, Lannes thought, he had indeed developed some regard for him, respect at least. They thought differently, as he had said. De Grimaud was a man of the Right, even the far-Right, even perhaps a Fascist, though it was likely that he despised the petit-bourgeois agitators who dominated the ever-shifting French Fascist parties. More probably he was a Cagoulard, a member of that aristocratic and haut-bourgeois secret society that in the years before the war had murdered and sought to provoke violence from the Left in an attempt to undermine, even destroy, the Republic. He had been responsible for that attempt on Lannes' life, an attempt which had so nearly succeeded, and his tools, Sigi and Sombra, had tortured Gaston in an attempt to extract information which Lannes was certain Gaston had never possessed, and then murdered him. It was vile and unforgivable, and yet Lannes couldn't bring himself to dislike the man. Perhaps I'm as morally corrupt as he is, he thought. What would Marguerite say if she knew? Or the children? And had Lannes in effect signed Sombra's death warrant? He hadn't mentioned the BMA, but de Grimaud must suspect he had enemies in the secret world, probably knew who they were. Lannes had made clear his suspicion that de Grimaud could no longer trust Sombra. If he was found with a bullet in his head, would he hold himself responsible? He remembered how Sombra had looked when he threatened him with the guillotine.

He returned to his hotel, and slept for two hours.

And now it was a beautiful June evening and lovers were strolling the streets hand in hand. The war was far away, not even in another country, for there was no war, certainly not one in which France was engaged. And nothing was simple.

Dominique joined him for dinner. He brought Maurice with him to serve as a buffer. The conversation was general. Maurice talked enthusiastically of the important work that was being done with the Chantiers de Jeunesse. 'You would be amazed, sir,' he said, 'in the transformation of these city boys after a few weeks' work in the country. It's not only a physical transformation, it's a moral one too.'

It was only as the boys rose to take their leave that Dominique's resentful reserve was breached.

'Speak to Maman, please,' he said. 'Don't shut her out.'

And then, 'Do you think Alain will be all right? Give Maman my love and say I'm happy. And Clothilde too.'

XLVII

He slept badly, as he almost always did in hotels, and woke from a wretched disturbing dream of which he could remember little. He had found himself in a deserted house, wandering through rooms where dust lay thick on every surface, and when he called out, 'Is there anyone here?' heard only the echo of his own words. Each door he opened took him further towards something fearful.

He dressed, paid his bill, and stepped out into the sunshine. It was still very early. At the café next door to his hotel, the waiters were unhooking the chairs on the terrace. He went into the bar and had a coffee standing at the counter. He had two hours to kill before his train.

'Superintendent Lannes.'

He turned round. The speaker was in shadow and for a moment

he didn't recognise him. Then he moved forward and Lannes saw it was the BMA spook – what was his name? Villepind? No, Villepreux, that was it.

'So: what do you think of the news?'

'What news?'

'Hitler has repeated Napoleon's error.'

'You mean?'

'Yes, it's just come through. At dawn this morning the first troops of the Wehrmacht were launched against the Soviet Union.'

Lannes' first reaction: enormous relief, this is marvellous, Germany will lose the war. Then, he said, 'Napoleon reached Moscow.'

'The USSR stretches a long way east of Moscow.'

He laid his hand on Lannes' arm.

'Come for a walk. You have time before your train, I think.'

He led Lannes past the Hôtel du Parc, so incongruously the seat of government.

'The Marshal rarely appears before mid-day,' Villepreux said, 'and sleeps in the afternoon. He has to husband his strength. I wonder if they have yet told him the news. I wonder if he will realise its significance.'

'Whatever that may be,' Lannes said.

'Ah, you understand. It changes everything, but the immediate changes will be different from the long-term ones.'

'As you say.'

'There will be talk of a crusade against atheistic Bolshevism.'

'Only talk?'

'Perhaps. We must certainly hope so, don't you think?'

They came to the Parc des Sources. At this hour of the morning there was a coming-and-going of officials and secretaries criss-crossing the park on the way to their offices, many of them in hotels requisitioned by the State. Most would have heard the news on their radios, but they were going to work as if it was an ordinary day, rather than one on which the campaign that would decide the outcome of the war, and therefore the fate of France and the regime, was beginning.

Villepreux stopped by a bench under the canopy of a plane tree.

'This'll do,' he said, 'pleasant spot, nobody within hearing.'

He began to fill his pipe. Lannes lit a cigarette and waited. He wasn't going to make the running in this conversation which certainly hadn't been brought about by chance.

'Then there are our own Reds,' Villepreux said. 'They've been no trouble so far, not as long as Hitler and Stalin were in a loving embrace or, if that's putting it too strongly, then at least nominally allies. Things will be different now. My organisation will be required to keep an even closer eye on them. They're patriots of course, but are they patriots for France or patriots for the Soviet Union?'

'They might be both.'

'But which comes first? You know they've been denouncing the general who is currently in London as a Fascist. They're wrong of course. De Gaulle's an old Action Française man, who might have found himself here if he had a different temperament and hadn't fallen out with the Marshal over that book he wrote, but he's no Fascist, too old fashioned for that. What was in the envelope you handed over to de Grimaud, superintendent?'

An aeroplane passed over, heading south. Lannes waited till the sound of its engine had died away. Pierre, he thought, the barman at the Ambassadeurs – it was natural that the spooks would have their man there. He took a chance.

'You wouldn't need to ask if Sombra had got it for you,' he said.

Villepreux paused to re-light his pipe. Lannes watched a squirrel leap from branch to branch of the tree.

'That wretched Spaniard,' Villepreux said. 'He didn't kill your Red professor, you know.'

'I know. Are you sure he was working only for you?'

'One can be sure of nothing these days. I'm certainly not sure of you, superintendent. Who else might he be working for?'

'Oh, there are several possibilities,' Lannes said. 'I wouldn't even exclude the Boches. He's a twister. Then there's the murdered man's brother, a lawyer. Sombra's certainly had dealings with him. And of course, as you certainly know, there's de Grimaud himself, indirectly perhaps, directly for de Grimaud's nephew Sigi, who sometimes calls himself Marcel, and who certainly was the first person to commission him to get the envelope. You'll know about him, I daresay.'

'You're avoiding my question, superintendent.'

'Not at all. It's simply that I don't know the answer. I handed the envelope to de Grimaud unopened.'

Villepreux frowned.

'Why should I believe you?'

'It's no matter to me whether you do or not,' Lannes said. 'Nevertheless that's what I did. As you know he arranged for my son to be repatriated. We had an arrangement, a deal if you like. I was keeping my side of the bargain.'

'You're very old-fashioned, superintendent. Or are you playing both sides?'

'Not how I would put it,' Lannes said.

*　　*　　*

The spook's question was a fair one, perplexing too. He looked out of the train window and pondered it. Why was de Grimaud so apparently eager to be on good relations with him? There was no satisfactory answer to that.

XLVIII

He climbed the stairs slowly. He didn't want to be home, to be received by Marguerite with reproaches or, worse, icy and hostile silence. He was in the position of so many Frenchmen, of France itself indeed, unable to do what was right, because the alternative courses open to him were between bad and worse. Consequently he was condemned to behave badly, and not only in his treatment of Marguerite or in making no move to re-open the case of Aristide's death, now that he knew who was responsible. He couldn't have done so, certainly. Though St-Hilaire had not deigned to suggest that he was offering a quid pro quo, nevertheless that was indeed the case: he had arranged for Alain and Léon to get to Algiers, and in exchange had provided the solution to the case in such a manner that Lannes could not honourably act on the information. And now there was the matter of his recruitment by Vincent of the TR as an agent, if a sleeping one, and the complication of his relations with Edmond de Grimaud. To say nothing of his difficulties with Kordlinger . . .

He unlocked the door of the apartment. The sitting room was dark and for a moment he wondered if Marguerite had left him. Then Clothilde came through from the kitchen with a mug in her hand.

'Where's your mother?'

'At Grandma's. She's ill and was getting in a state, apparently. So Maman went round to look after her.'

Lannes was ashamed to feel a stab of relief at his wife's absence.

'I don't think it's serious,' Clothilde said.

'And you're all alone?'

'I'm grown up, Papa, almost anyway. How was your trip? How was Dominique?'

'Happy, I think. As for the trip, I did what I had to do.'

Alain's cat came and rubbed against his legs.

'Poor No Neck,' Clothilde said, 'I think he's really missing Alain badly.'

'We're all missing him, but . . . '

'Oh I understand, even if Maman doesn't. Maybe if I was a boy I would think like him.'

'I think she does understand. It's just that she disapproves.'

'You look tired. Are you hungry?'

'No, only tired. Have you eaten, darling?'

'Maman left a vegetable stew. There's plenty for you too.'

'No, it's all right. I'll have a glass of wine and then bed.'

Clothilde stretched out on the couch, dangling her fingers for the cat to play with.

'It's nice being alone together,' she said.

Then she sat up.

'But this news,' she said. 'What does it mean?'

'It'll be months before we can know the answer to that,' Lannes said. 'But I think Hitler may have bitten off more than he can chew.'

He went through to the kitchen for the wine. When he returned, Clothilde said, 'Michel's sure it means we must join the war against Bolshevism . . . '

'Michel? Oh, your new boy. I hope we'll do no such thing.'

'So do I.'

'Tell me about him.'

Clothilde blushed.

'Your mother approves of him,' he said. 'That's good. When am I to be allowed to meet him? Or am I too disreputable?'

'Actually he says you've already met. Apparently you know his grandfather, Professor Lazaire.'

Lannes paused, pretending to think, then said, 'I remember, he was playing chess with the professor when I had occasion to call on him. A nice-looking boy, good manners as your mother says.'

He sipped his wine, lit a cigarette.

'Have you told him about Alain?'

'No, I didn't know what to say.'

'Best to say nothing. You know nothing about where he's gone, what he's doing.'

*   *   *

In bed, unable to sleep, acutely aware of Marguerite's absence, he thought, that boy, Sigi's disciple, what should I have said? But she looks so happy, and, as Marguerite said, she's denied so much that she should have at her age. Perhaps he is indeed charming and intelligent and certainly he's a handsome boy, it's easy to see why she's fallen for him – and him for her? but, but . . . They're young, it won't last, perhaps it won't last, but if it does . . .

Soon after dawn he gave up trying to sleep. He left a note for Clothilde and went to the Bar du Marché for his coffee which, as usual, he improved with a dash of marc. Beside him at the counter people were talking about the Nazi invasion of the Soviet Union.

One market porter said, 'I don't care who hears me. I hope Stalin gives the little bastard a bloody nose.'

'Not much chance of that,' the man beside him said. 'The Russians couldn't even beat the Finns. They've no chance against the Boches. Mark my words, little Adolf will be in Moscow before the autumn to take the surrender. And then what?'

'Might be the end of it all,' another said.

'I don't know about that. If you ask me, it's going to be bad whatever. We'll still be stuck in the shit.'

'You're all wrong,' the first speaker said, 'and I'll tell you why. The future belongs to Communism. Like I say, I don't give a damn who hears me. Stalin's victory is what they call historical necessity. That's a fact.'

'Give over,' his companion said. 'As for me, I know nothing about your historical necessity, but in my opinion the only thing to do is get on with our work.'

*   *   *

'The boss wants to see you,' old Joseph said. 'He's in a right stew, God knows why.'

The Alsatian didn't offer Lannes his hand. Instead, immediately after telling him to sit down, he got up himself and crossed to the window where he stood for a couple of minutes with his back to Lannes.

When at last he turned round, he smoothed his hair and said, 'I'm embarrassed. You've embarrassed me. I thought I could rely on you.'

Lannes waited.

'You've let me down,' Schnyder said. 'I trusted you to keep Kordlinger happy.'

'Difficult job,' Lannes said.

'Shouldn't have been. What you were required to do was simple enough.'

'Not my opinion.'

'You weren't required to have a opinion, merely to find these delinquents and hand them over. Instead . . . '

'Instead what?' Lannes said.

'Instead you've defied him.'

'We're policemen,' Lannes said. 'Our job is to investigate crime and arrest criminals. I carried out the investigation as required, and found no crime had been committed. So there were no criminals to arrest.'

Schnyder sat down behind his desk. A nerve in his right cheek twitched.

'Don't play at being obtuse,' he said. 'I can't believe you don't understand, don't understand the reality of the position we're in. You aren't that naïve. You know where the power lies, and you know that we can keep our independence only if we respect the wishes of the Occupying forces and do as they require.'

'Some independence, that,' Lannes said. 'Kordlinger demanded that boys or young men, who may be deplorable characters – that's none of my business – but who have committed no crime, should be handed over to him or the Gestapo. I didn't like that, but I carried out the investigation as I was ordered to. However, fortunately or unfortunately, I was unable to identify them. So there was nobody to arrest, and in any case, as I say, I have found no evidence of a crime. I've reported all this to Bracal by the way, and discussed it with him. That's how it stands then. I admit I'm not sorry.'

'You're not?'

'No. You can't think it right yourself that we should deliver young Frenchmen to the Gestapo.'

'God give me strength,' Schnyder said. 'Of course I'd rather not, even if they are what Kordlinger calls degenerates, rent-boys, pansies, scum, but my duty – yes, my duty, Jean – is to protect the PJ, to enable us to continue to function. There are times when sacrifices have to be made in the name of a Higher Good.'

'Sacrifices of other people?'

'Yes. I wouldn't put it like that, but if you insist. The people we're talking about are of no significance, except in so far as they have got up the nose of the Boches. I've had to apologise to Kordlinger. Do you think I liked that? To apologise abjectly.'

Lannes thought, so what? You'll eat any shit if you're told to. Vichy will eat any shit if it's told to. He had hoped for better from the Alsatian, not much better, but a bit better.

'And it wasn't enough,' Schnyder said. 'Because of you I humiliated myself, I grovelled, and it wasn't enough. Kordlinger went straight to the Prefect to express his displeasure. The Prefect had me on the carpet, upbraided me for failing to ensure that my subordinates did their duty as instructed by the Occupying Power. He railed on for half an hour. The upshot, Jean, is that you're suspended. I'm sorry.

I'll do what I can of course to get you reinstated, we've got on well and you've been helpful since my arrival. Actually you can thank me you're only suspended, not dismissed.'

'I can thank you?' Lannes said. 'Really?'

'I've seen to it that you are still on full pay till the matter is resolved. I've done the best I can for you, believe me.'

It was probably true. That was the ridiculous thing.

*　　*　　*

It was strange, abruptly, to be in the sunshine with nothing to do. Moncerre was right; he had been a fool to twist Kordlinger's tail. Yet he didn't regret it. He ought to go home, tell Marguerite he had been suspended, ask how her mother was. He couldn't bring himself to do so.

The sky was a deep blue, free of any cloud. The sun beat down. Thousands of miles to the east the Panzers would be rolling over the vast plains that stretched to the Ural Mountains. And Alain and his friends? Had they made contact with the Gaullists? He hoped they had gone to the beach and were soaking up the sunshine. He turned away from home, stopped off in the Place Gambetta for a beer on the terrace of the Café Régent. There were women all around, some of them pretty. He thought of Yvette stretched out on her bed and saying 'needing?' Why not? What harm could it do? But he lacked the energy. A sentence formed in his head: 'Superintendent Lannes, having been suspended from duty, found he lacked the energy to betray his wife with a tart.' But it wasn't only that. It was also that in defying Kordlinger he had regained his self-respect, even his honour. Honour? Wasn't it a sense of honour that animated Alain and his friends, the belief that to acquiesce in Vichy and the Occupation was dishonourable? Alain might even use the word. He wasn't so sure of Léon and really knew nothing of what prompted Jérôme. But Alain had been brought up on d'Artagnan. He wished he could speak to him now. Alain would understand his defiance of Kordlinger, and approve of it. So, he was sure, would young René. In a crumbling world what remained to a man but his sense of honour? Tarnished, certainly, but not entirely lost.

233

The beer was beautifully cold. He flicked a hand to the old waiter he had known for years who understood and brought him another demi.

'On days like this you can almost forget how things are.'

'Almost, Georges.'

Lannes gestured across the square where a group of German soldiers was gathered by the fountain.

'I did say "almost", superintendent. We must make the best of things and take such pleasures as present themselves. Enjoy your beer.'

Such pleasures as present themselves? Yes, except such as young Yvette with her bedroom eyes, which honour forbids you. She had been kind to old Aristide in his loneliness and fear – though it wasn't those he had feared who killed him. Had his commitment to the Communist cause been an attempt to regain his honour, the honour he had lost when he betrayed his young daughter?

Damn the word. There was some character in fiction – in a novel or play, he couldn't remember – who had dismissed it as just that, a mere word.

Meanwhile there was an Italian proverb, Neapolitan, he thought: *dolce far' niente* – sweet to do nothing.

For the moment, yes. But nothing? Only nothing? Was that what they were condemned to now, in their humiliated France?

He sat there for a long time and didn't order another beer. It seemed to him that his suspension from duty was a blessing; it gave him the freedom to reflect. He had taken a first step, but the first step counts only if others follow. There was the man Vincent of TR to whom he had made some sort of a commitment. Blessing or not, the suspension would make it difficult, even impossible, to act on that. So he must get it lifted. Perhaps Bracal could help. The hot sun was making him sleepy. He closed his eyes.

*   *   *

When he woke it was as if his mind had cleared. He went into the bar and telephoned the house in the rue d'Aviau. When old Marthe answered he said, 'I need to speak to Sigi. Is he in Bordeaux? . . . Good. I know you refuse to have dealings with him for the reason you've told me, but this is urgent. Tell him I must see him. This evening, seven o'clock in the Café des Arts, cours du Marne, where we met before. He'll understand . . . '

*   *   *

As soon as he turned his key in the door of their apartment he knew Marguerite was home. If anyone had asked him how he knew, he might have replied, 'Twenty-five years of marriage.' He had never thought of it before, but now it came to him that no matter how strained relations between them might be, these twenty-five years couldn't be wiped away. They had contributed to making each of them what they were. If Marguerite lived only for their children and their home and refused to take an interest in his work or the world beyond her immediate circle, wasn't this because he had himself chosen to shut her out of so great a part of his life?

'Why are you home so early?' she said.

'How's your mother? Better, I trust?'

'It was nothing really, as usual,' she said. 'Just in need of attention and reassurance. How did you leave Dominique?'

'Well and happy, I think. As for being home now, I have to tell you I've been suspended from duty.'

He hadn't been sure he would tell her. Then it seemed impossible not to.

'It's a long story,' he said. 'Do you want to hear it?'

For a moment it seemed as if she was about to turn away. Then she sat down. He stood looking out of the window, at nothing really.

'You know we're required to collaborate with the Germans,' he began.

He told her everything from his meeting with the spook Félix, about Léon, not concealing that he was one of Alain's companions, the wretched Schussmann's suicide, the Café Jules and the boy Karim, Fernand's role, Kordlinger's demand and his defiance of it. Everything, even details which he knew would disgust her.

'So?' he said. 'Have I been a fool?'

She laid aside the knitting to which she had attended throughout his recital.

235

'Why do you ask me that?'

'Because I have to, just as I decided I had to tell you the whole story. So: have I been a fool?'

'You know you have. You must also know I wouldn't have wished for you to behave otherwise. The boys you speak of – well, what you say they are disgusts me, you know that, insofar as I understand it, and I'm sorry to think that one of them is Alain's friend as you say he is, but they have mothers and if some policeman was to hand over any of our children to that German, what would I think? I'd want to tear his eyes out.'

'Thank you.'

For the first time in days she smiled to him.

'There's a postcard from Alain,' she said. 'It hadn't occurred to me that he might be able to write to us, that there was still a postal service with North Africa.'

She got up to fetch it. A photograph of the Marshal.

'All well and happy,' Alain had written. 'Don't worry. Lots of Love. A.'

'It makes me feel better,' she said.

A photograph of the Marshal, Lannes thought; it was as if d'Artagnan had sent a card with the image of the Cardinal.

XLIX

Of course he was late. His arrogance, characteristic in Lannes' experience of the natural killer, wouldn't permit him to be the one to arrive first. Doubtless it wasn't only arrogance; there was wariness too. He would want to make sure Lannes was alone before he presented himself. When he arrived, looking like a fashionable man about town in a newly pressed biscuit-coloured linen suit with silk shirt and silk tie, he was all smiles.

'What's this you are drinking?' he said, 'a *petit vin blanc*, super-intendent? How modest.'

'Have what you please,' Lannes said. 'I wasn't sure old Marthe would give you my message.'

Sigi continued to smile, but the smile did not reach his eyes.

'Poor old woman,' he said, 'she suffers from delusions, you know. And have you solved the case of that poor professor who got his head bashed in?'

'The case is closed,' Lannes said.

'So you have decided my poor friend Sombra is innocent? Your inspector was rather rough with him.'

'No rougher than he deserved. You haven't spoken to Edmond recently?'

'Why should you think that?'

'Because you still refer to Sombra as your friend.'

'And why not?'

'We had him in custody. Someone applied pressure to have him released. It wasn't Edmond. So who was it? It's a question that should interest you, Sigi.'

Sigi caught the waiter's attention.

'Bring us a bottle of champagne,' he said, 'the best you have.'

'He's been turned,' Lannes said. 'You can't rely on him now. There are people in Vichy, even in Vichy, who don't like Edmond. I don't suppose they much care for you either.'

'Are you threatening me, superintendent?'

'Threatening you? I'm in no position to threaten anyone. Call it rather a warning. There's nothing simple or straightforward in Vichy. You should know that.'

The waiter popped the champagne.

'Your health, superintendent.'

He leaned back in his chair, holding his glass aloft and watching the bubbles dance.

'Should I be grateful?' he said. 'I don't think so. That poor Sombra, he's nothing really, a nothing man. And as for what you say about Vichy, it's true of course, but of no importance. I was surprised, I don't mind telling you, to receive your message, and even curious. After all, our previous dealings have not always been agreeable. But if it was only to warn me against Sombra, it's of no significance. Do you remember, superintendent, when we met here in this café a year ago – or perhaps when we had that other conversation in the public garden? I told you that there are two kinds of people in the world, Masters and Slaves, and two kinds of morality, that of the Masters – the *Herren*, as Nietzsche puts it, and that of the *Sklaven* – the Slaves. Poor Sombra is a Slave, I'm afraid. But what about you, superintendent? I invited you, as I recall, to be one of the *Herren*. It's not too late. You must see now that the game is going our way. France must play its part in the battle against Bolshevism, which will see us rewarded with a leading role in the New Order of Europe.'

'Russia stretches a long way,' Lannes said, 'and there are more Russians than Germans. Russia can lose many battles and still win a war.'

'Germany beat them in the last war and the Third Reich is stronger than the Kaiser's. Moreover, this time France will be fighting alongside Germany, not against her. I assure you, my dear superintendent, it's not too late for you to attach yourself to the winning side.'

'We shall see,' Lannes said.

It wasn't to listen to this nonsense that he had invited Sigi to meet him, but now that he was there, he found it difficult to broach the subject of Clothilde and the boy Michel who hero-worshipped this scoundrel. He knew what he wanted to demand of him, and knew he would have to abase himself.

'You tried to kill me,' he said. 'There's no point denying it . . . I accept that you were acting under orders.'

'Certainly, superintendent, there was nothing personal, I assure you.'

'Quite so, and since then your uncle or half-brother – for he is both, isn't he? – Edmond and I have reached an understanding. For the time being, anyway. We have done each other a service. You probably know of this. Now there is the boy Michel, your – what should I call him? – your disciple? – I don't know. Whatever he is, he thinks you are wonderful, you're a hero to him. His grandfather, Professor Lazaire, confirms this. It fills him with anxiety. And now Michel and my daughter.'

'Who is charming, I'm told.'

'Whom I love dearly. There, I've confessed a weakness. You tried, as I said, to kill me. Now I ask you to break your hold on the boy. You can only harm him.'

There, he thought, I've said it. I've made my plea to this killer with his talk of *Herrenmoralitie*, and he'll reject it.

'Clothilde tells me he talks of fighting agaist Bolshevism. Spare him that nonsense. Let him be a boy and only a boy.'

'You don't understand, superintendent. The world is a battlefield. I've had to fight all my life to maintain a foothold. Life is struggle. Nobody can escape that reality. Michel recognises this and welcomes it.'

I've failed, Lannes thought. It was stupid even to try to penetrate his crazy egoism. Clothilde will be hurt and I have revealed my own vulnerability. Whoever forms a tie, gives his heart to another, exposes himself.

Sigi picked up his glass and smiled.

'You never replied to my notes, superintendent.'

'What notes?'

'Don't you want to know who your real father was?'

'Oh that? More nonsense. My father was the man who brought me up, and as for you – you killed your own father, didn't you?'

'The old man fell downstairs. You mustn't believe everything old Marthe tells you. The old woman is losing her wits, and besides she has hated me for years. But what if he was your father too?'

'That's ridiculous.'

'Really? Before she married the man you call your father she was a maid in my father's household. Ask Marthe. You believe everything else she says, after all. And ask yourself two more questions. Why did the old man ask for you personally to investigate the matter of these anonymous letters, and why has Edmond become your protector in Vichy? He has a strong sense of family, Edmond. You know so much less than you think you do, superintendent. Now let us finish this bottle, and, as for young Michel, why should I do as you ask? He has chosen the side of the Future, and it belongs to him.'

L

The knock on the door came in the hour before dawn. Lannes was already up, dressed and drinking coffee in the kitchen. Everything in that conversation with Sigi had disturbed him. He had been foolish to appeal to what probably didn't exist, certainly wasn't to be found – the man's better nature. As for the suggestion that he was himself another of the old count's bastards, it was ridiculous. Malicious too. He knew of course that his mother had gone into service as a maid when she came to the city from her father's farm in the Landes. But she had never mentioned the Comte de Grimaud and his father had never given him any reason to suppose he wasn't his son. In any case it didn't matter. It was all so long ago.

The knock was repeated, more loudly. Why not ignore it? He was suspended from duty, wasn't he? He didn't want to see anyone. All the same, he sighed and got up to answer it before it woke Marguerite or Clothilde.

There were three men on his doorstep, a lieutenant and two private soldiers. They wore the uniform of the SD – the *Sicherheits-Dienst* or Nazi Security Service . . .

'Superintendent Lannes?'

'Yes.'

'You are required to accompany us to headquarters.'

It was the officer who spoke, a young man not much older than Dominique. Lannes looked him in the eye.

'Am I under arrest?'

'You are required to accompany us. I am told there are questions you are required to answer.'

Lannes thought, how often I've spoken that line. And now it's addressed to me.

Then, like so many to whom he had made that request, he said, 'Very well. You'll permit me to inform my wife?'

The lieutenant hesitated a moment, then nodded.

'Two minutes,' he said. 'Please don't do anything stupid.'

Lannes woke Marguerite gently, told her what was happening.

'I'm not entirely surprised, but don't worry.'

'How can I not?'

'I'm confident I can clear things up,' he lied, as so many of those he had himself arrested must have lied to their wives. 'But if I'm not back in a few hours, telephone this number and ask for Judge Bracal.'

He scribbled the number on a piece of paper and laid it on the table by the bed.

'And don't worry, I'll be all right.'

She lifted her head. He bent forward and kissed her on the lips, held her close for a moment and turned away.

The two privates descended the stairs ahead of him, the lieutenant behind. One of the privates held the car door open for him. The lieutenant joined him in the back seat. Nobody spoke. The car had tinted windows, and it was only half-light outside. Lannes did not try to see where they were going. The men who had arrested him were merely obeying orders. They probably had no idea why the orders had been given. Lannes pulled out a packet of cigarettes.

'You permit?'

The lieutenant made no objection. Lannes drew the smoke deep into his lungs and felt better.

The car turned into the rue de Cursel and stopped. Again one of the privates held the door open. The lieutenant took Lannes by the elbow as they entered the building. He saluted an officer who called out an order. Two sergeants came forward, each taking one of Lannes' arms. They hustled him down a stair. The door of a cell was standing open. With a practised move they threw Lannes forward so that he stumbled and would have hit the stone floor if his outstretched arms hadn't broken his fall on a camp-bed. Then the door slammed shut. The only other piece of furniture in the cell was a straight-backed chair. Lannes sat on the bed. He lit another cigarette. A bluebottle buzzed round the naked bulb hanging from the ceiling. Nobody would come for some time. He was sure of that. Arresting a man in near-silence, without a charge, flinging him into a cell and leaving him alone – he knew the score. Well, the longer the wait, the more chance there was of Marguerite getting in touch with Bracal, but even if he acted at once, it would take time for the judge to learn where he was. He stubbed out his cigarette on the floor, lay back on the bed, and closed his eyes.

Eventually he heard footsteps. The door opened and Kordlinger came in, accompanied by the sergeants who had thrust him into the cell.

'Get up, superintendent,' Kordlinger said, 'and sit on the chair.'

Lannes did as he was bid. One of the sergeants stepped forward with a rope in his hand. The other seized Lannes' arms and held them behind the chair while the first one tied him to it.

'I'm sorry you made this necessary,' Kordlinger said. 'You know what I want. Give me the names.'

Lannes shook his head.

'You're being foolish,' Kordlinger said.

Lannes made no reply. Whatever he said straightaway would not be believed. Kordlinger nodded to one of the sergeants who stepped forward and with his fist clenched struck Lannes on the mouth. The chair rocked and he tasted blood. The other sergeant kicked the chair hard. It fell over and Lannes' head hit the concrete floor. They picked the chair up and then kicked it over from the other side. Again his head struck the floor and there was a ringing noise in his ears.

Kordlinger said, 'Well?'

Lannes spat out blood.

'Again,' Kordlinger said, and over the chair went.

Again and again and again.

'The names,' Kordlinger said. 'I want the names.'

Lannes shook his head.

'Don't have them,' he said.

'Again.'

This time he hit the floor even harder and the fall left him dazed and dizzy. He wondered how much more he could take. When the chair was upright one of the sergeants produced a rubber truncheon and hit him first on one shoulder, then on the other. Then his companion seized Lannes by the hair and pulled his head back, while the first one forced his mouth open and poured something from a bottle down his throat. Castor oil. He began to retch.

'You don't have to suffer this,' Kordlinger said. 'You are really being very stupid, superintendent. I am sure you have enough experience of interrogations to know that you will speak in the end. Everybody does. You know that. And you know that we have scarcely begun. There's much more and a lot worse we can do to you. So why not be sensible, and tell me what I need to know, without suffering more pain. No? Again.'

Over he went and this time they let the chair lie where it fell. The bigger of the sergeants stepped forward and kicked Lannes hard in the crotch. Then he hauled the chair upright while Lannes felt the pain run through his body and gasped for breath. The smaller sergeant gave him a backhander to the face.

'Fucking Frenchman, fucking obstinate Frehchman,' he said. 'We can go on for a long time, me and my mate.'

His colleague dangled the truncheon before Lannes' eyes.

'You want more of this chappie?' he said, and smacked him across the cheek with it.

Then he stepped back. Lannes' mouth was again full of blood and this time when he spat it out, a tooth came with it.

'All right,' he said. 'I'll talk. Alone, Kordlinger.'

Kordlinger hesitated a moment, then snapped out an order and the two heavies cut the rope that bound Lannes to the chair and withdrew. Lannes flexed his arms, wiggled his fingers and then took a handkerchief from his pocket. He ran it over his mouth and spat twice into it.

'Lucky I've a good dentist,' he said.

'What makes you think you'll ever visit him again?'

'I'm always hopeful.'

'Names . . . '

'I don't have any names for you,' Lannes said. 'I told you that before. How's your grandmother? Is she still alive?'

Kordlinger clenched his fist and took a step forward. Lannes held up his hand, palm toward the German. He smiled. It hurt him to move his mouth, but he managed the smile.

'Your Jewish one of course. That's the one who interests me.'

'I don't know what you're talking about.'

'Now it's you that's being stupid,' Lannes said. 'Your Jewish non-Aryan grandmother. That's who I mean.'

He smiled again, fished a crumpled packet of Gauloises from his pocket and extracted a cigarette. It had been crushed in one of his falls, but he lit it and drew in the smoke happily.

'Why don't you sit down?' he said. 'I've given you a shock. Think about it. Think about her.'

Kordlinger didn't move. Lannes read uncertainty in his face.

'Of course,' he said, 'you could call in your thugs again and have them beat me to death, but you can't suppose I'm the only person who knows about Granny. Who do you think told me? A spook of course. He was interested in you, knew I was too. Come, Kordlinger, face up to it. You know why Schussmann killed himself? Because one of our spooks put the boy up to seduce him, so that he could be turned. He took what he considered to be the honourable way out. I don't think that's your style. Is it? You'd rather be useful to us. Wouldn't you? Of course there are other courses open to you. As I said, you can have your thugs kill me, but when the word of my disappearance, or death, gets out, the spook who told me about Granny will put two and two together. Spooks can do their sums. So he'll get the right answer, and you'll be faced with the same question I'm putting to you. Exposure or co-operation. Co-operation? Let's call it collaboration. Alternatively you could volunteer for the Eastern Front and fight the Bolsheviks. But I don't think that's your style either. So there you are. Long speech, sorry. It hurts me to talk after the roughing-up I've had.'

Kordlinger had turned away while Lannes spoke and stood facing the wall.

'You bastard,' he said.

'You were the one who started playing rough,' Lannes said. 'So are you going to collaborate or do you prefer that your superiors learn about Granny? Not today – not if you have your thugs bump me off or send me to a camp. But some day, and you'll meanwhile live wondering when that day comes and the spook approaches you. You'll have long anxious hours, lots of them.'

'I never even knew her,' Kordlinger said.

'So what? You missed knowing your Jewish granny. Doesn't alter facts. You won't be asked for much, you know. Just a little information now and then. Like you said, collaboration is important. Say "yes" and I'll help you, give you something, save your face. After all it's in my interest to do so. You wanted names. I'll give you two. First, Ahmed Benazzi – yes, an Arab, a rent-boy whom Schussmann picked up in one of these bars I told you about. He's given us the slip, I'm afraid, and is somewhere in the Free Zone, the so-called Free Zone, Marseilles probably, he has family there. One of his other German clients procured an ausweis for him when he ran blubbering to him. Blackmail again, I'm afraid.'

'And the other?'

'The one who was set up to seduce Schussmann? Daniel Matthieu. He's got away too. It was one of our spooks set him up, but I've since learned he was also working for British Intelligence and they've got him out. He's probably in London and it doesn't look, does it, as if the Wehrmacht is going to get to England, not now that you have this business with the Soviet Union. But there you are. You've got two names to pass on to your superiors and another Wehrmacht officer – the one who got that ausweis for the Arab boy to investigate. To say nothing of the activity here in Bordeaux of British Intelligence. I've given you enough to interest your superiors, may even win you some credit. So is it a deal?'

Kordlinger turned round to face him.

'You bastard,' he said again.

'Sure I'm a bastard, just like you. You're wondering why I let your gorillas beat me up before I spoke? Aren't you? You don't understand it. You will if you think about it. I did it for your sake, Kordlinger, to let you come out of this well. Your bosses are more likely to believe what you tell them if they think you got it the hard way. And it's in our interest that they do. Maybe you'll get a promotion. Good for you and good for us. So, do we have a deal?'

'I'll think about it.'

'That's right. Think about it. By the way Bracal will know by now I was picked up this morning. And that's not all he knows. He'll be asking questions, politely of course because he's a judge.'

Kordlinger said, 'I should have let them finish you off.'

'That wouldn't have helped you,' Lannes said. 'Meanwhile, as long as you collaborate, Granny's secret's safe. By the way, Schussmann's boy-friend, Daniel Matthieu, the English spy, is a Jew. Just like you, Kordlinger, just like you.'

Kordlinger took a step forward. His hand went to the gun in its holster. For a moment Lannes thought he was going to draw it. Then he turned away, and the cell door slammed behind him.

Lannes lay down on the bed. He felt terrible. God knows what my face looks like, he thought. He took out the crushed packet of cigarettes and counted them. Twelve left. He lit one. He had better ration himself. It might be some time before Kordlinger accepted the reality of his position. He might wait till Bracal arrived. But he would accept it. Lannes was sure of that. He drew on his cigarette. The man wasn't a fool. And he was frightened, just frightened enough to see sense, not so frightened that he would go wild. Thank God Bracal told me to go to see his friend in Vichy, he thought. It was a mad world in which having a Jewish grandmother could destroy a man. But that's how it was.

Lannes lay back on the bed, smoking, and looked at the cell door. Sometime it would open again. It might not do so for a few hours, but it would open and he would walk free. Hobble free anyhow. His suspension would be lifted. He was sure of that too. How would the Alsatian take it? He would guess that levers had been pulled, and he wouldn't want to know who had done so. He would smile and say, 'Welcome back, Jean,' but he would be worried too. So what? Let him worry.

He kept his gaze fixed on the door, waiting for the moment of liberation. Waiting, like France itself.